Anything can happen when love is in the air
and there's mistletoe hanging up above...

Three couples are about to discover
exactly how magical the Christmas season
can be and each will experience their own

Mistletoe Miracles

Three of your favorite authors invite you
to share these extra-special, brand-new novellas
about the miracle of love under the mistletoe!

Merry Christmas!

Betty Neels spent her childhood and youth in Devonshire before training as a nurse and midwife. She was an army nursing sister during the war, married a Dutchman and subsequently lived in Holland for fourteen years. She now lives with her husband in Dorset, and has a daughter and grandson. Her interests are reading, animals, old buildings and writing. Betty started to write on retirement from nursing, incited by a lady in a library bemoaning the lack of romantic novels!

Catherine George was born in Wales, and early on developed a passion for reading, which eventually fueled her compulsion to write. Marriage to an engineer led to nine years in Brazil, but on her husband's later travels, the education of her son and daughter kept Catherine in the U.K. And instead of constant reading to pass her lonely evenings, she began to write the first of her romantic novels. When not writing and reading, she loves to cook, listen to opera, browse in antiques shops and walk the Labrador.

Marion Lennox is a country girl, born on a south-east Australia dairy farm. She moved on—mostly because the cows just weren't interested in her stories! Married to a "very special doctor," Marion also writes hugely popular Medical Romance™ stories for Mills & Boon®. In her other life she cares for kids, cats, dogs, chickens and goldfish, she travels, she fights her rampant garden (she's losing) and her house dust (she's lost)—oh, and she teaches statistics and computing to undergraduates at her local university.

BETTY NEELS
CATHERINE GEORGE
MARION LENNOX

Mistletoe Miracles

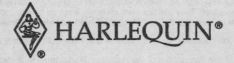

HARLEQUIN®

TORONTO • NEW YORK • LONDON
AMSTERDAM • PARIS • SYDNEY • HAMBURG
STOCKHOLM • ATHENS • TOKYO • MILAN • MADRID
PRAGUE • WARSAW • BUDAPEST • AUCKLAND

ISBN 0-373-83475-6

MISTLETOE MIRACLES

Copyright © 2000 by Harlequin Books S.A.

The publisher acknowledges the copyright holders
of the individual titles as follows:

DEAREST EULALIA
Copyright © 2000 by Betty Neels

THE EXTRA-SPECIAL GIFT
Copyright © 2000 by Catherine George

THE DOORSTEP BABY
Copyright © 2000 by Marion Lennox

Visit us at www.eHarlequin.com

Printed in U.S.A.

CONTENTS

DEAREST EULALIA

Betty Neels

Dear Reader,

Isn't it a comforting thought that whatever happenings the year has brought with it, Christmas is the time we all look forward to? Families gather together, small differences are forgotten, friends send their yearly letters and the children are in their own little seventh heaven.

And as for romance, there must be many of you who remember being kissed under the mistletoe—a kiss that may have led to your own romance and, even if it didn't, is a memory never quite forgotten.

I do hope that this Christmas—with or without the mistletoe—will be a romantic one for you!

A very happy Christmas!

Betty Neels

CHAPTER ONE

THE two men talking together at the back of the hospital entrance hall paused to watch a young woman cross the vast floor. She was walking briskly, which suggested that she knew just where she was going, but she paused for a moment to speak to one of the porters and they had the chance to study her at their leisure.

She was worth studying: a quantity of dark brown hair framed a beautiful face and the nylon overall she was wearing couldn't disguise her splendid figure.

'Eulalia Langley,' said the elder of the two men, 'runs the canteen in Outpatients. Good at it, too. Lives with her grandfather, old Colonel Langley—your father knew him, Aderik. No money, lives in a splendid house somewhere behind Cheyne Walk. Some family arrangement makes it impossible for him to sell it—has to pass it on to a nephew. A millstone round his neck; Eulalia lives with him, keeps the home going. She's been with us for several years now. Ought to have married by now but I don't suppose there's much chance of that. It's a full-time job here and there isn't much of the day left by the time the canteen shuts down.'

His companion said quietly, 'She's very beautiful,' and then added, 'You say that my father knew Colonel Langley?'

He watched the girl go on her way and then turned to his companion. He was tall and heavily built, and towered over his informative colleague. A handsome man in his thirties, he had pale hair already streaked with grey, a high-bridged nose above a thin mouth and heavy-lidded blue eyes. His voice held only faint interest.

'Yes—during the Second World War. They saw a good deal of each other over the years. I don't think you ever met him? Peppery man, and I gather from what I hear that he is housebound with severe arthritis and is now even more peppery.'

'Understandably. Shall I see more of you before I go back to Holland?'

'I hope you'll find time to come to dinner; Dora will want to see you and ask after your mother. You're going to Edinburgh this evening?'

'Yes, but I should be back here tomorrow—I'm operating and there's an Outpatient clinic I must fit in before I return.'

'Then I'll give you a ring.' The older man smiled. 'You are making quite a name for yourself, Aderik, just as your father did.'

Eulalia, unaware of this conversation, went on her way through the hospital to the Outpatients department, already filling up for the morning clinic.

It was a vast place, with rows of wooden benches and noisy old-fashioned radiators which did little to dispel the chill of early winter. Although a good deal of St Chad's had been brought up to date, and that in the teeth of official efforts to close it, there wasn't enough money to spend on the department so its walls remained that particular green so beloved by authority, its benches scuffed and stained and its linoleum floor, once green like the walls, now faded to no colour at all.

Whatever its shortcomings, they were greatly mitigated by the canteen counter which occupied the vast wall, covered in cheerful plastic and nicely set out with piles of plates, cups and saucers, soup mugs, spoons, knives and paper serviettes.

Eulalia saw with satisfaction that Sue and Polly were filling the tea urn and the sugar bowls. The first of the patients were already coming in although the first clinic wouldn't open for another hour, but Outpatients, for all its drawbacks, was for many of the patients a sight better than cold bedsitters and loneliness.

Eulalia had seen that from the first moment of starting her job and since then, for four years, she had fought, splendid white tooth and nail, for the small comforts which would turn the unwelcoming place into somewhere in which the hours of waiting could be borne in some degree of comfort.

Since there had been no money to modernise the place, she had concentrated on the canteen, turning it by degrees into a buffet serving cheap, filling food, soup and drinks, served in brightly coloured crockery by cheerful, chatty helpers.

With an eye on the increasing flow of patients, she sent two of the girls to coffee and went to check the soup. The early morning clinic was chests, and that meant any number of elderly people who lived in damp and chilly rooms and never had quite enough to eat. Soup, even so early in the morning, would be welcome, washed down by strong tea...

One clinic succeeded another; frequently two or more ran consecutively, but by six o'clock the place was silent. Eulalia, after doing a last careful check, locked up, handed over the keys to the head porter and went home.

It was a long journey across the city but the first surge of home-goers had left so she had a seat in the bus and she walked for the last ten minutes or so, glad of the exercise, making her way through the quieter streets down towards the river until she reached a terrace of imposing houses in a narrow, tree-lined street.

Going up the steps to a front door, she glanced down at the basement. The curtains were drawn but she could see that there was a light there, for Jane would be getting supper. Eulalia put her key in the door and opened the inner door to the hall, lighted by a lamp on a side table—a handsome marble-topped nineteenth-century piece which, sadly, her grandfather was unable to sell since it was all part and parcel of the family arrangement...

There was a rather grand staircase at the end of the hall and doors on either side, but she passed them and went through the green baize door at the end of the hall and down the small staircase to the basement.

The kitchen was large with a large old-fashioned dresser along one wall, a scrubbed table at its centre and a Rayburn cooker, very much the worse for wear. But it was warm and something smelled delicious.

Eulalia wrinkled her beautiful nose. 'Toad-in-the-hole? Roasted onions?'

The small round woman peeling apples at the table turned to look at her.

'There you are, Miss Lally. The kettle's on the boil; I'll make you a nice cup of tea in a couple of shakes. The Colonel had his two hours ago.'

'I'll take a cup of tea with me, Jane; he'll be wanting his whisky. Then I'll come and give you a hand.'

She poured her own tea, and put a mug beside Jane. 'Has Grandfather had a good day?'

'He had a letter that upset him, Miss Lally.' Jane's nice elderly face looked worried. 'You know how it is; something bothers him and he gets that upset.'

'I'll go and sit with him for a bit.' Eulalia swallowed the rest of her tea, paused to stroke Dickens, the cat, asleep by the stove, and made her way upstairs.

The Colonel had a room on the first floor of the house at the front. It was a handsome apartment furnished with heavy mahogany pieces of the Victorian period. They had been his grandparents' and although the other rooms were furnished mostly with Regency pieces he loved the solid bulk of wardrobe, dressing table and vast tallboy.

He was sitting in his chair by the gas fire, reading, when she tapped on the door and went in.

He turned his bony old face with its formidable nose towards her and put his book down. 'Lally— jut in time to pour my whisky. Come and sit down and tell me about your day.'

She gave him his drink and sat down on a cross-framed stool, its tapestry almost threadbare, and gave him a light-hearted account of it, making much of its lighter moments. But although he chuckled from time to time he was unusually silent, so that presently she asked, 'Something's wrong, Grandfather?'

'Nothing for you to worry your pretty head about, Lally. Stocks and shares aren't a woman's business and it is merely a temporary setback.'

Lally murmured soothingly. Grandfather belonged to the generation which considered that women had nothing to do with a man's world, and it was rather late in the day to argue with him about that.

She said cheerfully into the little silence, 'Jane

and I were only saying this morning that it was a waste of gas and electricity keeping the drawing room open. I never go in there, and if anyone comes to call we can use the morning room...'

'I'll not have you living in the kitchen,' said the Colonel tetchily.

'Well, of course not,' agreed Lally cheerfully, and thought how easy it was to tell fibs once she got started. 'But you must agree that the drawing room takes a lot of time to get warm even with the central heating on all day. We could cut it down for a few hours.'

He agreed reluctantly and she heaved a sigh of relief. The drawing room had been unheated for weeks and so, in fact, had most of the rooms in the house; only her grandfather's room was warm, as was the small passage leading to an equally warm bathroom. Lally wasn't deceitful but needs must when the devil drove...

She went back to the kitchen presently and ate her supper with Jane while they planned and plotted ways and means of cutting down expenses.

It was ridiculous, thought Eulalia, that they had to go on living in this big house just because some ancestor had arranged matters to please himself. Her grandfather couldn't even let it to anyone; he must live in it until he died and pass it on to a nephew who lived on the other side of the world. The family solicitor had done his best but the law, however quaint, was the law. Trusts, however ancient, couldn't be overset unless one was prepared to spend a great deal of money and probably years of learned arguing...

Eulalia ate her supper, helped Jane tidy the kitchen and observed with satisfaction that tomorrow was Saturday.

'I'll get Grandfather into his chair and then do the shopping.'

She frowned as she spoke; pay day was still a week away and the housekeeping purse was almost empty. The Colonel's pension was just enough to pay for the maintenance of the house and Jane's wages; her own wages paid for food and what Jane called keeping up appearances.

What we need, reflected Eulalia, is a miracle.

And one was about to happen.

There was no sign of it in the morning, though. Jane was upstairs making the beds, the Colonel had been heaved from his bed and sat in his chair and Eulalia had loaded the washing machine and sat down to make a shopping list. Breast of chicken for the Colonel, macaroni cheese for Jane and herself, tea, sugar, butter... She was debating the merits of steak and kidney pudding over those of a casserole when the washing machine, long past its prime, came to a shuddering stop.

Usually it responded to a thump, even a sharp kick, but this morning it remained ominously silent. Extreme measures must be taken, decided Eulalia, and searched for a spanner—a useful tool she had discovered when there was no money for a plumber...

Mr van der Leurs, unaware that he was the miracle Eulalia wished for, paid off his taxi and made his way to the Colonel's house. A man esteemed by the members of his profession, renowned for his brilliant surgery, relentlessly pursued by ladies anxious to marry him, he had remained heart-whole, aware that somewhere on this earth there was the woman he would love and marry and until then he would bury his handsome nose in work. But his patience had been rewarded; one glimpse of Eulalia and he knew that he had found that woman. Now all he had to do was to marry her...

He reached the house and rang the bell and presently the door was opened and Eulalia stood there in a grubby pinny, looking cross. She still had the spanner in her hand, too. He saw that he would need to treat her with the same care with which he treated the more fractious of his small patients.

His 'Good morning' was briskly friendly. 'This is Colonel Langley's house? I wondered if I might visit him? My father was an old friend of his—van der Leurs.' He held out a hand. 'I am Aderik van der Leurs, his son.'

Eulalia offered a hand rather reluctantly. 'Grandfather has talked about a Professor van der Leurs he met years ago...'

Mr van der Leurs watched her face and read her thoughts accurately.

'I'm visiting at St Chad's for a few days,' he told her. 'Mr Curtis mentioned that the Colonel was housebound with arthritis and might be glad to have a visit. I have called at an awkward time, perhaps…'

He must be all right if Mr Curtis knew him, decided Eulalia.

'I think Grandfather would be pleased to see you. Come in; I'll take you to his room.'

She led him across the hall but before she reached the staircase she turned to look at him.

'I suppose you wouldn't know how to make a washing machine start again?'

He had been wondering about the spanner. He said with just the right amount of doubt in his voice, 'Shall I take a look?'

She led him into the kitchen and Mr van der Leurs gave his full attention to the machine just as though it were one of his small patients on the operating table awaiting his skill. After a moment he took the spanner from her hand, tapped the dial very very gently and rotated it. The machine gave a gurgle and when he tapped it again—the mere whisper of a tap—it came to life with a heartening swish.

Eulalia heaved a sigh of relief. 'Thank you very much. How clever of you, but I dare say you know something about washing machines.' She added doubtfully, 'But you're a doctor.'

He didn't correct her. 'I'm glad I could be of

help,' he said, and then stood looking at her with a look of faint enquiry.

She said quickly, 'I'll take you to see Grandfather. He loves to have visitors.'

She took off her pinny and led the way into the hall and up the graceful staircase. It was a cold house—although there were radiators along the walls, none of them gave warmth. Outside the Colonel's door Eulalia stopped. 'I'll bring coffee up presently—you'll stay for that?'

'If I may.'

She knocked and opened the door and then led him into the large room, pleasantly warm with a bright gas fire. There was a bed at one end of the room, bookshelves and a table by the wide window and several comfortable chairs. The Colonel sat in one of them, a reading lamp on the small table beside him, but he looked up as they went in. He eyed Mr van der Leurs for a moment. 'The spitting image of your father,' he observed. 'This is indeed a surprise—a delightful one, I might add.'

Mr van der Leurs crossed the room and gently shook the old hand with its swollen joints. 'A delight for me too, sir; Father talked of you a great deal.'

'Sit down if you can spare an hour. Lally, would you bring us coffee? You have met each other, of course?'

'Yes, Grandpa, I'll fetch the coffee.'

Mr van der Leurs watched her go out of the room. She wasn't only beautiful, he reflected, she was charming and her voice was quiet. He sat down near the Colonel, noting that the radiators under the window were giving off a generous warmth. This room might be the epitome of warmth and comfort but that couldn't be said of the rest of the house.

Eulalia, going back to the kitchen, wondered about their visitor. He had said that he was at St Chad's. A new appointment? she wondered. Usually such news filtered down to the canteen sooner or later but she had heard nothing. In any case it was most unlikely that she would see him there. Consultants came to Outpatients, of course, but their consulting rooms were at the other end and they certainly never went near the canteen. Perhaps he was visiting to give lectures.

She ground the coffee beans they kept especially for her grandfather and got out the coffee pot and the china cups and saucers, and while she arranged them on a tray she thought about Mr van der Leurs.

He was a handsome man but not so very young, she decided. He had nice blue eyes and a slow smile which made him look younger than he was. He was a big man and tall but since she was a tall girl and splendidly built she found nothing unusual about that. Indeed, it was pleasant to look up to someone instead of trying to shrink her person.

She found the Bath Oliver biscuits and arranged them on a pretty little plate and bore the tray upstairs and found the two men in deep conversation. The Colonel was obviously enjoying his visitor and she beamed at him as she handed him his coffee and put the biscuits where her grandfather could reach them easily. She went away then, nursing a little glow of pleasure because Mr van der Leurs had got up when she had gone in and taken the tray and stayed on his feet until she had gone.

Nice manners, thought Eulalia as she went downstairs to have her coffee with Jane.

'I heard voices,' observed Jane, spooning instant coffee into mugs.

Eulalia explained. 'And Grandfather was pleased to see him.'

'He sounds all right. I remember his dad; came visiting years ago.'

'He got the washing machine to go again.'

'That's a mercy. Now, Miss Lally, you do your shopping; I'll hang out the washing—see if you can get a couple of those small lamb cutlets for the Colonel and a bit of steak for us—or mince. I'll make a casserole for us and a pie if there's enough…'

Eulalia got her coat from the hall and fetched a basket and sat down at the table to count the contents of her purse. A week to pay day so funds were low.

'It had better be mince,' she said. 'It's cheaper.' And then she added, 'I hate mince…'

She looked up and saw that Jane was smiling— not at her but at someone behind her. Mr van der Leurs was standing in the doorway holding the coffee tray.

'Delicious coffee,' he observed, 'and I was delighted to meet the Colonel.'

Eulalia got up and turned round to face him. 'Thank you for bringing down the tray. This is Jane, our housekeeper and friend.'

He crossed the room and shook hands with her and smiled his slow smile so that she lost her elderly heart to him.

'Miss Lally's just going to do the shopping,' she told him.

'Perhaps I may be allowed to carry the basket?'

And very much to her surprise Eulalia found herself walking out of the house with him and down a narrow side street where there was a row of small shops, old-fashioned and tucked discreetly behind the rather grand houses.

She asked, 'Don't you have to go back to the hospital? I mean, this is kind of you but you don't have to.'

'It's more or less on my way,' said Mr van der Leurs, and since she was too polite to ask where he was going and he had no intention of telling her she made polite small talk until they reached the shops.

The grocer's was small and rather dark but he sold everything. Mr van der Leurs, without appearing to do so, noted that she bought Earl Grey, the finest coffee beans, Bath Olivers, farm butter, Brie and Port Salut cheese, Cooper's marmalade and a few slices of the finest bacon; and, these bought, she added cheap tea bags, a tin of instant coffee, a butter substitute, sugar and flour and streaky bacon.

It was the same at the butcher's, where she bought lamb cutlets, a chicken breast, lamb's kidneys and then minced beef and some sausages. He hadn't gone into the shop with her but had stood outside, apparently studying the contents of the window. At the greengrocer's he followed her in to take the basket while she bought potatoes and a cabbage, celery, carrots and a bunch of grapes.

'We make our own bread,' said Eulalia, bypassing the baker.

Mr van der Leurs, keeping his thoughts to himself, made light-hearted conversation as they returned to the house. It was evident to him that living was on two levels in the Colonel's house, which made it a sensible reason for him to marry her as quickly as possible. There were, of course, other reasons, but those, like his thoughts, he kept to himself.

At the house he didn't go in but as he handed over the basket he said, 'Will you have lunch with me tomorrow? We might drive out into the country. I find the weekends lonely.'

It was a good thing that his numerous friends in London hadn't heard him say that. He had sounded very matter-of-fact about it, which somehow made her feel sorry for him. A stranger in a foreign land, thought Eulalia, ignoring the absurd idea; he seemed perfectly at home in London and his English was as good as her own.

'Thank you, I should like that.'

'I'll call for you about eleven o'clock.' He smiled at her. 'Goodbye, Eulalia.'

Jane thought it was a splendid idea. 'Time you had a bit of fun,' she observed, 'and a good meal out somewhere posh.'

'It will probably be in a pub,' answered Eulalia.

She told her grandfather when she carried up his lunch.

'Splendid, my dear; he's a sound chap, just like his father was. I've asked him to come and see me again. He tells me he is frequently in England although he has his home in Holland.'

Eulalia, getting the tea later while Jane had a rest, spent an agreeable hour deciding what she would wear. It was nearing the end of October but the fine weather had held although it was crisply cold morning and evening. She decided on a short jacket, a pleated skirt and a silk jersey top, all of them old but because they had been expensive and well cut they presented an elegant whole. He had said that they would drive into the country, which might mean a pub lunch, but if it were to be somewhere grander she would pass muster...

When he called for her he was wearing beautifully cut tweeds, by no means new but bearing the hallmark of a master tailor, and his polished shoes were handmade. Even to an untutored eye he looked exactly what he was—a man of good taste and with the means to indulge it. Moreover, reflected Eulalia happily, her own outfit matched his.

He went to see her grandfather, to spend ten minutes with him and give him a book they had been discussing, and then stopped to talk to Jane, who was hovering in the hall, before he swept Eulalia out of the house and into the dark grey Bentley parked on the kerb.

'Is this yours?' asked Eulalia.

'Yes. I need to get around when I'm over here.' He glanced at her. 'Comfortable? Warm enough? It's a lovely morning but there's a nip in the air.'

He took the M4 out of London and turned off at Maidenhead. 'I thought the Cotswolds? We could lunch at Woodstock and drive on from there. A charming part of England, isn't it? You don't need to hurry back?'

'No. Jane likes to go to Evensong but I expect we shall be back long before then. Do you know this part of England well?'

'Not as well as I should like but each time I come here I explore a little more.'

He had turned off the A423 and was driving along country roads, through small villages and the quiet countryside to stop presently at North Stoke, a village by the Thames where they had coffee at a quiet pub. He talked quietly as he drove, undemanding, a placid flow of nothing much. By the time they reached Woodstock, Eulalia was wishing the day would go on for ever.

The Feathers was warm and welcoming, with a

pleasant bar and a charming restaurant. Eulalia, invited to choose her lunch, gulped at the prices and
then, urged by her companion, decided on lobster
patties and then a traditional Sunday lunch—roast
beef, Yorkshire pudding, roast potatoes, vegetables…and after that a trifle to put to shame any
other trifle. Eulalia finally sighed with repletion
and poured the coffee.

'What a heavenly meal,' she observed. 'I shall
remember it for years.'

'Good. The Cotswolds are at their best in the
autumn, I think.'

He drove to Shipton-under-Wychwood, on to
Stow-on-the-Wold and then Bourton-on-the-Water
where he obligingly stopped for a while so that she
might enjoy its charm and the little river running
through the village. At Burford he stopped for tea
at a hotel in its steep main street, a warm and cosy
place where they sat in a pleasant room by the fire
and ate toasted teacakes oozing butter and drank
the finest Assam tea.

'This is bliss,' said Eulalia, mopping a buttery
mouth. She smiled at him across the little table.
'I've had a heavenly day. Now we have to go back,
don't we?'

'I'm afraid so. I'll settle up and see you at the
car.'

Eulalia, powdering her beautiful nose, made a
face at her reflection.

This has been a treat, she told herself. It isn't
likely to happen again and so I mustn't like him

too much. Even if I were to meet him at St Chad's it wouldn't be the same; he might not even recognise me. He'll go back to Holland and forget me.

It was already getting dusk and this time Mr van der Leurs took the main roads, travelling at a steady fast pace while they carried on an easy flow of small talk. But for all that, thought Eulalia as they were once more enclosed by the city's suburbs, she still knew almost nothing about him. Not that that mattered since she was unlikely to see him again. She hadn't asked him when he was going back to Holland but she supposed that it would be soon.

At the house, he came in with her. They were met by Jane in the hall.

'You'll have had your tea, but the kettle's boiling if you'd like another cup. The Colonel's nicely settled until supper time. I'm off to church.'

She smiled at them both. 'You've had a nice day?'

'Oh, Jane, it was heavenly.'

'I thought it might be. I'll get my hat and coat.'

'I don't suppose you want more tea?' Eulalia asked Aderik.

'I'd love a cup. While you are getting it may I have five minutes with the Colonel?'

'He'd like that. Do you want me to come up with you?'

'No, no. I know my way. I won't stay more than a few minutes.'

He went up the staircase, tapped on the Colonel's door and, bidden to enter, did so.

The Colonel was sitting in his chair doing a jig-saw puzzle but he pushed it to one side when Mr van der Leurs went in.

'Aderik. You had a pleasant day? Where did you go?'

Mr van der Leurs sat down beside him and gave him a succinct account of the day.

'You found Lally good company? She goes out so seldom. Never complains but it's no life for a girl. I do wonder what will happen to her when I am no longer here. She can't stay here—the place has to go to a nephew. A good chap but married with children.'

'Perhaps I can put your mind at rest about that, sir. I intend to marry Eulalia.'

The Colonel stared at him and then slowly smiled. 'Not wasted much time, have you?'

'I'm thirty-eight. Those years have been wasted romantically. I fell in love with her when I first saw her at St Chad's a day or two ago. I see no reason to waste any more time. You have no objection?'

'Good Lord, no. And your father would have liked her, as I'm sure your mother will.' He paused to think. 'She has no idea of your intentions?'

'None.'

'Well, I'm sure you know how you intend to go about that. You have lifted a load off my mind,

Aderik. She's a dear girl and she has a loving heart.'

Mr van der Leurs got up and the Colonel offered a hand. 'You'll stay for supper?'

'No. I think not; enough is as good as a feast. Is that not so?'

The colonel rumbled with laughter. 'You're very like your father. Goodnight, my boy.'

Eulalia was in the kitchen. She and Jane were to have jacket potatoes for their supper but it was hardly a dish to offer to a guest. She hadn't asked him to stay to supper but she expected him to. She made the tea and when he entered the kitchen gave him a worried look.

'Shall we have tea here? Would you like to stay for supper?' She didn't sound at all eager and he hid a smile.

'Thank you but I mustn't stay. I've an appointment this evening. Tea would be fine.'

He drank his tea, waved aside her thanks for her day out, bade her a brisk goodbye and drove himself away. Eulalia shut the door as the Bentley slipped away, feeling hurt and a little peevish. He could at least have waved; it was almost as if he couldn't get away fast enough.

She poured herself another cup of tea. Of course he might be late for his appointment—with a girl? She allowed her imagination to run riot and then told herself sternly to stop being a fool. He was almost a stranger; she had only met him a couple of times; she knew nothing about him... So why was it that she felt so at ease with him, as though she had known him all her life?

If she had hoped to see him at the hospital the next day, she was disappointed. Her journeys into the hospital proper were limited to her visits to the supply department, the general office for requisitioning something for the canteen or taking money from the canteen at the end of the day to one of the clerical staff to lock away, but those trips took her nowhere near the wards and, since she had no idea as to what he actually did, even if she had the opportunity she had no idea where to look for him.

Filling rolls with cheese as the first of the day's patients began to surge in, she told herself to forget him.

Since it was the haematology outpatients clinic the benches were filling up fast. She recognised several of the patients as she poured tea and offered rolls. Anaemia in its many guises took a long time to cure, and if not to cure at least to check for as long as possible...

The clinic was due to start at any moment. She glanced towards the end of the waiting room to the row of consulting rooms and almost dropped the teapot she was filling. Mr van der Leurs, enormous in a white coat, was going into the first room, flanked by two young doctors and a nurse.

'But he's a mister,' said Eulalia to the teapot. 'A surgeon, so why is he at this clinic?' She had picked up quite a bit of knowledge since she had been working at St Chad's, not all of it accurate but she was sure that haematology was a medical field. He had disappeared, of course, and he wouldn't have seen her.

In this she was mistaken.

When the clinic was finally over she was at the back of the canteen getting ready for the afternoon's work and didn't see him leave.

It was six o'clock by the time she had closed the canteen, checked the takings and locked up. She got into her coat, picked up the bag of money and went through to the hospital. The clerk on night duty would lock it away and she would be free to go home. It was a pity that she had seen Mr van der Leurs again, she reflected. It had unsettled her.

She handed over the money and made for the main door. With any luck she wouldn't have to wait too long for a bus and the rush hour was over.

She pushed open the swing doors and walked full tilt into Mr van der Leurs.

He said easily, 'Ah, Eulalia, I was on my way to look for you. I have a book for your grandfather and I wondered if you would like a lift?'

She said slowly, 'I saw you in Outpatients this morning. I thought you were a surgeon—Mr, you know?'

He had taken her arm and was leading her to where the Bentley was parked.

'I am a surgeon, but I do a good deal of bone marrow transplanting and I had been asked to take a look at several patients who might benefit from that.'

He popped her into the car, got in beside her and drove away.

Eulalia said, 'Oh, I see,' which wasn't very adequate as a reply but it was all she could think of, and she answered his casual enquiry as to her day just as briefly; she hadn't expected to see him again and it had taken her by surprise.

He went straight up to the Colonel's room when they reached the house and when he came down again after ten minutes or so she was in the hall. There wasn't a fire in the drawing room. If he accepted her offer of coffee he would have to drink it in the kitchen; the drawing room would be icy…

He refused her offer. 'I'm leaving for Holland in the morning,' he told her, then he smiled down at her, shook her hand, and was gone.

CHAPTER TWO

JANE came to the kitchen door. 'Gone, has he? Well, it was shepherd's pie for supper; I doubt if he would have fancied that. I'll get a tin of salmon in the house; if he comes again, unexpected, like, I can make fishcakes.'

Eulalia said quietly, 'No need, Jane; he's going back to Holland in the morning.'

'You'll miss him...'

'I don't really know him, but yes, I shall miss him.'

Which was exactly what Mr van der Leurs had hoped for.

She was pouring tea for the thirsty queue towards the end of Thursday's afternoon clinic when she looked up and saw him. She put the teapot down with a thump and hoped that she didn't look as pleased as she felt; he had, after all, bidden her goodbye without a backward glance...

The queue parted for him to watch and listen with interest.

'I'll be outside the entrance,' he told her, smiled impartially at the queue and went on his way.

''E was 'ere last week,' said a voice. 'Looking at my Jimmy—ever so nice 'e was, too.'

'A friend of yours, miss?' asked another voice.

'An acquaintance,' said Eulalia in a voice which forbade confidences of any sort, her colour somewhat heightened. The queue dissolved, the last few patients were called, she began to clear up, and presently, the hall empty, Sue and Polly gone, she closed down for the day.

The clerk kept her talking when she took the money to the office. He was an elderly man and night duty was a lonely job and she was too kind and polite to show impatience while he talked. Perhaps Mr van der Leurs would think that she didn't intend to meet him. She hadn't said that she would, had she? And if it had been a casual offer made on the spur of the moment, he might not wait.

He was there, leaning against the Bentley's bonnet, oblivious of the chilly evening. He opened the door for her as she reached him and got in beside her.

'Could we go somewhere for a cup of coffee? I haven't much time...'

'You can have coffee at home—' began Eulalia, and was cut short by his curt,

'There's a café in the Fulham Road; that is the quickest way.'

She said tartly, 'If you are so pressed for time you had no need to give me a lift.'

He didn't answer but drove through the city. The café he ushered her into was small and half empty. He sat her down at a table away from the other customers, ordered coffee and observed in a matter-of-fact voice, 'This isn't quite what I intended but it will have to do. I got held up.'

The coffee came and Eulalia took a sip. 'I thought you were in Holland.'

'I was; I came over on the fast ferry this afternoon. I must go back on the ferry from Dover in a couple of hours' time.'

'You mean you're only here for an hour or two? Whatever for?'

'I wanted to see you and as I'm going to be away for a few days…'

'But you could have seen me at home or at the hospital.'

'Don't interrupt, Eulalia; there isn't time. It is enough to say that I wanted to see you alone.'

He smiled then and sat back, quite at his ease. 'Will you marry me, Eulalia?'

She opened her pretty mouth and closed it again and stared at him, sitting there asking her to marry him in a manner one would use to ask for the sugar.

'No,' said Eulalia.

He didn't look in the least put out. 'There are a dozen reasons why you should say no. Perhaps you will think about them while I'm away and when I see you again we can discuss them.' He smiled at her. 'I shall see you again, you know, and next time we can talk at our leisure. Now I'm afraid I must take you home.'

Eulalia could think of nothing to say; she tried

out several sensible remarks to make in her head but didn't utter them. She could, of course, tell him that she didn't want to see him again but somehow she didn't say so. Later she would think of all kinds of clever replies to make but he wouldn't be there to hear them. And she musn't see him again.

He drove the short distance to the Colonel's house, got out and went with her to the door.

'Well, goodbye,' said Eulalia, and offered a hand.

'Not goodbye; we say *tot ziens*.' He shook her hand briefly and opened the door for her.

As he turned away she asked, 'Where are you going?'

'Albania.'

'But that's… Oh, do take care!'

He stood looking down at her for a moment, his eyes half hidden under their heavy lids. Just for a moment Eulalia had let her heart speak for itself.

Driving down to Dover and once on the other side of the Channel, taking the long road home, Mr van der Leurs allowed his thoughts to dwell on a pleasant future.

October became November and brought cold wind and rain and grey skies, none of which lightened Eulalia's mood. Mr van der Leurs had been gone for a week and she worried about him, and although she told herself that he was old enough and large enough to take care of himself she scanned the papers and listened to the news and wished that there was some way of finding out if he was back home…

The Colonel, expressing a wish to see him again, had to be told.

'He'll be back. Miss him, do you, Lally?'

Arranging his bedside table just so for the night, she admitted that she did, kissed him fondly and bade him sleep well.

The Colonel, waiting for sleep, thought contentedly that he had no need to worry about Lally's future; Aderik would take care of it. He drifted off gently and died peacefully as he slept.

Somehow or other Eulalia got through the next few days. There was a great deal to do—not least the nephew to notify. There were no other family but old friends had to be told, notices printed in *The Times* and *Telegraph*, the bank manager, his solicitor informed, arrangements for the funeral made. The nephew arrived after two days, a middle-aged kindly man who needed to be housed and fed.

There was no question of Eulalia leaving the house until she had made her own arrangements, he told her. He had a wife and four children who would be coming to England shortly but the house was large enough—he had no intention of turning her out of her home. She thanked him, liking him for his concern, and listened politely to his plans. He was an artist of some repute and was delighted to return to London; the house was large enough to house his family in comfort, and there were attics which could be turned into a studio.

His wife and children arrived in time for the funeral so that Eulalia, opening rooms again, getting ready for their arrival, had little time to grieve. After the funeral he would return to sort out his affairs but his wife and children would remain.

Tom and Pam couldn't have been kinder to her, and the children, although circumstances had subdued them, brought the house alive. Somehow, the funeral which she had been dreading turned into a dignified and serene occasion, with the Colonel's old friends gathered there, making themselves known to Tom and Pam, shaking Eulalia by the hand, asking about her job, telling her in their elderly voices that she was a pretty girl and wasn't it time she married.

However, there were still the nights to get through; there was time to grieve then and wonder what the future held for her. She would have to leave the house, of course, despite Pam's kind insistence that she could stay as long as she wanted to. But at least Jane's future was safe; she was to remain as housekeeper.

The Colonel had left Eulalia his small capital— enough to supplement her wages so that she could rent somewhere. But London was expensive; she would have to find somewhere nearer the hospital and even then she would be eating into her bank balance with little chance of saving. Perhaps she should move away from London, find a job in a small town where she could live cheaply...

She was on compassionate leave from her work but she continued to get up early to go down to the kitchen and help Jane. Still in her dressing gown, her hair hanging tangled down her back, she made tea for them both, laid the breakfast table, fed Dickens and cut the bread while Jane made porridge and collected bacon, eggs and mushrooms.

The new owners of the house enjoyed a good breakfast and Jane, now that she had a generous housekeeping allowance, was happy to cook for hearty eaters. After the skimping and saving she and Eulalia had lived with, it was a treat to use her cooking skills once more. And her future was secure. The one thing which troubled her was Miss Lally, brushing aside her worried questions as to where she was to go and how she would manage, assuring her that she would have no trouble in finding a nice little flat and making lots of friends.

She looked across at Eulalia now, a worried frown on her elderly face. She was beautiful even in that elderly dressing gown with her hair anyhow, but she was pale and too thin. She said, 'Miss Lally...' and was interrupted by the front door knocker being thumped.

'Postman's early,' said Eulalia, and went to open it.

Mr van der Leurs stood there, looking larger than ever in the dim light of the porch lamp.

Eulalia stared up at him, burst into tears and flung herself into his arms. He held her close while she sobbed and snuffled into his cashmere overcoat, unheeding of the early morning wind whistling around them. But when she had no more tears, sucking in her breath like a child, he swept her into the house, shut the door and offered her his handkerchief, still with one arm around her.

'Grandfather died,' said Eulalia into his shoulders. 'I'm sorry I've cried all over you but, you see, I didn't know it was you and I was so glad…'

A muddled speech which Mr van der Leurs received with some satisfaction. 'Tell me about it, Eulalia.' He propelled her gently into the kitchen, nodded pleasantly to an astonished Jane and sat Eulalia down at the table.

'You don't object to me coming into your kitchen? Eulalia is rather upset. If I might just stay and hear what has happened…'

'It's a blessing that you've come, sir.' Jane was already pouring boiling water into a teapot. 'You just sit there for as long as you like and don't mind me.'

So he pulled out a chair and sat down beside Eulalia. Nothing would ever dim her beauty, he reflected: tousled hair, pink nose, childish sniffs and wrapped in a garment which he supposed was a dressing gown, cut apparently with a knife and fork out of a sack. He asked quietly, 'When did the Colonel die, Eulalia?'

She gave a final sniff and sipped some tea and

told him. Her voice was watery but she didn't cry again and he didn't interrupt her. Only when she had finished he said gently, 'Go and get dressed, Eulalia. Tell Tom that you are going out to have breakfast with me and will be back later.'

When she hesitated he added, 'I'm sure Jane thinks that is a good idea.'

Jane said at once, 'Just what she needs—to get away from us all for a bit, talk about it, make a few plans.'

She gave Mr van der Leurs a sharp look and he smiled. 'Just so, Jane!'

Lally went to the door. She turned round when she reached it. 'You won't go away?'

He got up and opened the door for her. 'No, I won't go away, but don't be long; I'm hungry.'

A remark which made everything seem perfectly normal. Just as it seemed perfectly normal to find the Bentley outside. It was only as they were driving through the early morning traffic that Eulalia asked, 'How long have you been back?'

'I got to Schiphol late last night, went home and got the car and took the late night ferry from Ostend.'

'But you haven't been to bed. You haven't got to go to St Chad's and work...?'

'No. No, I wanted to see you.'

She said faintly, 'But don't you want to get some sleep?'

'Yes, but there are several things I want to do first. We'll go to Brown's and have breakfast.'

It seemed that he was known there. The door-man welcomed them with a cheerful 'Good morning', summoned up someone to park the car and held the door open for them. It was quiet, pleasantly warm inside and for the moment free of people. They sat at a table by a window and an elderly waiter assured them that the porridge was excellent and did they fancy kedgeree?

It wasn't until they were eating toast and marmalade and another pot of coffee had been brought that Mr van der Leurs made any attempt at serious conversation. Only when she asked him how long he would be in London did he tell her that he would be returning to Holland that evening.

When she protested, 'But you can't—you've not been to bed; you must be tired,' he only smiled.

One or two people had come to eat their breakfasts, exchanging polite 'Good mornings' and opening their newspapers. Eulalia leaned across the table, anxious not to be heard.

'Why have you brought me here?'

'To eat breakfast,' he said promptly, and smiled when she said crossly,

'You know that isn't what I mean.'

He said, suddenly serious, 'You know that if I had known about the Colonel I would have come at once?'

'Yes. I don't know quite how I know that, but I do.'

'Good. Eulalia, will you marry me?'

'You asked me once already…'

'In somewhat different circumstances. Your grandfather knew of my intentions and thought it was a good idea.'

She stared at him. 'After I told you I wouldn't...'

'Yes.'

'You mean you were going to ask me again?'

'Of course.' He sounded matter-of-fact. 'Shall we go for a walk and talk about it?'

When she nodded, he added, 'I'll book a table for lunch here. I'll drive you back on my way to the ferry afterwards.'

It was as if he had lifted all her worries and doubts onto his own shoulders, she reflected.

They walked to Hyde Park. There were few people there: dog owners and joggers and a few hardy souls who had braved the chilly November morning. Mr van der Leurs hardly spoke and Eulalia, busy with her chaotic thoughts, hardly noticed. They had walked the length of the Serpentine before he said, 'It is high time that I married, Eulalia, but until I met you I hadn't given it much thought. I need a wife—a professional man does—but I want a friend and a companion too, someone sensible enough to see to my home, to be a hostess to my friends, and cope with the social side of my life. You know nothing of me but if we marry you may have all the time you wish for to get to know me.'

Eulalia said gravely, 'But doesn't love come into it?'

'Later, and only if you wish it...'

'You mean you would be quite happy to have me as—as a friend until I'd got used to you?'

He hid a smile. 'Very neatly put, Eulalia; that is just what I mean. And now let us look at the practical side. You have no home, no money and no prospects, whereas I can offer you a home, companionship and a new life.'

He stopped walking and turned her round to face him. 'I promise you that I will make you happy.'

She looked up into his face. 'I believe you,' she told him, 'but have you considered that you might meet a woman you could fall in love with?'

'Yes, I have thought about that too. I am thirty-eight, my dear; I have had ample time in which to fall in love a dozen times—and out again.'

'I've never been in love,' she told him. 'Oh, I had teenage crushes on film stars and tennis players but I never met any young men once I'd left school and gone to live with Grandfather. I know almost everyone at St Chad's. But I'm just the canteen lady; besides, I'm twenty-seven.'

Mr van der Leurs restrained himself from gathering her into his arms and hugging her. Instead he said, 'It is obvious to me that we are well suited to each other.'

He took her arm and walked on. Since he was obviously waiting for her to say something, Eulalia said, 'You asked me to marry you. I will.'

And she added, 'And if it doesn't work out you must tell me...'

He stopped once more and this time took her in his arms and kissed her gently, a very light, brief kiss. He said, 'Thank you, Eulalia.'

They walked on again with her arm tucked under his. Presently he said, 'I shall be away for several days after which I can arrange for a day or so to be free. Would you consider marrying by special licence then? I know it is all being arranged in a rush and in other circumstances I wouldn't have suggested it. But I can see no good reason for you to remain any longer than you must at Tom's house. I'm sure he would never suggest that you should leave before you are ready but you can't be feeling too comfortable about it.'

'Well, no, I'm not. Tom is very kind and so is Pam but I'm sure they'll be glad to see me go. I shall miss Jane...'

'Is she also leaving? She may come with you, if you wish.'

'Tom has asked her to stay as housekeeper and she has agreed. She's lived there for years.'

They were retracing their steps. She glanced up at him and saw how tired he was. She said warmly, 'I'll be ready for whatever day you want us to marry. Must I do anything?'

'No... I'll see to everything. If you would give me the name of your local clergyman and his church, as soon as everything is settled I'll let you know.' He added, 'It will be a very quiet wedding, no bridesmaids and wedding gown, no guests...'

'I wouldn't want that anyway. It would be a

sham, wouldn't it? What I mean is we're marrying for…' She sought for words. 'We're not marrying for the usual reasons, are we?'

He reflected that his reasons were the same as any man in love but he could hardly say so. He said merely, 'I believe that we shall be happy together. And now let us go back and have our lunch…'

They had the same table and the same waiter— a dignified man who permitted himself a smile when Mr van der Leurs ordered champagne.

'The lobster Thermidor is to be recommended,' he suggested.

So they ate lobster and drank champagne and talked about this and that—rather like a married couple who were so comfortable in each other's company that there was no need to say much. Eulalia, spooning Charlotte Russe, felt as though she had known Aderik all her life, which was exactly what he had intended her to think. She liked him and she trusted him and in time she would love him but he would have to have patience…

He drove her back to the house presently and spent ten minutes talking to Tom before leaving. He bade Eulalia goodbye without wasting time and drove away, leaving her feeling lonely and all of a sudden uncertain.

'What you need,' said Pam, 'is a cup of tea. We're delighted for you—Tom and I would never have turned you out, you know, but you're young and have your own life and he seems a very nice man. I'm sure you'll be happy. What shall you wear?'

'Wear?'

'For the wedding, of course.'

'I haven't any clothes—I mean, nothing new and suitable.'

'Well, I don't suppose you'll need to buy much; your Aderik looks as though he could afford to keep a wife. Tom told me that his uncle has left you a little money. Spend it, dear; he would have wanted you to be a beautiful bride.'

'But it'll be just us…'

'So something simple that you can travel in and wear later on. You go shopping tomorrow; he might be back sooner than you think and you must be ready.'

So the next morning Eulalia went to the bank and, armed with a well-filled purse, went shopping. It wasn't just something in which to be married that she needed; she was woefully short of everything. She went back at the end of the day, laden with plastic bags, and there were still several things which she must have. But she was satisfied with her purchases: a wool coat with a matching crêpe dress in grey and a little hat in velvet to go with them, a jersey dress, and pleated skirt and woolly jumpers and silk blouses, sensible shoes and a pair of high-heeled court shoes to go with the wedding outfit.

Tomorrow she would get a dressing gown and undies from Marks & Spencer. The question of something pretty to wear in case Aderik took her out for an evening was a vexatious one. She had spent a lot of money and there wasn't a great deal left, not sufficient to buy the kind of dress she thought he might like—plain and elegant and a perfect fit. She had seen such a dress but if she bought it it would leave her almost penniless and she had no intention of asking Aderik for money the moment they were married.

This was a tricky problem which was fortunately solved for her. Tom and Pam gave her a cheque for a wedding present, explaining that they had no idea what to give her. 'I'm sure Mr van der Leurs has everything he could possibly want, so spend it on yourself, Lally.'

It was a handsome sum, more than enough to buy the dress, and what was left over she could spend on something for Aderik and tell him it was from Tom and Pam.

Trying the dress on, Eulalia smiled at her reflection in the long mirror. It was exactly right; the colour of old rose, silk crêpe, its simple lines clinging to her splendid shape in all the right places. Perhaps she would never wear it; she had no idea if Aderik had a social life but it would be there, hanging in her wardrobe, just in case…

She displayed it to Tom, Pam and Jane, and packed it away in the big leather suitcase which had belonged to her grandfather. She was quite ready now. Aderik hadn't phoned or written but she hadn't expected him to do so. He was a busy man; he had said that he would let her know when he was coming and it never entered her head to doubt him.

He phoned that evening, matter-of-fact and casual. He would be with her in two days' time and they were to marry on the following morning and travel back to Holland that evening. 'You are well?' he wanted to know. 'No problems?'

'No, none, and I'm quite ready. The Reverend Mr Willis phoned to say he was coming to see me this evening. I don't know why.'

'I asked him to. I don't want you to have any doubts, Eulalia!'

'Well, I haven't, but it will be nice to talk to him. I've known him a long time.'

'I'll see you shortly. I'm not sure what time I'll get to London.'

'I'll be waiting. You're busy? I won't keep you. Goodbye, Aderik.'

She could have wished his goodbye to have been a little less brisk...

Mr Willis came that evening; they had known each other for a number of years and it pleased her that he was going to marry them. 'I would have liked to have met your future husband before the wedding, Lally, but in the circumstances I quite understand that it is not possible. We had a long talk over the phone and I must say I was impressed. You are quite sure, aren't you? He has no doubts but perhaps you have had second thoughts?'

'Me? No, Mr Willis. I think we shall be happy together. Grandfather liked him, you know. And so do I...'

'He will be coming the day after tomorrow? And I understand you will be returning to Holland on the day of the wedding?'

'Yes, it all seems rather a scramble, doesn't it? But he has commitments at the hospital which he must keep and if we don't marry now, in the next day or so, he wouldn't be free for some time. Tom and his wife have been very kind to me but you can understand that I don't want to trespass on their hospitality for longer than I must.'

'Quite so. Both you and Mr van der Leurs are old enough not to do anything impetuous.'

Eulalia agreed, reflecting that buying the rose-pink dress had been impetuous. She didn't think that Mr van der Leurs had ever been impetuous; he would think seriously about something and once he had decided about it he would carry out whatever it was in a calm and unhurried manner...

Mr Willis went away presently after a little talk with Tom, and Eulalia went upstairs and tried on the pink dress once more...

Mr van der Leurs arrived just before midnight. Tom and Pam had become worried when he didn't arrive during the day but Eulalia was undisturbed. 'He said he would be here today, so he'll come. It may be late, though. You won't mind if I stay up and see him? We shan't have time to talk in the morning.'

So she sat in the kitchen with Dickens for company and everyone else went to bed. She had the kettle singing on the Aga and the coffee pot keeping warm. If he was hungry she could make sandwiches or make him an omelette. The house was very quiet and she had curled up in one of the shabby armchairs, allowing her thoughts to wander.

She had lived with the Colonel ever since she had been orphaned, gone to school, lived a quiet life, had friends, gone out and about until her grandfather had lost most of his money. It had been tied up in a foreign bank which had gone bankrupt. He had then been stricken with arthritis of such a crippling nature that there was little to be done for him. It was then that she had found a job. She supposed that if Aderik hadn't wanted to marry her she would have stayed there for the rest of her working life, living in a bedsitter, unwilling to accept Tom's offer of help.

'I'll be a good wife. It will be all right once I know more about him. And we like each other.' She addressed Dickens, sitting in his basket, and he stared at her before closing his eyes and going to sleep again.

He opened them again at the gentle knock on the door and Eulalia went to open it.

Mr van der Leurs came in quietly, dropped a light kiss on her cheek and put down his bag and his overcoat. 'I've kept you from your bed, but I couldn't get away earlier.'

'I wasn't sleepy. Would you like a meal? Come into the kitchen.'

'Coffee would be fine. I won't stay; I just wanted to make sure that everything was all right.'

She was warming milk. 'Have you got somewhere to stay?'

'Brown's. I'll be at the church at eleven o'clock. I've booked a table at Brown's for all of us afterwards. I arranged that with Tom. We can collect your luggage from here later and be in plenty of time for the evening ferry.'

'And when we get to Holland will you be able to have a few days' holiday?'

'A couple of days. You won't see a great deal of me, Eulalia, but as soon as it's possible I'll rearrange my work so that I can be home more often.'

They sat opposite each other at the table, not saying much. She could see that he was tired and she was pleasantly sleepy. Presently he got up, put their mugs tidily in the sink and went with her to the door, put on his coat and picked up his bag. Then he stood for a minute, looking down at her.

He had no doubts about his feelings for her; he had fallen in love with her and he would love her for ever. Now all he needed was patience until she felt the same way.

He bent and kissed her, slowly and gently this time. 'Sleep well, my dear.'

She closed the door behind him and went up to her room and ten minutes later was asleep, her last thoughts happy ones.

She was wakened by Jane with a breakfast tray.

'Brides always have breakfast in bed, Miss Lally, and Mrs Langley says you are to eat everything and no one will disturb you until you're dressed and ready.'

So Eulalia ate her breakfast and then, since it was her wedding day, took great pains with her hair and her face before getting into the dress and coat, relieved to see that they looked just as nice as they had done when she had bought them. And finally, with the little hat crowning her head, she went downstairs.

They were all there, waiting for her, ready to admire her and wish her well, and presently Pam and Jane and the children drove off to the church, leaving Eulalia and Tom to wait until it was time for him to get his own car from the garage and usher her into the back seat.

'Why can't I sit in the front with you?' asked Eulalia.

'Brides always sit in the back, Lally...'

The church was dimly lit, small and ancient and there were flowers. That much she noticed as they reached the porch. She clutched the little bouquet of roses which Aderik had sent that morning and took Tom's arm as they walked down the aisle to where she could see Mr Willis and Aderik's broad back. There was another man there too. The best man, of course. She dismissed him as unimportant and kept her eyes on Aderik. If only he would turn round…

He did, and gave her a warm, encouraging smile which made everything perfectly all right, and since there was nothing of the pomp and ceremony of a traditional wedding to distract her thoughts she listened to every word Mr Willis said and found them reassuring and somehow comforting. She wondered if Aderik was listening too and peeped up into his face. It was calm and thoughtful, and, reassured, she held out her left hand so that he could slip the ring on her finger.

Leaving the church with him, getting into the Bentley with him, she touched the ring with a careful finger, remembering the words of the marriage service. She had made promises which she must keep…

Mr van der Leurs glanced at her serious face. 'The advantage of a quiet wedding is that one really listens, don't you agree?'

'Yes. I—I liked it.'

'And you looked delightful; I am only sorry that we have to hurry away so quickly. You still have to meet my best man—an old friend, Jules der Huizma. We see a good deal of each other. He's married to an English girl—Daisy—you'll meet her later and I hope you'll be friends.'

'Do they live near you? I'm not sure where you do live…'

'Amsterdam but I was born in Friesland and my

home is there. When I can arrange some free time
I'll take you there to meet my family.'

'It's silly really, isn't it? I mean, we're married
and I don't know anything about you.'

'True, but you know me, don't you, Eulalia?
And that's important.'

She nodded. 'I feel as if I've known you for a
very long time—you know? Like very old friends
who don't often meet but know how the other one
is feeling.'

Mr van der Leurs knew then that he had his
heart's desire, or most of it. Perhaps he wouldn't
have to wait too long before Eulalia fell in love
with him. He would leave no stone unturned to
achieve that.

The luncheon party at Brown's hotel was all that
a wedding breakfast should be—champagne, lobster patties, chicken à la king, sea bass, salads, red
onion tartlets, garlic mushrooms in a cream sauce
and then caramelised fruits and ice cream and finally the wedding cake. When it was cut and
Eulalia and Aderik's health had been drunk, he
made a speech, gave brief thanks and offered regret
that they couldn't stay longer and enjoy their
friends' company. Then the best man, wishing
them well, said he was delighted that he would see
more of them in the future.

He seemed nice, thought Eulalia, and wondered
why his Daisy wasn't with him—she must remember to ask...

Then it was time to go. She was kissed and

hugged and Jane cried a little for they had been through some difficult years together. 'But I'll be back to see you,' said Eulalia. 'Aderik is often over here and I shall come with him.'

She turned and waved to the little group as they drove away. She was leaving a life she knew for an unknown future.

CHAPTER THREE

THEY travelled over to Holland on the catamaran from Harwich and were driving through the outskirts of Amsterdam before midnight. The crossing had been choppy and Eulalia was glad to be on dry land again. The lights of the city were welcoming and she felt a surge of excitement. They hadn't talked much, though Aderik had pointed out the towns they bypassed, but there was no way of seeing them in the dark night.

They had talked about the wedding and he had promised that he would show her as much as possible of Amsterdam before he went back to his usual working day. Now he said, 'I live in the centre of the city; we're coming to a main street—Overtoom—which leads to one of the main squares—Leidseplein—and a little further on I'll turn right onto the Herengracht; that's one of the canals which circle the old part of the city. The house is in a quiet street just off the canal and has been in my family for many years.'

There was plenty to see now. The streets were still bustling with people, cafés were brightly lighted, there were trams and buses and cars. Mr van der Leurs turned into a street running beside a canal bordered by trees and lined with tall narrow houses with steep gables and important-looking front doors.

Eulalia, wide awake by now despite the lateness of the hour, said happily, 'Oh, it's like a painting by Pieter de Hooch...'

'True enough since they might have been painted by him. They knew how to build in those days; all these houses are lived in still.'

He crossed a bridge and turned into a narrow street beside another, smaller canal also lined with trees and a row of gabled houses. The street was short and there was another bridge at its end, too small for cars, spanning yet another canal. It was very quiet, away from the main streets with only the bare trees stirring in the night wind, and as he stopped before the last house Eulalia asked, 'Is this where you live?'

'Yes. Are you very tired? I think that Ko and Katje will be waiting up for us.'

She assured him that she was wide awake as he opened her door and they crossed the street to his front door—a handsome one with an ornate transom above it—and it was now flung open wide as they mounted the two steps from the pavement.

Eulalia hadn't known what to expect. Aderik had scarcely mentioned his home, and she had supposed that it would be a solid, comfortable house, the kind of house she imagined a successful man might live in. But this was something different. She was ushered in and the door was shut behind them before Mr van der Leurs spoke, and that in his own language to the stout, middle-aged man who had admitted them. Then he took her arm. 'Eulalia, this is Ko, who runs our home with his wife. Come and meet everyone.'

She shook hands with Ko who welcomed her in English and then shook hands with his wife, Katje, as stout as her husband, beaming good wishes which Aderik translated. Then there was Mekke, young and buxom, adding her good wishes in hesitant English, and lastly Wim, a small, wizened man 'who has been in the family for as long as I can remember', said Mr van der Leurs. 'He drives the car when I'm not around and sees to the garden.' He looked around him. 'Where is Humbert?'

They had taken the precaution, explained Ko, of putting him in the garden in case *mevrouw* was nervous of dogs.

Aderik looked at her. 'Are you nervous of dogs, Eulalia?'

'No, I like them. May he not come in and meet me? He must be wanting to see you again.'

Ko had understood her and trotted off through a door at the back of the hall.

'Koffie?' asked Katje, and trotted after him, taking Mekke and Wim with her.

Mr van der Leurs turned Eulalia round, unbuttoned her coat and cast it on one of the splendid chairs flanking a console table worthy of a museum.

'Then come and meet Humbert.'

He opened a door and led her into a high-ceilinged room with an ornate plaster ceiling, tall narrow windows and a wide fireplace with a great hood above it. There was a splendid fire burning in the fire basket below, adding its light to the sconces on the walls hung with crimson silk. It was a magnificent room and Eulalia stood in the doorway and gaped at it.

But she wasn't allowed to stand and stare. 'This way,' said Aderik, and crossed the floor to another door at the end of the room, opposite the windows. This led to a little railed gallery with steps down to another room. A library, she supposed, for its walls were lined with shelves filled with books and there were small tables and comfortable chairs. But she had no chance to do more than look around her; the room led into a conservatory with a profusion of greenery and elegant cane furniture, and that opened onto the garden, which was narrow and high-walled and surprisingly large.

The dog that rushed to meet them was large too, a great shaggy beast who gave a delighted bark and hurled himself at his master. Then, at a word from Aderik the dog offered a woolly head for her to scratch. Mr van der Leurs switched off the outside lights and closed the door to the garden, then led the way back to the library, through another door in the further wall. Here there was a veritable warren of small rooms until he finally opened the last door which brought them back into the hall.

'Tomorrow,' he assured her, 'you will be given a leisurely tour of the house. You must be tired;

come and have a drink and something to eat and Katje will take you to your room.'

The Stoelklok in the hall chimed the hour as they went back into the drawing room where, on a small table by the fire, Ko was arranging a tray of coffee and a plate of sandwiches. Eulalia, half asleep now but excited too, drank her coffee, and, suddenly discovering that she was hungry, ate several sandwiches.

'What time do you have breakfast?'

'Since I am free tomorrow and we have all day before us, would half past eight suit you?'

She nodded. 'What time do you usually breakfast?'

'Half past seven. I walk to the hospital. If I have a list it starts at half past eight. If you would rather have your breakfast in bed that can easily be arranged.'

'I've only ever had breakfast in bed this morning and I like getting up early…'

'Splendid.' He got up and tugged the bell-pull by the fireplace and when Katje came said, 'Sleep well, my dear. I'll see you at breakfast.'

Eulalia got up, longing now for her bed. She lifted her face for his kiss, quick and light on her cheek, and followed Katje up the oak staircase to the landing above. It was ringed by several doors and another staircase but Katje led her to the front of the house and opened a door with something of a flourish.

The room was already lighted and heavy brocade curtains were drawn across the windows. There was a pale carpet underfoot and a Georgian mahogany and satinwood four-poster flanked by mahogany bedside tables faced the windows between which was a satinwood table with a triple mirror. There was a tapestry-covered stool before it and there were two Georgian armchairs on either side of a mahogany tallboy.

Eulalia caught her breath at the room's beauty as Katje bustled past her and opened the door in a wall, revealing a vast closet; she could see her few clothes hanging forlornly there; someone had unpacked already. Another door led to a bathroom, which Katje crossed to open yet another door, revealing a second room, handsomely furnished but simple.

Katje trotted back, smiling and nodding, and went away. Eulalia lost no time in undressing and bathing before tumbling into bed. The splendid room must be explored thoroughly but not tonight. She was asleep as her head touched the pillow.

She woke as Mekke was drawing back the curtains; the girl wished her a good morning and put a tea tray beside her. She said in English, 'Breakfast soon, *mevrouw*,' and went away. There was an ornate green enamel and gilt clock on the tallboy striking eight o'clock as she drank her tea.

Eulalia nipped from her bed and dressed quickly in a skirt, blouse and sweater, wasted time hanging out of the window in the cold morning air to view the quiet street outside and the canal beyond, then hurried downstairs. The house was alive with cheerful, distant voices and Humbert's deep bark as she reached the hall, uncertain where to go.

Aderik opened a door and then crossed the hall to her, kissed her cheek and wished her a good morning. 'You slept well? Come and have breakfast.'

He ushered her into a small room, very cosy with a small table laid ready for them, and Humbert came prancing to have his head scratched and grin at her.

Eulalia found her voice. 'What a dear little room. Did I see it last night?'

'We came through it but I doubt whether you saw it; you were asleep on your feet, weren't you?'

He smiled at her and pulled out a chair for her before sitting down himself. 'There's tea or coffee; you must let Ko know which you prefer to have.' He added kindly, 'It's all strange, isn't it? But you'll soon find your feet.'

Eulalia said slowly, 'I have the feeling that I shall wake up presently and find that none of this is happening.'

She buttered toast. 'It all happened so quickly...'

'Indeed it did, but now you can have all the time you want to adjust—it is merely that you will be doing it after we are married and not before. I imagine that you would have given your future a good deal of thought if we had waited to marry. You may still do so, Eulalia, and I hope that if you have doubts or problems you will tell me.'

'Yes, I will but I shan't bother you more than I must for you must be very occupied. What else do you do besides operating?'

'I have an outpatients clinic once a week, ward rounds, private patients at my consulting rooms, consultations—and from time to time I go over to St Chad's and occasionally to France or Germany.'

He saw the look on her face. 'But I am almost always free at the weekends and during the week there is the odd hour...'

Waiting for Eulalia in the hall presently, he watched her coming down the stairs. She was wearing a short jacket and no hat; a visit to a dress shop would have to be contrived; a warm winter coat was badly needed and some kind of a hat. It was obvious to him that his dearest Lally was sorely in need of a new wardrobe. He said nothing; he was a man who had learned when to keep silent. In answer to her anxious enquiry he merely assured her that Humbert had had a long walk before breakfast.

'We will come home for lunch and take him for a walk in one of the parks,' he suggested. 'But now I'll show you something of Amsterdam.'

Mr van der Leurs loved his Amsterdam; his roots went deep for a long-ago ancestor had made a fortune in the Indies—a fortune which his descendants had prudently increased—and built himself the patrician house in the heart of the city. The house in which he had been born and grown to manhood. He had left it for long periods—medical school at Leiden, years at Cambridge, a period of Heidelburg—but now he was firmly established in his profession, making a name for himself, working as a consultant at St Chad's, travelling from time to time to other countries to lecture or examine or attend a consultation.

He wanted Eulalia to love Amsterdam too and, unlike the tours arranged for sightseers, he walked her through the narrow streets away from the usual sights. He showed her hidden canals away from the main *grachten*, old almshouses, houses built out beside the canals so that their back walls hung over the water. He showed her churches, a street market, the flower barges loaded down with colour, gave her coffee in a crowded café where men were playing billiards and the tables were covered with red and white checked cloths, and then wove his way into the elegant streets where the small expensive dress shops were to be found.

Before one of those plate-glass windows he paused.

'The coat draped over that chair…it would suit you admirably and you will need a thick topcoat; it can be so cold here in the winter. Shall we go inside and see if you like it?'

He didn't wait for her to answer but opened the door. Five minutes later Eulalia and he returned to the pavement and this time she was wearing the coat. It was navy blue cashmere and a perfect fit, while on her head was a rakish little beret. The jacket, the friendly saleslady had promised, would be sent to the house.

Eulalia stood in the middle of the pavement, regardless of passers-by. 'Thank you, Aderik,' she said. 'It's the most beautiful thing I've ever possessed.' Her eyes searched his quiet face. 'I—I haven't many clothes and they're not very new.' She looked away for a moment and then gave him a very direct look. 'I hope you're not ashamed of me?'

Mr van der Leurs realised the danger ahead. He said in a matter-of-fact voice, 'You look elegant in anything you wear, my dear, and you are beautiful enough to wear a sack and still draw interested glances. And no, I am not ashamed of you, but I don't want you catching cold when all that are needed are warmer clothes.'

He took her arm and walked on. 'I think that you must get a few things before winter really sets in.'

Put like that, it seemed a sensible suggestion. He glanced down at her face and saw with satisfaction the look of delighted anticipation on it.

They went back to a main street and caught a tram. It was in two sections and both of them were packed. Eulalia stood with his arm around her, loving every minute of it, and then scrambled off when they reached the point where the street intersected the Herengracht. They walked back home from there so that she could find her way back on her own.

They lunched in the small room where they had breakfasted with Humbert sitting between them, happy now that they were home, knowing that presently he would be taken for a walk.

They went to Vondel Park, a long walk which took them past the Rijksmuseum and through a tangle of small streets to the park. Here Humbert raced to and fro while they walked the paths briskly in the teeth of a cold wind.

'Tomorrow we will take the car,' said Mr van der Leurs cheerfully, 'so that you may get a glimpse of Holland. This is not the time of year to see it, of course, but the roads will be empty and we can cover a good deal of ground. You know of St Nikolaas, of course? You must see him with Zwarte Piet riding through the streets. It was once a great day but now we celebrate Christmas much as you do in England. All the same, we exchange small presents and the children have parties.'

He turned her round smartly and started the walk back to the park's gates. 'And after St Nikolaas there will be parties and concerts and the hospital ball and the family coming for Christmas.'

'The family?' asked Eulalia faintly. 'You have a large family?'

'Mother, brother and sisters, nieces and nephews, scattered around the country.'

'You didn't tell me. Do they know you have married me?'

'Yes, and they are delighted. I should have mentioned it; it quite slipped my mind.'

She didn't know whether to laugh or be angry. 'But you should have told me; I might have changed my mind…'

'No, no. You married me, not my family. You'll like them. We don't see much of each other but we like each other.'

'This is a ridiculous conversation,' said Eulalia severely.

He tucked her hand under his arm. 'Yes, isn't it? Let us go home for tea and then I must do some work, much though I regret that. You can make a list of your shopping while I'm doing that and I'll tell you where the best shops are.'

They had tea in the drawing room by the fire— English tea and crumpets.

'Can you get crumpets here?' asked Eulalia, licking a buttery finger.

'There is a shop which sells them, I believe. We don't, as a nation, have afternoon tea, only if we go to a café or tea room.'

'Am I going to find life very different here?'

He thought for a moment. 'No, I think not. You will soon have friends, and there are any number of English living here. I shall take you to the hospital and introduce you to my colleagues there and their wives will invite you for coffee.'

'Oh—but not before I've got some new clothes…'

'No, no. In any case I shall be away for a couple of days next week; I have to go to Rome.'

'Rome? To operate?'

'To examine students. Ko will take care of you.'

He had sounded casual and for some reason she felt hurt. Surely she could have gone with him or he could have refused to go?

An unreasonable wish, she realised.

He went away to his study presently and she found pencil and paper and made a list of the clothes she might need. The list got longer and longer and finally she became impatient with it and threw it on the table by her chair. What was the use of making a list if she had no idea of how much money she could spend?

She curled up in her chair and went to sleep. It had been an active day and, besides that, her thoughts were in a muddle.

When she awoke Aderik was sitting on a nearby chair with Humbert pressed close to him, reading the list.

He glanced at her and finished his reading. 'You will need more than two evening frocks and a good handful of what my sisters call little dresses. There will be coffee mornings and tea parties. You'll need a raincoat and hat—there's a Burberry shop.'

He took out his pen and added to the list. 'If you'd rather not go alone Ko will go with you, show you where the best shops are and wait while you shop.'

'The best man,' said Eulalia. 'You said he had a wife—Daisy...'

'They had a son two weeks ago. When I get back from Rome we'll go and visit them. I dare say she will go shopping with you if you would like that.'

'If she could spare the time, I would.'

'We will have a day out tomorrow, if you would like that, but will you come to church with me after breakfast?'

'Yes, of course I will. Is it that little church we pass on the way here?'

'Yes; there is service at nine o'clock. I think you may find it not so very different from your own church.'

Eulalia, standing beside him in the ancient, austere little church, reflected that he was quite right. Of course she couldn't understand a word but somehow that didn't matter. And afterwards the *dominee* and several people gathered round to meet her, making her feel instantly at home. That Aderik was well liked and respected among the congregation was obvious, and it struck her anew how little she knew about him.

They went back home for coffee and then, with Humbert on the back seat, set off on their tour.

Mr van der Leurs, a man of many parts, had planned the day carefully. He took the road to Apeldoorn and then by side roads to Zwolle and then north for another twenty miles to Blokzijl, a very small town surrounding a harbour on the inland lakes of the region. It was hardly a tourist centre but the restaurant by the lock was famous for its food. He parked the car and as Eulalia got out she exclaimed, 'Oh, how Dutch! Look at the ducks and that little bridge over the lock.'

She beamed up at him. 'This is really Holland, isn't it?'

'Yes. In the summer there are yachts going to and fro and it can be crowded. Would you like to have lunch here?'

'Oh, yes, please…'

They had a table in a window overlooking the lock in a room half full of people, and Eulalia, with one eye on the scene outside, discovered that she was hungry and ate prawns, grilled sole and Charlotte Russe with a splendid appetite, listening to Aderik's gentle flow of conversation, feeling quietly happy.

They didn't hurry over their meal but presently they drove on, still going north in the direction of Leeuwarden, driving around the lakes and then to Sneek and Bolsward before bypassing Leeuwarden and crossing over to North Holland on the other side of the Ijsselmeer. The dyke road was almost empty of traffic, just over eighteen miles of it, and Mr van der Leurs put his well-shod foot down. Eulalia barely had time to get her bearings before they were on land again, and making for Alkmaar.

They stopped for tea then but they didn't linger over it. 'I'm going to take the coast road as far as Zandvoort. If it's not too dark we'll take a look at the sea.'

The road was a short distance from the sea but very soon he turned off to Egmond aan Zee, a small seaside town, very quiet now that it was winter. He parked the car and together they went down to the beach. It was dusk now, with a grey sky and a rough sea. Eulalia could see the sands stretching away north and south into the distance. 'You could walk for miles,' she said, then added, 'I like it; it's lonely…'

'Now it is. In the summer the beach is packed.'

He took her arm. 'Come, it will be dark very soon. We'll be home in half an hour.'

It was quite dark by the time they got home, to sit by the fire and then eat their supper while Aderik patiently answered her questions about everything she had seen during the day.

It was lovely, she reflected, sitting there in the beautiful drawing room with Aderik in his chair and Humbert sprawled between them. Despite the grandeur of the room, she felt as though she belonged. She was sleepy too and presently he said, 'Go to bed, my dear; we've had quite a long day.'

'When do you have to go tomorrow?'

'I must leave the house by half past seven.'

'May I come and have breakfast with you? You won't mind if I'm in my dressing gown?'

'That would be delightful. Shall I tell Mekke to call you at seven o'clock?'

'Yes, please, and thank you for a lovely day.' They went to the door together. 'I feel as though I've been here for years and years.' She gave a little laugh, 'That's silly, isn't it? We've only been married a couple of days.'

He smiled and kissed her cheek. 'Sleep well.'

The house was quiet when she went down in the morning but there were lights on in the dining room and a shaded lamp in the hall. She slid into her chair opposite Aderik, wished him 'Good morning' and told him not to get up. She was wearing the same worthy dressing gown, he saw at once, and her hair was hanging down her back and she was flushed with sleep and very beautiful. He hoped it wouldn't be too long before she fell in love with him...

She asked about his trip and he answered her briefly, promising to phone her that evening. When he got up to go his goodbye was cheerful and brief; nothing of his longing to stay with her showed in his face, which was very calm. She had been happy with him during their two days together: he had seen that in her expressive face—now she would be alone and have time to think about them and realise how happy they had been—and miss him.

It was a gamble, and Mr van der Leurs wasn't a gambling man. But he had faith in his own judgement and a great deal of patience.

He said, 'Ko will take care of you,' and kissed her swiftly, leaving her standing in the hall feeling quite lost.

But not for long. When she came down presently, dressed and ready for the day ahead, Ko was waiting for her. He handed her an envelope and went away to fetch some coffee and she sat down and opened it. There was a great deal of money inside. There was a note too from Aderik. 'Buy as much as you want; if you need more money, ask Ko who will know where to get it.'

She began counting the notes. It seemed like a fortune; she would have to make another list and plan what she could buy. Whatever she did buy would have to be of the best quality. Her coat was of the finest cashmere and she guessed expensive, but Aderik hadn't quibbled over its price. Whatever she bought must match it. She stowed the money away carefully and, seen on her way by a fatherly Ko, left the house.

Years of penny-pinching had taught her to be a careful shopper and that stood her in good stead now, as she stifled an impulse to enter the first elegant boutique she saw and buy everything which might take her fancy. Instead she sought out some of the bigger stores, inspecting their windows, and presently chose one bearing a resemblance to one of the fashion houses in London and went inside.

She had made a wise choice; the underwear department had everything a well-dressed girl would want. She choked over the prices but even though Aderik was never likely to see her purchases she would feel right. And there was no reason why he shouldn't see a dressing gown—she bought a pink quilted silk garment almost too charming to keep hidden in the bedroom and added it to the pile of silk and lace.

When she had paid for them and asked for them

to be delivered to the house, there was still a great deal of money left...

Aderik had told her to buy a Burberry. She found the shop, bought it and added a matching rain hat, paid for those too and arranged to have them delivered. With the bit firmly between her teeth, she went in search of the boutique where Aderik had bought her coat.

The saleslady recognised her at once. She was alone? she enquired of Eulalia. 'Perhaps *mevrouw* is looking for something special to wear of an evening, ready for the festive season?'

'Well, yes, but first I'd like to see some dresses for the day. Thin wool or jersey?'

'I have just the thing.' The saleslady raised her voice and said something unintelligible to a young girl hovering at the back of the boutique, who sped away and returned presently with several dresses.

'A perfect size twelve,' said the saleslady in her more or less fluent English, 'and a figure to make other women envious, *mevrouw*. Try this jersey dress, such a good colour—we call it mahogany— very simple in cut but elegant enough to wear later in the day.'

An hour later, Eulalia left the boutique, considerably lighter in purse but possessed of a jersey dress, a cashmere twin set, a tweed suit, its skirt short enough to show off her shapely legs, a dark red velvet dress which she was advised could be worn on any occasion after six o'clock, and a pleated skirt, all of which would be delivered to the house. She had tried on several evening gowns too, uncertain which to buy. It was the saleslady who suggested that perhaps she might like to return when it was convenient and bring her husband with her.

Eulalia had agreed although she doubted if he would have the time or the inclination to go with her, but at least she could describe them to him and he could advise her.

She went home for her lunch then; tomorrow was another day and she needed to sit down quietly and check her list and count her money. But first of all after lunch she would put on her coat again and go with Ko and Humbert to Vondel Park and walk there for an hour while Humbert nosed around happily.

There weren't many people about when they got there for it was cold and the day was closing in but she enjoyed it; Ko had ready answers to all her questions, giving gentle advice, telling her a little about the household's routine.

'And Katje hopes that you will come to the kitchen when you wish; she is anxious that you should know everything. You have only to say when you wish it.'

'I'd like that very much, Ko. When is the best time? I mean, Katje has her work to do.'

'That is thoughtful of you, *mevrouw*. Perhaps in the afternoon after lunch?'

'Tomorrow? You will be there, Ko, to translate...?'

'Naturally, *mevrouw*. Now it is time for us to return.'

The parcels and boxes had been delivered while they had been in the park; Eulalia had her tea by the fire and then went upstairs and unpacked everything and put them in drawers and cupboards. She would go to bed early, she decided, and try on everything then.

It was as she was sitting in the drawing room with Humbert pressed up against her that she began to feel lonely. The excitement of shopping had kept her thoughts busy all day but now she wished that Aderik was there. Even if he was working in his study, just to know that he was at home would be nice. They really got on very well, she reflected. Of course they had to get to know each other, and since it seemed that he was away from home a good deal that may take some time. In the meantime she must learn her way around and be the kind of wife he wished for. He would be home again tomorrow—late in the evening, he had said, but she would wait up for him as any good wife would.

He phoned later that evening and she gave a sigh of relief at the sound of his voice.

'You have had a happy day?' he wanted to know.

She told him briefly. It would have been nice to have described her shopping to him in some detail but after a day's work he might not appreciate that. 'I've had a lovely day and Ko took me and

Humbert to Vondel Park this afternoon. Have you been busy?'

'Yes. I shall have to stay another day, I'm afraid. I'll ring you tomorrow and let you know at what time I'll be home.'

She tried to keep the disappointment out of her voice. She said, 'Take care, won't you?'

'Yes, and you too. *Tot ziens.*'

It was raining the next morning but that couldn't dampen Eulalia's determination to do some more shopping. In the Burberry and the little hat she went in search of boots and shoes. She had seen what she wanted on the previous day in a shop in the Kalverstraat—boots, soft leather with a sensible heel, and plain court shoes, black, and, since she could afford it, brown as well. She would need more than these but the boots were expensive and she needed gloves...

Her purchases made, she went into a café and ordered coffee and then walked home, getting lost on the way. Not that she minded; she was bound to miss her way until she had lived in Amsterdam for some time. She had a tongue in her head and everyone seemed to speak English...

After lunch she went to the kitchen and sat down at the big scrubbed table with Ko and Katje. It was a room after her own heart, with a flagstone floor, old-fashioned wooden armchairs on either side of the Aga and a great wooden dresser with shelves loaded with china. There were cupboards too and Katje showed her the pantry, the boot room and the laundry and a narrow staircase behind a door in the wall.

It was a delightful room, and she sat there feeling very much at home, realising that it was her home now.

The afternoon passed quickly, looking into cupboards with Katje, going round the house once more, examining piles of linen stacked in vast cupboards, being shown where the keys of the house were kept, the wine cellar, the little room where Ko kept the silver locked up.

She had her tea presently, had a long telephone talk with Tom and Pam and then had her dinner. Aderik had said that he would phone and she went back to the drawing room to wait for his call. When he did ring it was almost eleven o'clock and he had little to say, only that he would be home in the late afternoon.

Eulalia put the phone down feeling let down and then she told herself that she was being a fool. Aderik had probably had a hard day; the last thing he wanted to do was to listen to her chatter. And he was coming home tomorrow.

Just before she slept she decided to wear the jersey dress. 'It will really be very nice to see him again,' she muttered sleepily. 'I hope he feels the same about me.'

She woke in the night with the terrible thought that he might not like having her for his wife after all but in the sane light of morning she had forgotten it.

CHAPTER FOUR

IT WAS wet and cold and very windy in the morning. Eulalia was glad that she had done all the shopping she had planned to do and needed little persuasion from Ko to stay indoors. She peered out at the dismal weather and hoped that Aderik would have a good journey home. It was a pity that he hadn't told her if he was likely to arrive earlier. She got into the jersey dress, did her face with extra care and arranged her hair just so before going to the library to wander round its shelves with Humbert for company. She drank her coffee, going every now and then to look out of the window to see if the Bentley was outside.

There was still no sign of it as she ate her lunch and since sitting around waiting was pointless she set off to explore the house again. This time she went to the very top floor and discovered the attics—two rooms under the gabled roof with tiny windows back and front. They were filled with tables and chairs, old pictures, boxes of china and glass and long-forgotten children's toys. There were great leather trunks too; she hauled on their lids and discovered dresses of a bygone age carefully wrapped in tissue paper.

Someone had left a pinny hanging on a door and

she put it on for the rooms were dusty and sat down on one of the trunks to examine a large box filled with toys, while Humbert, bored, went to sleep on a pile of rugs.

Mr van der Leurs, coming silently into his house, got no further than the hall before Ko came to meet him, took his coat and his overnight case and offered him coffee or a meal. He wanted neither but took his briefcase to his study and asked, '*Mevrouw* is home? It seems very quiet...'

'She was in the library but I believe she went upstairs.' He added, 'Humbert was with her—devoted he is, already.'

Mr van der Leurs went up the staircase; for such a big man he was light on his feet and quiet. He paused on the landing for his ear had caught a faint sound from somewhere above him. He went on up to the next floor and then opened the small door in a wall which led to the narrow stairs to the attics. It was cold up there, for which reason Eulalia had closed the door at the top of the stairs, and as he opened it Humbert hurled himself at him. Mr van der Leurs stood for a moment, the great dog in his arms, staring over his head at Eulalia, getting to her feet, hampered by the armful of dolls she was holding. She put them down carefully, beaming at him.

'Aderik, you're home...' She took off the pinny. 'I meant to be sitting in the drawing room looking welcoming, only you didn't come so I came up here to pass the time and now I'm a bit dusty.'

Words which brought a gleam to his eye but all he said was, 'How very nice you look; is that a new dress?' He crossed the room and kissed her, a friendly kiss conveying nothing of his feelings. 'How delightful it is to be home again.'

'It's almost tea time but would you like a meal? Did you have a good flight and was the visit to Rome successful?'

'Shall we have tea round the fire and I'll tell you about my trip?'

'Oh, please. I'll just put these dolls back…'

They went back down to the drawing room with Humbert at their heels and found Ko arranging the tea tray before the fire. Since Katje had a poor opinion of the meals Mr van der Leurs was offered when he was away from home, there was a splendid selection of tiny sandwiches, hot crumpets in their lidded dish, currant bread and butter and a Madeira cake—Katje considered that she made the finest Madeira cake in Amsterdam.

Over tea and for an hour or more after, he told her where he had been and why, what he had done and where he had stayed. Listening to his quiet voice gave her the pleasant feeling that they had been married for years, completely at ease with each other and like any other married couple.

'I don't need to go to hospital today,' said Aderik. 'Would you like to meet Daisy? Jules will probably be at home too.'

'Yes, please. Jules looked very nice and I'd like to meet Daisy.'

The der Huizmas lived less than ten minutes' walk away and it was bright and cold. Walking through narrow streets, crossing canals by narrow bridges with Humbert walking sedately beside them, Eulalia asked, 'They don't mind Humbert coming too?'

'No, they have a dog—Bouncer; he and Humbert are the greatest of friends.'

As they mounted the steps to the front door Eulalia saw that the house was very similar to Aderik's but she had no time to look around before the door was opened.

'Joop,' Mr van der Leurs greeted the severe-looking man, who stood aside so that they might enter. 'We're expected? Eulalia, this is Joop who runs the house with Jette, his wife.

'My wife, Joop.'

Eulalia offered a hand and watched the severe elderly face break into a smile before he led the way across the hall to a door which was flung open before they reached it.

The girl who came to meet them was small, with no pretensions to good looks, but her smile was lovely.

Aderik gave her a hug and kissed her soundly. 'Daisy, I've brought Eulalia as I promised.' He turned to greet Jules who had followed his wife.

Daisy took Eulalia's hand. 'You're as beautiful as Aderik said you were. I do hope we shall be friends...'

'I'm sure we shall.' Eulalia was kissed in her

turn by Jules who took her coat and hat and urged her into the drawing room. All this while Humbert had been sitting, quivering with impatience, and once in the room he went to greet the rather odd-looking dog who came trotting to meet him. 'Bouncer,' explained Daisy.

Jules added, 'A dog of many ancestors but devoted to all of us as well as Humbert. Come and sit by the fire and tell us what you have been doing since you arrived.'

They talked over their coffee and biscuits and then the two men went to Jules's study and the dogs with them.

'So now shall we go and see Julius? He's three weeks old today. He'll be asleep because I've just fed him. Jules's sister's nanny came to help me for a while but I want to look after him myself—and Jules is marvellous with him.'

She led the way upstairs into a large airy room. There was an elderly woman sitting in a chair knitting who smiled and nodded at them as they went in to bend over the cot.

Julius was sleeping, a miniature of his father, and Daisy said, 'Isn't he gorgeous? We had to call him Julius after Jules's father but it's a nice name, don't you think?'

'Just right for him; he's a lovely boy. You must be so proud of him.'

Eulalia looked at the sleeping baby, thinking she would like one just like him...

Perhaps in a while Aderik would become fond

of her—she knew he liked her otherwise he wouldn't have married her, but he treated her as a dear friend and that wasn't the same. He hadn't mentioned love—it was she who had done that and his answer had been almost casual.

Later, on their way back to the house, Eulalia said, 'They're happy, aren't they? Jules and Daisy—how did they meet?'

'Daisy came to Amsterdam to see about some antiques and fell into a canal, and Jules fished her out—they had met in England at her father's antiques shop but I imagine her ducking started the romance.'

'He must love her very dearly—I mean, I don't suppose Daisy looked too glamorous...'

He said evenly, 'I don't imagine that glamour has much to do with falling in love.'

'Well, no, but I should think it might help...'

Next morning they had breakfast together and he left the house directly they had finished, saying he wasn't sure when he would be home. She decided she would go to the shops and get something to do—knitting or tapestry work. Until she knew some people time would hang heavily on her hands. Of course when Aderik had the time he would introduce her to his family and friends...

A question which was partly settled when he got home that evening.

'It will be the feast of St Nikolaas in a day or two,' he told her. 'You will have seen the shops... St Nikolaas comes to the hospital and perhaps you would like to come and see him? It would be a good opportunity for you to meet some of my colleagues there with their wives and children. It's something of an occasion, especially for the children.'

'I'd like that. What time does he come?'

'Eleven o'clock. I'll come and fetch you about half past ten.' He smiled at her. 'I think you'll enjoy it. The day after tomorrow.'

She saw him only briefly the next day for he left the house directly after breakfast. It was evening before he came home and then after dinner he went to his study. When, feeling peevish, she went to wish him goodnight he made no effort to keep her talking.

At breakfast he reminded her to be ready when he came for her.

'You are sure you want me to come?' She sounded tart and he looked up from the letter he was reading to stare at her.

'Quite sure,' he told her mildly. 'Everyone's looking forward to meeting you.'

Which she decided wasn't a very satisfactory answer.

But she took care to be ready for him and she had taken great pains with her appearance—the new coat, one of the new dresses, the little hat just so on her dark hair, good shoes and handbag. She hoped that she looked exactly as the wife of a respected member of the medical profession should look.

It seemed that she did for when Aderik came into the house he gave her a long, deliberate look and said quietly, 'I'm proud of my wife, Lally.'

She said breathlessly, 'Oh, are you really, Aderik? What a nice thing to say. I'm feeling a bit nervous.'

'No need.' He spoke casually, popped her into the car and drove to the hospital.

Its forecourt was filled with people, mostly children. He parked in the area reserved for the senior consultants and took her into the vast foyer through a side door. There was a crowd round the entrance but there were small groups of people standing and chatting at the back. Eulalia reminded herself that she was no longer the canteen lady and took comfort from Aderik's hand under her elbow and found herself shaking hands with the hospital director and his wife and then a seemingly endless succession of smiling faces and firm handshakes. And Daisy was there with Jules.

'Hello, you do look nice. What did you think of the director and his wife?'

'Friendly; he looks awfully nice and kind and so does his wife.'

'They are. You do know that she is English?' And at Eulalia's surprised look Daisy added, 'Husbands do forget things, don't they? She came over here to nurse, oh, years ago, and they got married and they're devoted to each other. They've got four children, three boys and a girl. Her name's

Christina. She's forty-five. She gives lovely dinner parties and we all like her very much.'

She beamed at Eulalia. 'You will be very happy here and Aderik is a dear. We're all so glad that he's found you. You will get asked out a lot, you know.'

The men had joined them and everyone was moving forward to get a good view. St Nikolaas was approaching; they could hear the children shouting and clapping and a moment later Eulalia saw him seated on his white horse, in his bishop's robes, riding into the forecourt with his attendant, Zwarte Piet, running beside him, the sack into which he would put all the naughty children over his shoulder.

The noise was terrific as he got off his horse and stood in the forecourt, an impressive figure who presently addressed his audience in a long speech. Eulalia didn't understand a word but she found it fascinating and when he had finished clapped and cheered as loudly as anyone there.

St Nikolaas came into the foyer then, making his stately way towards the children's wards. He paused to speak to the director, nodded graciously to everyone as he passed and disappeared into one of the lifts with the director and his wife.

Aderik took her arm. 'He will be about half an hour and then he comes back to the courtyard and throws sweets to the children there. We're going to have lunch now—another opportunity for you to get to know everyone.'

He glanced down at her happy face. 'Enjoying it?'

'Oh, yes. Does he go anywhere else?'

'The other hospitals in Amsterdam. Of course there is a St Nikolaas in every town and village. It's a great occasion for the children for he leaves presents for them by the fireplace in their homes and if a grown-up finds a gift by his plate he mustn't ask who it is from but thank St Nikolaas for it. Now if you're ready we'll go and have lunch.'

A buffet had been set up in the consultants' room, a vast apartment furnished solidly with a great deal of brown leather and dark wood. Chairs and tables had been set up and everybody fetched their food and found places to sit with friends.

Mr van der Leurs piled a plate of food for Eulalia, settled her at a table with Daisy, the casualty officer's wife and two younger doctors, promised to be back shortly and went away. The doctors were friendly, only too pleased to tell her about St Nikolaas and Zwarte Piet, and she began to enjoy herself.

Presently they were joined by an older man who introduced himself as Pieter Hirsoff, one of the anaesthetists. He was charming to Eulalia and she responded rather more warmly than she realised. It was pleasant to be chatted up... When he suggested that she might like to see one of the many museums in the city, she agreed readily. 'But not the Rijksmuseum,' she told him. 'Aderik has promised to take me there.'

'I know just the right one for you—a patrician house furnished just as it was when it was first built. It's on one of the *grachten*. Suppose I come for you tomorrow afternoon? I'm sure you will enjoy it.'

He excused himself then and Eulalia joined in the general talk, wondering where Aderik had got to.

He came presently with Jules. They had been up to their wards, they explained, and St Nikolaas was about to leave.

'I'll drive you home,' he told Eulalia, 'but I must come back here for a while.'

Daisy said quickly, 'Come back with us, Eulalia, and have tea. Jules has to come back here and I'd love a gossip. Aderik can fetch you when he's finished here.'

So Eulalia went back to the der Huizmas' and had tea with Daisy and talked about the morning's events. Baby Julius was brought down to be fed and then lay placidly sleeping on Eulalia's lap while they discussed Christmas.

'We go to Jules's family home and so do the rest of his family. It's great fun. I dare say you'll go to Aderik's family. You haven't met them yet?'

'No. There wasn't much time to arrange anything before we married and Aderik doesn't have much free time.'

'Oh, well,' said Daisy comfortably. 'You'll see

them all at Christmas. Now you've met everyone at the hospital you'll make lots of friends, but I hope we'll be friends, real friends, you and me.'

It was later that evening as Eulalia and Aderik sat together after dinner that she told him she was going to spend the afternoon with Dr Hirsoff.

Mr van der Leurs had been reading his paper, but now he put it down.

'Which museum are you going to?' He sounded only mildly interested, and when she told him he said, 'Ah, yes, an interesting place. You liked him?'

'Yes. He's very amusing and easy to talk to.' She looked up sharply. 'You don't like him?'

'My dear girl, what has that to do with it? You are free to choose your friends and I would never stand in your way. We are both, I trust, sensible people, tolerant of each other's tastes and wishes. I hope you will have a very pleasant afternoon.'

He turned a page and returned to his reading, leaving her seething although she had no idea why she was put out. She knew that their marriage wasn't quite like the normal matrimonial state but surely he should show some interest, concern even, in the friends she made.

Pieter Hirsoff came for her after lunch and, since Aderik had phoned to say that he wouldn't be home until the evening and she had spent the morning painstakingly discussing household matters with Katje and Ko, Eulalia was quite ready to enjoy his company. And he was good company, guiding her expertly through the museum and then suggesting that they might have a cup of tea before he drove her home. He took her to a large hotel on the Leidseplein and ordered tea and cakes, and it wasn't until she told him that she would like to go home that he put a hand over hers on the table and smiled across it at her.

'Eulalia, we must meet again. This afternoon has been delightful. We are two lonely people, are we not? My wife doesn't care to live in Amsterdam and Aderik is so engrossed in his work, I doubt if he is home as often as he might be.'

She was too surprised to speak for a moment. She might be twenty-seven years old but there hadn't been much chance to gain worldly experience behind the canteen counter... She quelled a desire to lean over and box his ears; that would never do! He was a colleague of Aderik's. She said in a matter-of-fact voice, 'I'm sorry you're lonely, but I'm not; I'm very happy. Aderik is a marvellous husband and I love living here. I know I shall make lots of friends—his friends too—and I'm sure you'll be one of them. It was kind of you to take me out and I've enjoyed it but now I really must go home.'

'I hope Aderik knows what a treasure he's married.' They were walking to the car. 'I'm a persistent man, Eulalia.'

In the car she said, 'You're being silly now. Aderik and I have only been married for little more than a week; can you not understand that life for us is perfect?'

Which wasn't quite true but surely she would be forgiven for the lie so that she could convince the man? She had thought she liked him, but now she wasn't so sure...

Mr van der Leurs didn't get home until almost dinner time. He came into the drawing room with Humbert, who had gone into the hall to meet him, and bade Eulalia a cheerful hello.

'Did you enjoy your afternoon with Hirsoff?' he wanted to know.

'Since you ask,' said Eulalia tartly, 'I didn't.'

He handed her a drink and asked, still cheerfully, 'Oh? Why not?'

'He got a bit, well, a bit intense...'

'What did you expect? You're a beautiful young woman. It's only logical that he would chat you up.'

She tossed off her sherry. 'What a simply beastly thing to say. And if you knew that he was that kind of a man, why didn't you tell me not to go out with him?'

He had picked up the first of his letters and slit the envelope carefully before he answered.

'When we married—before we married—I told you that you might have all the time you needed to get to know me and settle into your new life. I hope by now that you know that I meant what I said. The fact that we are married and like each other enough to live together doesn't mean that I have any right to dictate to you.'

'You mean that you would never interfere in anything I might want to do or with the friends that I might make?'

'That is what I mean.'

'You don't mind?' she began angrily, and was interrupted by Ko telling them that dinner was served.

After that there was no chance to go on talking about it. Mr van der Leurs, keeping his thoughts to himself, rambled on about this and that, making it impossible for Eulalia to argue with him. After dinner he told her that he had some phone calls to make and it was an hour or more before he came back to sit by the fire with Humbert at his feet.

Eulalia sat with her newly bought tapestry frame before her, stabbing the needle in and out of the canvas, regardless of the havoc she was making. They were quarrelling, she reflected, or rather she was trying to quarrel; Aderik was being most annoyingly placid. She wondered what she would have to do to ruffle that smooth manner. She couldn't think of anything at the moment so she bade him a chilly goodnight and went to bed, her dignified exit rather spoilt by the kiss he dropped on her cheek as he opened the door for her.

She took a long time to go to sleep. She would have liked someone to confide in but the only person who would have done nicely was Aderik and he, she had to admit, seemed placidly indifferent, rather like an elder brother who didn't want to be bothered but was tolerant of her.

And how absurd, she reflected, half asleep by now, discussing her doubts and worries with the very person who was causing them.

An opinion that was strengthened at breakfast the next morning; Aderik was his usual amiable self but quite clearly he had neither the time nor the inclination to enter into a serious discussion.

He handed her an envelope addressed to them both. 'An invitation to the Christmas ball in a week's time. The invitation was delayed until we returned here but it was taken for granted that we would accept. Send a note to Christina ter Brandt, will you? It's a grand affair…'

'I haven't a dress…'

'Then we will go and buy one. Tomorrow directly after lunch.'

He was looking through his post. 'There are several invitations to dine and here's a letter for you inviting you to have coffee with Christina…'

He added warmly, 'You'll like her: everyone does.' He got up. 'I must go—I've a full day ahead of me so don't expect me until this evening. Why not do some Christmas shopping? Perhaps you can think of something to give Katje—and Mekke is getting engaged. I'll see to Ko.'

'And your family?'

'I'll take a morning off and we'll go shopping together.'

He kissed her cheek swiftly as he went.

Leaving her with a great deal to think about. His family would come to stay at Christmas, he had told her that, but somehow she hadn't thought any more about it. Now Christmas was less than three weeks away; there would be presents to buy and Katje to consult about meals and rooms. She choked back indignation; he had told her so little…

She sought out Ko. 'Christmas,' she said urgently. 'People will be coming to visit. How long do they stay, Ko? And do we have a tree and holly and give presents?'

He assured her that they did. Christmas, he told her in his careful English, had at one time been a rather solemn occasion, more a church festival, while St Nikolaas had been a more important feast. But Holland had adopted many English customs so that there would be turkey and Christmas pudding, a Christmas tree and decorations and the giving of presents.

'You will wish to consult with Katje, *mevrouw*, and decide on menus and beds for the guests. It will be a relief for *mijnheer* that he has you here to oversee the preparations.'

That evening after dinner, sitting comfortably together, it seemed a good time to her to broach the subject of Christmas.

'There is a great deal I need to know,' she began firmly, 'and I would like you to tell me.'

Mr van der Leurs put down his newspapers, the very picture of an attentive husband. 'Such as?'

'Well, your family. How many are coming to

stay and for how long?' A sudden surge of indignation made her voice shrill. 'I know nothing about
them.' She added pettishly, 'Probably they won't
like me.'

Mr van der Leurs, at his most reasonable, observed, 'How can you say that when you haven't
met them?' He saw that she was put out and added
in a quite different voice, 'My mother is the kind
of mother one hugs and kisses and who offers a
cosy shoulder if one wants comforting. My sisters
are younger than I am; Marijka is twenty-eight,
married and has two children—boys. Lucia is
thirty, married, also, with two girls and a boy. Paul
is the youngest, twenty-three, in his last year at
Leiden. He falls in and out of love so often I've
given up trying to remember their names.'

He smiled then. 'Contrary to your expectations,
they will like you and you will like them. They
will come on Christmas Eve and Katje will be able
to advise you as to where they will sleep and so
on. I'll get a free morning and we'll go shopping
together for presents. I believe that you will find it
a Christmas very much like the celebrations in
England.'

She had the lowering feeling that she had been
making a fuss about nothing but there was still
something. 'I have to buy a dress for the ball...'

'Tomorrow afternoon,' he reminded her placidly.

Not a very satisfactory conversation, she reflected; somehow she still felt that she had been making a fuss about nothing.

She went round the house in the morning with Katje, deciding which rooms should be made ready for their guests. There was time enough before Christmas but she wanted everything to be perfect...

Aderik was home punctually for lunch and while she went to put on her outdoor things he took Humbert for a brisk walk.

'And we'll walk too,' he told her. 'It's cold but dry and quicker than taking the car. Where do you want to go first?'

'The boutique where you bought my coat; there were some lovely dresses...'

She spent a blissful hour trying on one gown after another. It was hard to decide and she wanted to wear a dress which Aderik would like. Finally she was left with a choice between a pearl-grey chiffon which fitted perfectly but was perhaps not quite grand enough, and a pale pink taffeta with a square neckline, tiny cap sleeves and a wide skirt. She tried them on again in turn and stood rather shyly while Aderik studied her.

'Have them both,' he decided.

While the saleswoman had gone to supervise their packing, Eulalia said in a whisper, 'But we're only going to one ball...'

'There will be others,' he said. He had got up from the elegant little chair and was wandering around, to stop by a stand upon which a russet velvet dress had been artfully thrown. 'Now, I like that. Will you try it on?'

The saleslady was already at his elbow. 'It is *mevrouw's* size and a perfect colour for her.'

So Eulalia was swept back behind the silk curtains and helped into the velvet dress and, studying her reflection in the long mirror, had to admit that she really looked rather nice in it...

'But when will I wear it?' she wanted to know as they gained the street once more.

'Christmas Day. Now come and help me choose something for my mother...'

Eulalia had coffee with Christina ter Brandt on the following morning. The ter Brandts lived in a large house in a tree-lined road on the outskirts of den Haag. Aderik had told her that when they were first married Duert ter Brandt had been director of the main hospital there but the last few years had seen him holding the same position in Amsterdam. It was more than half an hour's drive between the two cities but neither of them wished to leave their home in den Haag and Duert enjoyed driving.

Aderik had driven her there, going first to the hospital and coming back for her during the morning, and she had worried that he was wasting his time.

'Not when I'm with you, Lally,' he had told her quietly, 'but it might be a good idea if we were to look around for a car for you. Can you drive?'

'No. We never had a car.'

'Then you shall have lessons. I like to drive you myself but there may be occasions when that's not possible.'

He had stayed only a few minutes at the house and Christina had told him that she would be going into Amsterdam to have lunch with Duert and would see Eulalia safely home.

Eulalia enjoyed her morning; Christina was the kind of person one could confide in. Not that she did that but she was sure if she ever needed help or advice Christina would give it without fuss. And during the course of the morning she offered tidbits of information about the small everyday problems Eulalia had encountered.

'Of course Aderik will have told you a great deal but men do tend to overlook the small problems—tipping and tram fares and whether to wear a long or short dress; that kind of thing.'

Which reminded Eulalia to ask about the ball.

'Quite an event,' said Christina. 'Long dresses and any jewellery you can lay hands on...' She glanced quickly at Eulalia's hands, bare save for her wedding ring. 'It's all rather dignified and stately but great fun. You have met quite a few of the wives at the hospital? You'll meet a lot more but you'll only need to smile and murmur. You're rather a nine days' wonder, you know. Aderik's family are coming for Christmas? They always do; they're all delightful so don't worry about meeting them.'

Christina poured more coffee. 'What do you

think of the shops in Amsterdam?' she asked, and the conversation moved on.

She drove Eulalia back presently. 'I don't suppose Aderik will be back for lunch? It's been fun meeting you; you must come again and perhaps we can meet Daisy one morning here and have coffee?'

She drove away and Eulalia, warmed by her friendliness, had her lunch and then sat down to write Christmas cards and make a painstaking list of people for whom she would need to buy presents.

It seemed a good idea to go shopping the next day. Aderik would be away until mid-afternoon but if she had an early lunch she would have time to do at least some of her shopping—the children's presents, perhaps.

She went down to breakfast ready to tell him, to find that he had left the house in the early hours of the morning. An emergency, Ko told her, but he hoped to be home during the afternoon, probably around four o'clock.

So after lunch she set out with her list and a nicely filled purse. She felt at home in the city now although she was familiar only with the main streets. That morning, while she had been in the kitchen, she had told Katje that she was going shopping; it was surprising how well they understood each other as long as they kept their conversation to basics. Mekke had been there too, helping them out when they reached an impasse.

Her English was only a smattering but she was quick to understand and quick to learn.

When Eulalia had mentioned that she wanted to buy toys for the children she had told Eulalia where to go: a large store near the Central Station. *Mevrouw* must take a tram to the station and then walk; the shop was close by and she would find all the toys she could wish for there. She had even drawn a map to make finding it easy.

Eulalia clutched it as she walked to the Leidsestraat and got into a tram. It took her a few minutes to find the street Mekke had written down and when she reached the shop it was packed with people so that it took her longer than she expected to find just what she wanted.

The final purchases made, she glanced at her watch. Aderik would be home in a short while and she wanted to be there. She joined the surge of people leaving the store and started walking briskly, confident of her direction.

She had been walking for several minutes when it dawned on her that she was in a street she didn't know. Somehow she must have missed a turning. Not a serious matter, she told herself, and turned to walk back the way she had come. It was a narrow street and there were few people in it and no shops.

She stopped the first person coming towards her and asked the way; her Dutch was negligible but 'Central Station' and an arm waved enquiringly should be enough. It seemed that it wasn't; she

tried two more people and was about to try again
when the faint drizzle became a downpour. She
was brushed aside; no one wanted to hang around
answering questions in such weather...

There was no shelter and she could hardly knock
on a door, while to try and find her way on her
own was a waste of time... She wasn't the
Colonel's granddaughter for nothing; she walked
on until she saw a telephone box.

It took time to find the right coins and decipher
the instructions, and, although there was no one
about, the street outside, its lights almost obscured
by the rain, looked menacing. She dialled and
heard Aderik's voice.

'It's me. I'm lost and it's raining...'

He was reassuringly calm. 'Do you know the
name of the street?'

'No, it's dark and—and empty.'

Mr van der Leurs, stifling a panic which astonished him, became all at once briskly reassuring.

'You're in a phone box? Tell me the number on
the dial. Did you tell anyone where you were going?'

'Yes, Mekke. To a big toy shop near the station...'

'Stay where you are, Lally. I'll be with you very
shortly.'

'I'm sorry to be a nuisance...' Her voice had a
decided squeak.

'You've been very sensible, my dear; just stay
where you are.'

*   *   *

Mr van der Leurs went into the hall and found Ko. 'Ask Mekke to come here, will you?'

When she came, he asked, 'Mekke, this shop you suggested *mevrouw* should visit—which street?' And when she told him he went on, 'And is there another entrance?'

'Yes, *mijnheer*, at the back of the shop.' She put her hand to her mouth. '*Mevrouw* has lost herself?'

'Only temporarily. Do you know the street? Is there a phone box in it?'

'Yes. Turn left as you leave the shop.'

Mr van der Leurs nodded, whistled to Humbert and went out to his car. The streets were jammed with traffic but he knew a number of back ways...

He slid to a halt by the phone box and got out, opened its door and took Eulalia in his arms.

'My poor dear, you're wet and cold...'

'I was getting frightened too,' muttered Eulalia into his shoulder. 'I don't know why I got lost...'

'There was another entrance at the back of the shop—a natural mistake.'

He gathered up her parcels and shoved her gently into the car. 'Humbert's in the back.'

The car was warm and comfortable and Humbert pushed his woolly head against her shoulder. Eulalia supposed it was relief which made her want to cry. She sniffed away the tears and Aderik, without looking at her, said cheerfully, 'Dry clothes and tea and then you can show me what you have bought.'

CHAPTER FIVE

BACK at the house, Aderik pulled off her wet gloves, took off her coat and gave it to a hovering Ko and tossed her hat into a chair while Katje and Mekke, both talking at once, urged her to get into something warm.

'I'm only a bit wet,' protested Eulalia, and shivered.

'You appear half drowned. Go and get into something dry; your feet are sopping. And don't be long; I want my tea.'

So she went up to her room with an emotional Mekke in attendance, declaring in a mixture of English and Dutch that it was all her fault; she should never have told *mevrouw* to go to that shop. If *mevrouw* caught cold she would never forgive herself...

Ten minutes later Eulalia went back downstairs. Mekke had taken away her wet shoes and damp skirt and she had got into a jersey dress, brushed her hair and done her face, none the worse for her soaking. She had been frightened; she hoped that Aderik hadn't noticed that...

But of course he had.

He was standing with his back to the fire, his hands in his pockets and Humbert lolling beside him, while Ko arranged the tea things on a small round table between the two armchairs drawn up to the blaze.

Eulalia heaved a sigh of contentment; it was lovely to be home and she told him so. 'I'll be more careful next time,' she told him earnestly.

'It's easy to get lost,' he said easily, 'but you will soon find your way around. I must arrange for you to have lessons in Dutch so that you can ask the way. There are parts of Amsterdam where English might not be understood. I'm sorry that you got so wet...'

She had hoped that he might have said more than that; that it had been sensible of her to phone, a word of praise for her good sense and lack of panic, but he began a casual conversation about Christmas, dismissing the whole thing as trivial, reflected Eulalia pettishly.

Mr van der Leurs, watching her expressive face from under his eyelashes, thought his own thoughts and presently asked her if she would like to go shopping with him in the morning. 'I'm free until two o'clock; we might get the family presents bought. You found what you wanted for the children?'

'Yes. I hope they'll do; I mean, I haven't seen the children yet, have I? I don't know what they like.'

He didn't answer that but asked abruptly, 'Are you happy, Eulalia?'

She was too surprised to say anything for a moment. She put down the toasted teacake she was on the point of eating and licked a buttery finger. She said composedly, 'Yes, I am happy. Why do you ask, Aderik?'

'When I asked you to marry me I promised that you could have all the time you needed to get to know me and adjust to a new way of life. Ours was hardly a traditional marriage, was it? There should be time to reflect on the future together before becoming man and wife and I gave you no time for that. You may have regrets or doubts. And I think that you like me well enough to tell me if that is the case?'

She said thoughtfully, 'I don't think I ever had any doubts or regrets. Perhaps I should have thought about it more…but I feel at home here although it's much grander than I had expected. And I miss Grandfather…but we get on well together, don't we? And in a little while, as soon as I've learnt to speak Dutch and become the kind of wife you want…'

'You are the kind of wife I want, Lally. Stay just as you are. Learn to speak Dutch by all means, but don't change.'

He got up and pulled her gently to her feet. 'And now that you are quite certain that you are happy here with me I think that it is time we became engaged!'

He had put his arm around her shoulders and she stared up at him.

'Engaged? But we are married!'

'So now we will be engaged as well.'

He took a little box out of his pocket and opened it. There was a ring inside—diamonds in an old-fashioned gold setting. 'My grandmother's ring—I had it altered to fit your finger.'

He picked up her hand and slipped it above her wedding ring and, before she could speak, bent and kissed her. A gentle, slow kiss which left her with a surge of delight, so unexpected that she lost her breath.

'Oh,' said Eulalia, and kissed him back.

Mr van der Leurs' arms tightened around her for a moment, then he let her go. 'Sealed with a kiss,' he said lightly. 'Now tell me, have you any ideas about these presents?'

Eulalia sat down again, feeling vaguely disappointed, telling herself that she had no reason to be; hadn't Aderik just given her a most beautiful ring? And the kiss—she refused to think about that for the moment. It hadn't been like the other brief kisses he had given her—brief tokens of affection; it had left her feeling unsettled.

Mr van der Leurs, sitting in his chair, Humbert's great head resting on his knee, watched her face, and because he loved her so deeply he guessed her thoughts and was satisfied. A little more time and a lot more patience, he reflected.

They went shopping in the morning and Eulalia, at Aderik's quiet direction, bought silk scarves, exquisite handbags, gloves as supple as velvet, earrings for his mother, thin gold bangles for his sisters, books for his brother, before having a cup of coffee while they decided what to get Katje, Ko and Mekke. Soft fleece-lined slippers for Ko, whose elderly feet would be glad of them at the end of the day, and silk-lined gloves for Katje. As for Mekke—a quilted dressing gown in one of the bright colours she loved…

They went home, well pleased with their purchases, and after an early lunch Aderik left for the hospital, leaving Eulalia sitting at the little writing desk in the small sitting room, carefully writing Christmas cards from the list he had given her. It was a long list, prudently updated from year to year so that all she had to do was copy names and addresses. Tomorrow, she decided, she would buy presents to send to England; the cards she had already sent. And she still had to find a present for Aderik.

The days passed surprisingly quickly, with last-minute presents to buy, Humbert to take for walks, and rather anxious preparations for the ball, now only a day or two away. And Aderik was seldom home before the early evening. So it was all the more delightful when she went down to breakfast on the morning before the day of the ball to be told that he was free until the afternoon and would she like to see more of Amsterdam?

'Not a museum; we'll save those for when we have hours of leisure. Suppose we just walk round some of the older streets? Most of them have little antique or book shops and the small houses are worth seeing.'

It was a day for walking: a cold blue sky, frost underfoot and the city bustling with preparations for Christmas. But the small streets to which Aderik led the way were quiet. The small gabled houses had their doors shut, spotless curtains shrouding their gleaming windows. From time to time they met a housewife, basket on arm, going to the shops, and exchanged good mornings, and they stopped frequently to look in the shop windows.

Eulalia found them fascinating—book shops galore and antiques shops, some with their goods spread out on the narrow pavement. Aderik bought her a small china bowl, patterned in the lavender colour, which was the first Delftware. It had a small chip and a hairline crack yet was none the less expensive, but since she didn't know the price and Mr van der Leurs paid without comment she accepted it with delight.

It was as they were on their way back, going down a narrow lane with a few shops and rather shabby cottages, that Eulalia stopped suddenly before a window. There was a kitten sitting in a cage there, a puny little creature with huge eyes. Attached to the cage was a card with 'Goedkoop' written on it.

Eulalia tugged at Aderik's sleeve. 'How could anyone be so callous?' she demanded. 'Writing "cheap" on that card, just as though the little creature is fit for nothing. And supposing no one wants him? He'll just die.'

Mr van der Leurs looked down at her furious face, flushed with rage, her eyes flashing. She looked so beautiful he could hardly keep his hands off her. He said, 'We want him; he's just the companion Humbert will enjoy.'

The smile she gave him was his reward. 'You'll buy him? I'll look after him; he won't be a nuisance…'

He opened the door and its old-fashioned bell tinkled rustily and an elderly man came through the curtain at the back of the shop. Eulalia couldn't understand what was said; the man sounded apologetic and had a great deal to say while Aderik listened silently. Presently he handed the man some notes and the kitten was fetched out from the window, removed from his cage and transferred to the inside of Aderik's topcoat, and they were ushered out of the shop with some ceremony.

'Oh, Aderik, thank you. I'm sure he'll grow into a splendid cat. That horrible man…'

'He had a so-called pet shop there but is moving away. He sold the animals he had, and the shop, but this small creature for some reason wasn't sold, so he put it in the window as a last hope before being drowned.'

He added, 'Don't be sad; he's going to be our family pet and he's too small to remember his unhappy start. We'll cut through here; there's a shop in the next street where we can buy him a basket and anything else he needs.'

Eulalia was struggling not to cry. She had no reason to do so; the kitten was safe, Aderik had dealt with the unhappy little episode with instant calm; for some reason she realised that was why she wanted to cry. And that was absurd. He was a man of unfailing kindness. She might not know him very well yet but of that she was sure. And she trusted him...

Back at the house the kitten was laid on a clean towel, given warm milk and gently examined. He was in poor shape but Aderik thought that with good food and tender loving care he had a good chance of growing into a handsome cat. All the same, he would take him to the vet when he got home later in the day. So the kitten was settled in the basket Aderik had bought for him, lined with paper and a blanket, before the warm hearth. Humbert, at first doubtful and puzzled, came and sat beside him and presently, to their delight, the kitten crawled out of his basket and curled up between Humbert's paws.

Mr van der Leurs was late home; the bone marrow transplant he had done that afternoon had had unexpected complications and he would have to go back to the hospital later on. Nevertheless he took the kitten to the vet before he sat down to his dinner.

'Nothing wrong with him,' he assured Eulalia.

'He's had his injections and a thorough overhaul; all he needs now is feeding up and warmth.'

'And to be loved,' said Eulalia. 'And he must have a name—an important one to make up for an unhappy start. Something grand...'

They were sitting in the drawing room with Humbert lying on Aderik's feet and the kitten half buried against the great dog's furry chest.

'Ferdinand,' said Eulalia, 'and we can call him Ferdie. Oh, Aderik, I'm so glad you saved him.'

'He's made himself at home; I hear that Katje is mincing chicken and keeping milk warm on the Aga and obviously Humbert is pleased to have him.'

He got up carefully from his chair. 'I have to go back to the hospital. I'll say goodnight, Lally, and see you at breakfast. Ko will see to Humbert and Ferdie.'

He brushed her cheek with a quick kiss, a brief salute which left her feeling lonely. 'How can I possibly feel lonely?' asked Lally of her two companions.

And indeed she had no leisure to feel lonely; the next day was spent attending to Ferdie's needs, taking Humbert for a walk and then getting down to the serious business of dressing for the ball. She had decided on the pink taffeta and when she was finally dressed she had to admit that she really looked rather nice. She had taken pains with her face and her hair, and the fine cashmere shawl which she had had the forethought to buy made a warm and dramatic wrap against the cold night. There remained nothing for her to do but go down to the drawing room and wait for Aderik.

He was late, she thought worriedly; perhaps there had been an emergency which would hold him up for hours, and they might have to miss the first part of the evening, even the whole evening. She sat there trying not to fidget in case it creased her dress, thinking how much she had been looking forward to the ball. She hadn't been to a dance for a long time; she had always refused invitations to the annual dance at St Chad's; she couldn't afford a dress for one thing and for another she had been afraid that no one would dance with the canteen lady... But now she had the right clothes and a husband to partner her, and she very much wanted to dance with Aderik.

She glanced at the clock once more, heard voices in the hall and just had time to compose her features into serenity as the door opened and Aderik came in.

Annoyingly unhurried. Eulalia bit back wifely admonishments to hurry up and change, smiled as though time were of no importance at all, and said, 'Hello, Aderik. Would you like a drink before you change?'

He had shut the door and was leaning against it looking at her.

'Eulalia, you leave me speechless. I was prepared to see an impatient virago hissing at me to hurry up and change and did I know the time?

Instead of which I find a charming vision in pink offering me a drink!'

He crossed the room and pulled her to her feet. 'You look beautiful and that is a most becoming gown.' He held her away so that he could study her at his leisure. 'My enchanting wife,' he said quietly and then dropped her hands and added briskly, 'Give me fifteen minutes,' and was gone...

He was as good as his word and returned the epitome of a well-dressed man with time on his hands.

Eulalia said uncertainly, 'You won't leave me alone, will you?'

He hid a smile. 'No, Lally, although I think that you will have more partners than you will be able to cope with. Shall we go?' When she got up and picked up her wrap, he added, 'Just a moment,' and took a long box from an inner pocket. 'I have never given you a wedding present, have I?'

He took the double row of pearls from the box and fastened it round her neck and bent to kiss her. 'I wanted you to feel free, Lally...'

She knew what he meant; he had wanted her to marry him without any strings attached. She said simply, 'Thank you, Aderik. You are so good to me and thank you for that too.'

She turned to look in the gilt wood mirror above a wall table and put a hand up to touch the pearls. 'They're very beautiful.'

* * *

The ball was being held in the assembly hall of the hospital and the place was packed. The ter Brandts were standing by the doors, shaking hands and exchanging greetings as the guests arrived. Christina kissed Eulalia and said warmly, 'You look lovely; Aderik must be so proud of you. He'll be lucky to have more than two or three dances with you. Daisy and Jules are here already; it's quite a crush but you'll find them when the dancing stops.'

She turned to Aderik and Duert kissed Eulalia's cheek. 'I shall want a dance with you later,' he told her.

They joined the dancers then—they were playing a waltz and she gave herself up to the delight of dancing; it was as though she and Aderik had danced together all their lives and for a moment she was oblivious of anything but his arm around her and her feet following his of their own volition. But presently he said, 'There are many people here whom you met when you came to see St Nikolaas, but you won't remember all of them.'

He was greeting other couples as they danced and she hastened to nod and smile too, feeling shy. When the dance ended and a rather pompous man and his wife approached them, Aderik said, 'You remember Professor Keesman, Eulalia? And his wife?'

Eulalia murmured politely and Mevrouw Keesman said kindly, 'You have met so many new faces, it must be difficult for you. You must come and visit me soon—after Christmas perhaps? I should like that.'

Eulalia barely had time to thank her before Professor Keesman danced her off into a slow foxtrot. He was a short stout man and she discovered quickly that he was self-important too, impressing upon her the high rank of his position in the hospital. She listened politely, making appropriate replies when necessary, thinking that Aderik never boasted about his work, nor did Duert, and she suspected that they were just as important as the professor. She hoped that Aderik wasn't a close friend of the Kessmans; she much preferred Duert and Jules.

But if she didn't much care for the professor there were any number of guests there who professed to be close friends of Aderik. She didn't lack for partners and from time to time she would find him at her elbow introducing her to one or other of them and claiming her for a dance.

They had supper with Daisy and Jules and half a dozen couples who obviously knew each other well and Eulalia got up from the supper table with enough invitations to fill her days for weeks to come. And when they went back into the ballroom Aderik whisked her onto the dance floor.

'Now we can dance together until the end,' he told her. 'My duty dances are done and you have had partners tumbling over each other to get at you; now we can behave like an old married couple and dance together.'

'Oh, yes, please,' said Eulalia. 'I feel so comfortable with you and I've run out of polite small talk!'

'But you are enjoying yourself? You have been much admired.'

'I've had a lovely time. I did my best to behave like a consultant's wife. I hope I didn't let you down. I mean, not remembering names and not being amusing or witty.'

She felt his arm tightening round her. 'My dear Eulalia, do not, I beg you, try to change in any way. You are delightful as you are, restful and soft-voiced and with the happy knack of knowing when to talk and when to keep silent.'

In other words, reflected Eulalia, dull. It was a depressing thought but if that was what he wanted in a wife then she would endeavour to be just that.

Somehow—she wasn't sure why—the pleasures and the excitement of the evening had evaporated. Which was absurd. She had had partners and compliments and there had been young women of her own age only too ready to make friends.

She watched Daisy and Jules dancing together and had a sudden pang of envy. And the ter Brandts, no longer in their first youth but obviously devoted... But of course they're in love, thought Eulalia wistfully.

The ball wound to a close and the guests began a leisurely departure, calling goodnights, stopping to chat with friends before going out into the cold night.

Back home, Aderik said, 'Shall we have a warm drink before we go to bed? Katje will have left something ready for us.'

The kitchen was cosy and neither Humbert nor Ferdie did more than open an eye as they went in.

'Hot cocoa?' suggested Eulalia, and fetched mugs from the dresser and the plate of sandwiches she had asked Katje to make. 'Supper seems a long while ago,' she observed. 'I asked Katje to make them with ham and there's cold chicken...'

'Bless you for being a thoughtful housewife,' said Aderik, and took a huge mouthful before sitting down at the table opposite her. 'What a pleasant way to end the evening.'

He smiled at her. 'And you looked lovely, Lally. I am a very much envied man.'

She thanked him gravely. 'I've never been to a grand ball before; it was exciting.' She put down her mug. 'I think I'll go to bed.'

He got up and went to the door with her. 'Shall we go and buy the Christmas tree in the morning? I've private patients to see in the afternoon but otherwise I'm free.'

'Oh, yes—and a little one for Katje and Ko and Mekke?'

'Of course. We'll go into the country. Goodnight, Lally.'

She went to her bed feeling deprived. A goodnight kiss would have set the seal on the evening.

* * *

It was mid-morning before they set out. Humbert had to have his walk, Ferdie needed to be fed and brushed and made much of and Katje needed to discuss what they should have for dinner that that evening...

'We'll have lunch out,' said Aderik. 'I need to be back soon after one o'clock.'

He drove out of Amsterdam and took the road to Hilversum, some twenty miles away, and then turned off the main road into a narrow country lane running between flat fields. There was wooded country ahead of them and when they reached it there was a small village, well hidden from the road.

Aderik parked by a small farm at the edge of the village and they got out and walked across the yard and round the back to find an old man surrounded by Christmas trees in all shapes and sizes. He shouted a greeting to Mr van der Leurs and came to shake hands and then shake Eulalia's. He had a great deal to say, too, in his gruff old voice, nodding and shaking his head and then leading them among the trees. They chose a splendid one for the house and a small one for the kitchen and Eulalia wandered off, leaving Aderik to pay and talk to the man. Presently he joined her.

'The trees will be delivered in two days' time. They'll be in tubs and his son will bring them and carry them into the house.'

'He'll need a tip? How much do I give him?'

'Ten guilden—I've paid for transport...'

'And a cup of coffee,' said Eulalia, very much the housewife.

Christmas was near now; Eulalia's days were filled wrapping presents, deciding on menus with Katje—a hilarious business with Ko patiently translating the more complicated remarks, although he was quick to tell her that her Dutch was improving each day. And then there was Humbert needing a walk even on a wet day, and Ferdie, still puny but beginning to look more like a kitten should.

There was Daisy to visit too and new-found friends phoning and Christina coming for coffee. Life was perfect, Eulalia told herself, ignoring the thought that all the same there was something not quite right... Perhaps it was because she didn't see much of Aderik: an hour or two in the evening, a brief half-hour at breakfast.

It was Christina who told her that he had agreed to take several teaching rounds. 'And I can't think why,' she added. 'Duert told him that they could be fitted in after the New Year so that he could be free instead of staying at the hospital in the afternoons.' She didn't say any more because she had seen the look on Eulalia's face. Had they quarrelled? she wondered, and dismissed the idea as absurd, sorry that she had said it.

Eulalia tried to forget about it. Aderik had his reasons for wanting to fill his days with work and when he was home he was as kind and friendly to her as he always was—only he was so seldom home...

She told herself she was worrying about nothing and flung herself into the final arrangements for the arrival of their guests.

Paul arrived first on the day before Christmas Eve, breezing into the house just before lunch, clapping Ko on the back, kissing Katje and Mekke, hugging Eulalia, demanding to know where Aderik was. He was almost as tall as his brother and very like him in looks, bubbling over with good spirits.

'I'm not supposed to be here until this evening, am I? But I couldn't wait to meet you. You're even more beautiful than Aderik said. Am I in my usual room? Is lunch at half-past twelve? I'm famished.'

Eulalia liked him. When he was ten years older he would be just like Aderik.

'How much longer will you be in Leiden?' she asked over lunch.

'Another year. I'm qualified but I want to specialise. I'd like to go to England, work in a hospital there and get some experience. Of course I'll never reach the heights Aderik has—he's top of the tree. I only hope I'll be half as good.'

They took Humbert for his walk presently and soon after they got back Aderik came home in time to greet the rest of his family, his arm around Eulalia as he introduced her to his mother who was unexpectedly small and plump with grey hair pulled severely back from a kind face, to his sisters, tall and good-looking, and their husbands and five children.

'It is too bad,' said Mevrouw van der Leurs, 'that you should have to meet all of us at once, and more so since Aderik tells me that you have no family. But we welcome you most warmly, Eulalia, and hope that you will adopt us as your own.' Eulalia, hugged and kissed and made much of, reflected that this was going to be a wonderful Christmas.

And so it was. The children were small enough to believe in Father Christmas and the old house rang with their small voices, and after tea everyone helped decorate the tree, glittering with baubles and with a magnificent fairy doll topping it, and then they all went to the kitchen while Katje and Ko decorated the smaller tree with the children's help.

Since it was Christmas time dinner was served earlier than usual so that the children could stay up for it, and Eulalia, looking round the table, thought how marvellous it was to belong to such a happy family. She caught Aderik's eye, sitting at the head of the table, and beamed at him, and he smiled back briefly as he turned to speak to his mother.

For a moment she felt chilled. But it was impossible to be downcast; Paul took all her attention and when they got up from the table she went upstairs with Lucia and Marijka and helped them put the children to bed. Afterwards they sat and talked over coffee and the delicious little biscuits Katje had made.

Mevrouw van der Leurs declared that she was tired and would go to bed—the signal for everyone else to do the same. Eulalia, kissed goodnight and complimented on the delicious dinner and pleasant evening, was left alone with Aderik, and she asked anxiously, 'Was it really all right? Just as you wanted it?'

'It was perfect, Eulalia.'

'Oh, good. Your mother is a darling, isn't she? And your sisters and brother and the children.' She gave a small sigh. 'They're all so happy.'

'Does that mean that you're not, Lally?'

'No, no, of course not. I was only thinking that I've missed so much. Although Grandfather and Jane were always so good to me.' She added sharply, 'I'm not whinging…'

'No, no; I never thought you were. I'm glad that you do like the family—your family as well as mine.'

'Well, I think it's very nice of them not to mind that you married me in such a hurry.' She got up. 'I'm going to bed. Will you make sure that Ferdie's comfortable when you take Humbert to his basket?'

He went to open the door for her. 'I'm going to the hospital in the morning but I'll be back for lunch. Would you like to go to the midnight service at the English church?'

'Oh, yes. Daisy told me about it. All of us?'

'No, just you and me. The family will go to morning service which will give us the chance to put the presents round the tree.'

Her eyes shone. 'It's like a fairy-tale Christmas,' she told him, and leaned up to kiss his cheek.

Mr van der Leurs went back to his chair. In fairy tales, he reflected, the prince always won the hand of the princess. Which was what he intended to do.

Christmas Eve passed in a happy bustle: last-minute talks with Katje, walking with Paul and the children and Humbert while Lucia and Marijka saw to the children's presents, Ferdie to feed and play with, chatting to her mother-in-law over coffee and then Aderik coming home and the house alive with children's voices. But all five had an early supper and were put to bed and dinner was a leisurely meal with easy talk and a lot of laughter.

The house was quiet when Aderik and Eulalia went out to the car. It was bitterly cold but there were stars and half a moon casting its icy light. The city was thronged with people and although the shops were long since shut their lighted windows rivalled the lighted Christmas trees in the squares. The church was in a small enclosure off Kalverstraat, surrounded by a ring of old houses, and was already almost full. Eulalia saw Christina and Duert ter Brandt almost at once, and then Daisy and Jules.

There was a Christmas tree and holly and flowers and a choir. It was all so English and she felt tears prick her eyelids. The congregation burst into the opening carol and after a moment she joined in.

It took some time to leave the church once the service was over, there were so many people to exchange good wishes with. The streets were quieter now and the shop windows dark, but as they reached the house she could see a glimmer of light through the transom over the door and inside it was warm and very welcoming.

'Coffee in the kitchen if you would like it,' she told Aderik, and went ahead of him to fill the mugs and get it ready.

He came into the kitchen presently, took the mugs from her and set them on the table. 'Happy Christmas, Lally. I'm cheating and giving you your present while we are alone together.'

It was earrings, gold and diamonds with a pearl drop.

Eulalia looked up at him. 'Aderik—they are so very beautiful; I've never seen anything as lovely. Thank you over and over again; you are so good and kind to me.' She kissed his cheek. 'May I try them on now?'

She slipped the hooks into her ears and went to look in the small looking-glass by the dresser, turning this way and that, her eyes shining.

It would be so easy, he thought, watching her, to play on her happiness and gratitude, but that wasn't what he wanted. If she came to love him it had to be of her own free will...

'Could I wear them to breakfast?'

He laughed then. 'Well, perhaps lunch would be a better choice. What dress are you wearing?'

'The russet velvet you chose.' She beamed at him as she sat down to drink her coffee. 'I'm so happy I could burst,' she told him, and presently, her coffee drunk, she wished him goodnight and went off to bed, still wearing the earrings.

Everyone was up early in the morning and breakfast was eaten to a chorus of seasonal greetings. The children could hardly eat for excitement and were presently borne away to church, leaving Aderik and Eulalia to collect up the presents and arrange them round the tree. They went to the kitchen first with the gifts for Katje, Ko and Mekke. Wim was there too, shaking hands and having a great deal to say to Eulalia, who didn't understand a word but made up for that by smiling a lot and looking interested. He was profuse in his thanks for the box of cigars and the envelope Mr van der Leurs gave him and went to sit by the Aga, for he was to spend the day there, joining in the festivities.

The presents arranged, Aderik took Humbert for his walk and Eulalia fetched Ferdie to sit in his little basket in the drawing room and then everyone was back from church to drink coffee.

Eulalia had decided that their traditional Christmas dinner should be eaten at midday so that the children could join in before the presents were handed out. She had taken great pains with the table and on her way upstairs went to check that everything was just so. It looked magnificent with the white damask cloth, silver and sparkling glass. She had made a centrepiece with holly and Christmas roses and gold ribbon and the napkins were tied with red ribbon. She went to her room then, got into the russet velvet dress and fastened the pearls, put in the earrings and went back to the drawing room.

That night curled up in her bed, waiting for sleep, Eulalia re-lived the day. It was one that she would always remember for it had been perfect. Christmas dinner had been a success; the turkey, the Christmas pudding, the mince pies, the wines and champagne had all been praised. And as for the presents, everyone had declared that everything they had received was exactly what they wanted.

She closed her eyes to shut out the thought that she and Aderik had had no time to be together, had exchanged barely a dozen words. If she hadn't been so sleepy she might have worried about that.

In Holland, she had discovered, there wasn't a Boxing Day but a second Christmas Day, only the names were different. The day was spent looking at presents again, going for a walk, playing games with the children and having friends in for drinks in the evening. She spent it being a good hostess, making endless light conversation with Aderik's friends and their wives, trying out her fragmented

Dutch on her sisters-in-law, being gently teased by
Paul and all the while wishing for Aderik's company.

Everyone went home the next day and the house
was suddenly quiet, for Aderik had gone to the
hospital in the early morning. She had slipped
down to sit with him while he had breakfast but
there was no time for a leisurely talk.

'I shall probably be late home,' he'd told her,
getting up to leave. 'I've a list this morning and a
clinic in the afternoon.'

She mooned around the house with Humbert
padding beside her and Ferdie tucked under one
arm. 'I do miss them all,' she told Humbert, and
then changed that to, 'I do miss Aderik.'

It was nearly lunchtime when Ko came looking
for her. He looked so anxious that she said, 'Ko,
what's the matter? Are you ill?'

'*Mevrouw*, there has been a message from the
hospital, from the director. There has been an ex-
plosion in one of the theatres and I am to tell you
not to worry.'

'Aderik,' said Eulalia—and, thrusting Ferdie at
Ko, flew past him and into the hall, to drag on an
elderly mac she kept for the garden. She dashed
out of the house, racing along the narrow streets,
oblivious of the cold rain and the slippery cobbles.
If he's hurt, I'll die, she told herself. She said
loudly, 'Oh, Aderik, I love you. I think I always
have and now perhaps it's too late and how silly
of me not to know.'

She glared at a solitary woman standing in her way and pushed past her. She was sopping wet and bedraggled when she reached the hospital and the porter on duty gave her a shocked look and started towards her, but she flew past him and belted up the stairs to the theatre unit. She had to pause then for the place was thronged with firemen and police and porters carrying away equipment. They were all too busy to notice her. She edged her way through, looking for someone who would know where Aderik was. He might even now be being treated for injuries—or worse, said a small voice in the back of her head.

She was dodging in and out of the various side rooms and then saw the main theatre at the end of the corridor, its doors off the hinges, everything in it twisted and smashed. She slithered to a halt and almost fell over when Aderik said from somewhere behind her, 'My dear, you shouldn't be here.'

She turned on him. 'Why didn't you tell me, phone me? You must have known I'd be half out of my mind. You could have been hurt—killed. I'm your wife.' She burst into tears. 'And it doesn't matter to you but I love you and I really will not go on like this.'

She stopped, aware that she was babbling, that that was the last thing she had meant to say to him. She wiped a hand across a tear-stained cheek and muttered, 'I didn't mean to say that.' She gave a great sniff and said in a small polite voice, 'I hope you haven't been hurt.'

Mr van der Leurs wasted a moment or so looking at her—hair in wet streamers, a tear-smeared
face, in an old mac fit for the refuse bin and thin
slippers squelching water. And so beautiful...!

He removed the wet garment from her and took
her into his arms.

'My darling,' he said gently, 'why do you suppose I married you?'

'You wanted a wife.' She sniffed again.

'Indeed I did. You. I fell in love with you the
moment I set eyes on you at St Chad's. I knew
that you didn't love me, but I was sure that if I
had patience you would find that you love me too.'

'You never said...' mumbled Eulalia.

'I cherished the thought that you would discover
it without any help from me.'

His arms tightened around her. 'I'm going to
kiss you,' he said.

'Oh, yes, please,' said Eulalia.

They stood there, the chaos around them forgotten, watched by silent onlookers: firemen, doctors, police and porters and the odd nurse, all of
them enjoying the sight of two people in love.

THE EXTRA-SPECIAL GIFT

Catherine George

Dear Reader,

In *The Extra-Special Gift*, I invite you to share in my own family Christmas, which takes place in a setting very like the one I describe in the story. Everyone comes home for the festivities, and long-standing traditions are observed in every detail, with log fires (regardless of the temperature outside), and holly, mistletoe and garlands everywhere. My husband insists on buying the tallest Christmas tree he can find as soon as December arrives, and the same winking lights and glittering baubles are hung from it, crowned by the ancient fairy with the tulle skirt, which gets more bedraggled every year.

There may be one or two minor crises in the kitchen, until the chef (yours truly) decides the turkey is done, and the serious business of the day can begin. But afterward comes the reward of watching the delight on faces young and not so young as lovingly chosen Christmas presents are given and received.

If you can find a little time to spare from your own festivities for reading, I hope you enjoy my story. Please look on it as my own "extra-special gift" to you.

Yours sincerely,

Catherine George

CHAPTER ONE

EVERY hotel employee sprang to attention as a commanding male figure, deep in discussion with the younger man hurrying by his side, strode through the crowded, elegant foyer. Lorenzo Forli halted impatiently as his cellphone rang, told his cousin he would join him later, and retired to an alcove.

'Lorenzo, can you talk?' asked an urgent voice.

'Isabella,' he said brusquely. 'What is it? I am very busy, so be quick, please.'

'Jess has gone,' said his sister unhappily. 'She came to see me before she went to the airport.'

Lorenzo Forli stood like a man turned to stone, staring blindly at the chattering crowd of guests making for the hotel restaurant.

'Lorenzo! Are you still there? Listen to me—'

'I am listening,' he said harshly, when he had command of his voice. He breathed in deeply. 'So. My wife has flown to England, to her family, of course. How did she seem, Isabella?'

'Very upset. Though she did not say so, of course. Or tell me why. Jess came to bring presents for everyone, and to apologise for not joining us in Lucca for Christmas. She asked me to say nothing to you. But I could not do this. You had to know.' Isabella hesitated, then blurted, 'What is *wrong* between you two?'

The light of battle gleamed in Lorenzo Forli's eyes. 'Nothing I cannot put right, Isabella, I swear.'

Later that same evening in Friars Wood, their home high above the Wye Valley in England, Tom and Frances Dysart were watching a Christmas concert on television, with the volume turned up to hear the music over the snores of the dog sleeping at their feet. In the kitchen their daughter Leonie, involved in her nightly telephone conversation with her husband, Jonah Savage, was reassuring him that she was fit as a fiddle, the lack of her husband's presence the only thing amiss.

'I've just been up to check on Fenny,' Leonie announced later, coming to join her parents. 'She's sleeping peacefully.'

Her father gently swung her feet up on the sofa. 'I used to do this for your mother,' he said, exchanging a smile with his wife.

'Only by the time I got to Dysart Mark Four I was a lot bigger than you, Leo,' said Frances, chuckling.

'I've still got time to expand yet!'

'How's Jonah?'

'Missing me, he says, but otherwise fine. He'll be here tomorrow afternoon.'

As the three of them settled down to watch the concert the retriever suddenly jumped up, ears cocked expectantly.

'What's up, Marzi?' said Frances. 'Was that the doorbell?'

'Carol singers, probably,' said Tom, and switched off the television so they could listen, but there was no sound. The bell rang again, so impatiently this time that the dog began barking, and Tom hurried out into the hall to investigate.

Frances heard her husband exclaim in surprise, exchanged a startled look with Leonie, then rose quickly as the study door flew open to admit a blonde vision in a creamy wool coat.

'Hi. I'm home for Christmas after all,' said Jessamy Forli, tears glistening in her dark eyes as she threw herself into her mother's arms.

'Get Jess a drink, Dad,' said Leonie, getting up as quickly as her bulk allowed. 'This is obviously an emergency,' she added, trying to calm the excited dog.

But Jess vetoed any alcohol. 'Just tea, please,' she said, sniffing hard. 'How I long for a strong cup of proper tea.'

'I'll go and make it, and take this hound out of here before he wrecks the place,' said Tom, intercepting a look of command from his wife. 'I'll take Jess's luggage up to her room while I'm at it.' Eyeing his younger daughter with deep concern, he went from the room, clicking his fingers for Marzi to follow.

'Now then, Jess,' said Frances without preamble. 'We're delighted to have you home, darling, as you know very well. But you're obviously miserable, and you've come alone. So what's wrong? Have you quarrelled with Lorenzo?'

Jess mopped her eyes with the tissue Leonie handed her. 'We—we had a bit of a disagreement, yes.'

'Before you say another word for heaven's sake let me put this coat away,' said her mother, and relieved her daughter of the garment, her eyes widening as she noted the label. Giving Leonie a look which meant 'find out what's wrong', she left her daughters alone together.

Jess embraced Leonie with care. 'Sorry to spring a shock on you like this, Leo,' she said ruefully, patting her sister's bulge. 'I hope it didn't upset the baby. How are you feeling?'

'The baby's great,' said Leonie impatiently. 'So am I. But you, Signora Forli, are obviously *not* great. So come on. Talk! I thought you were spending Christmas in Lucca with Lorenzo's sister.'

Jess blew her nose again, and sat down with Leonie on the sofa. 'We were. But Lorenzo had to take off for Venice yesterday. Some staffing crisis at his hotel there. Little brother couldn't deal with it, of course—'

'Because Roberto's making for the ski-slopes, as he does every Christmas!'

'Right. Lorenzo not only took off for Venice immediately, he couldn't even promise to join me at Isabella's house before Christmas Day.' Jess stared down at the heavy gold wedding band on her finger. 'Without him our new apartment felt very empty. And lonely. I felt so homesick I told Isabella I couldn't make it for Christmas at her house after all, and came home.'

'How on earth did you get a flight at this time of year?'

'I bought two tickets ages ago.' Jess sighed heavily. 'I wanted to come home for Christmas all along. Lorenzo knew this, but he said it wasn't possible because Roberto had already booked his holiday. Then the crisis blew up at the Forli hotel in Venice, and my husband decided that his hotels are more important than me. So here I am.'

By the time Tom and Frances returned with a teatray Jess was composed enough to repeat the bare bones of her story to her anxious parents, then very deliberately changed the subject to ask for news of her siblings.

'Adam's decided to stay in Virginia for Christmas, Kate's coming home tomorrow, and Fenny's recovering from croup,' Frances informed her.

'She's at the fractious stage now,' said Tom with feeling.

'Poor little thing! Has she been very poorly?' asked Jess with sympathy.

'She had a cough like a sea-lion, and didn't sleep or eat properly for days,' said Frances. 'But she's a lot better now.'

'By the time I was allowed here Fen was really down in the dumps because you and Adam wouldn't be home for Christmas,' said Leonie.

'And Kate's in her bad books because she went off to earn pocket money in a restaurant instead of coming straight home from Cambridge the minute term ended. Fenny can't see why everyone can't be in Friars Wood for Christmas at least, if not the rest of the time.'

'You missed out the worst bit,' said Frances dryly. 'Fen's croup kept her from the school fancy dress party, and her best friend's gone to Grandma's for Christmas.'

'Tragedy!' Jess managed a genuine smile for the first time since her arrival. 'Poor old Fenny.' She paused, and looked from one parent to the other. 'Look, you don't mind my turning up out of the blue like this, do you?'

'My dear child!' said her father. 'Of course we don't mind. I'd rather Lorenzo was with you, naturally—'

'So would I,' she said forlornly.

'In which case isn't it time you rang him to say you've arrived?'

Jess nodded meekly. 'Yes, Dad. I'll do it now.'

Alone in the big kitchen, Jess stood quietly for a moment, soothed by the comforting familiarity of it, then took out her address book and rang the hotel in Venice. Signor Forli, she was informed, had left for Florence earlier.

Florence? Why had he gone back there? To make up with her, perhaps? Jess brightened, and thanked the receptionist politely in Italian which had quickly grown fluent during the months of her marriage. She rang the apartment eagerly, then slumped into a chair, deflated, when she heard Lorenzo's recorded message. The mere sound of his voice sent such a sharp pang of longing through Jess her own voice was off-hand with disappointment as she informed him she was in Friars Wood, and he could ring back there. If he wanted to. Then, in case Lorenzo had gone to look for her at their country home outside Florence, she rang the Villa Fortuna, where Carla the housekeeper assured her that Lorenzo was neither there, nor expected. Finally Jess rang the Forli hotel in Florence, only to be told that her husband had arrived there earlier, but had gone out again. By this time utterly desperate to talk to Lorenzo, Jess told the receptionist there was no message, then went back to the study to join the others.

'Success?' demanded Leonie.

Jess shook her head disconsolately. 'I didn't manage to catch up with Lorenzo to speak to him personally, but I've left messages everywhere to say where I am.'

'Didn't you tell him you were coming here to Friars Wood?' demanded her father.

'No, I didn't.' Jess shrugged. 'He'll find one of my messages somewhere, so he won't be worried.'

'Lorenzo won't worry that this disagreement of yours was serious enough to send you running back home?' demanded Frances.

Jess flushed guiltily. 'I meant that he'll know where I am. If Isabella hasn't told him already. She probably rang him the moment I left her in Lucca.' Which had been part of her reason for calling in on Isabella before going to the airport. Too angry and hurt to contact him herself, Jess had hit on the one sure way to let Lorenzo know as soon as possible what she intended.

'You need something to eat, darling,' said Frances briskly. 'I'll make you some supper.'

'No, thanks, Mother. I'm not hungry.'

'Tell you what,' said Leonie, heaving herself to her feet. 'Mother always makes me a milky drink to take up to bed. You have one too, Jess, and come and drink it with me in my room. I feel a bit weary.'

'Good idea,' said Tom promptly. 'You two go off to bed, and I'll bring the drinks up. But for pity's sake don't wake Fenny. Your mother needs some sleep. She's had some bad nights with Fenny's croup.'

'Quiet as a mouse, I swear,' promised Jess. She gave her parents a hug, then pulled away quickly to hide the tears she'd been battling with ever since her arrival at Friars Wood.

'Mother and Dad are being so good about this,' said Jess thickly, once she was inside Leonie's bedroom with the door firmly closed. 'They must be dying to fire questions at me.'

'If you think I'm going to be so restrained you can think again!' said her sister promptly, and turned her back. 'Undo my zip, please.'

Jess complied, and helped her sister get ready

for bed. When Leonie was propped up against the pillows Jess curled up at the foot, looking at her enviously.

'You look remarkably well, Leo.'

'Probably because I *am* well. No swollen ankles, normal blood pressure. I'm very popular at the Chelsea and Westminster.'

'That's where you're producing Junior?'

Leonie nodded. 'I don't have another clinic there until after Christmas, and the baby's not due for at least three weeks. Even so I had quite a job to persuade Jonah to bring me down here for a few days.'

'I'm sure lots of people managed to produce babies successfully in these parts without the aid of a top London maternity hospital!'

'Of course they do. Jonah worries too much.' Leonie eyed her sister's creamy knit dress with envy. 'Shouldn't you get out of that? It looks frighteningly expensive.'

'I should. And it probably was.' Jess slid off the bed and peeled the clinging knitted fabric over her head, laid it on the back of a chair, then stretched wearily. 'Can I borrow your dressing gown for a minute?'

'You'd better. At the double, too, before Dad gets here with the drinks. You look like something from a girlie magazine, especially now your hair's longer again.'

Jess laughed, and sashayed across the room, model-fashion, in a flesh-tint silk teddy and knee-length suede boots the colour of milk chocolate. After a mocking pirouette she took Leonie's warm wool dressing gown from a hook behind the door, wrapped herself in it, then tugged off the boots and returned to her place at the foot of the bed. 'There. More respectable now?'

Leonie grinned. 'Has Lorenzo ever seen you rigged out like that?'

Jess flushed hectically, glad when her father's entry with a tray spared her a reply.

Frances followed Tom in and gave Jess a commanding look. 'I've made some toast, and I'd like you to eat it, please. And I've put a spot of something lively in your hot milk so you'll sleep. Just honey in yours, though, Leo.'

'Never mind. I'll sneak some of Jess's toast to make up,' said Leonie cheerfully.

After Tom and Frances Dysart had gone off to bed, Leonie fixed Jess with a ruthless eye over her steaming beaker.

'Right, then. What's this disagreement about?'

Jess slid off the bed and helped herself to some toast as a delaying tactic, found she was rather hungry after all, and munched for a while in silence. 'It's just personal stuff, Leo,' she said at last.

'You mean bed?'

'In a way.'

'Tell me to mind my own business, but in the past I got the impression you didn't care much for all that with the men you knew before Lorenzo.'

Leonie smiled cajolingly. 'Surely it's not the same trouble with him, too?'

Jess gave a short, mirthless laugh. 'No. Quite the reverse. We're so compatible in the sex department one touch—one look, sometimes—is all it takes for both of us.'

'So what's the problem?'

Jess sipped her drink, her eyes heavy. 'Lorenzo won't let me *do* anything with my life. A job, I mean. He just wants me to be his wife. For a while, at least. I pleaded to help him in the Florence hotels, use my experience in advertising. But nothing doing.'

'Why? Is it just a macho Italian thing, or does he have another reason?'

'A bit of both, probably. After the disaster of his first marriage, I think he just needs to feel I'm there for him all the time. And I can sympathise with that. But now I've got the new flat in shape the time hangs heavy, Leo. I don't know anyone in Florence other than Roberto. Isabella and her husband live in Lucca.' Jess drank down her hot milk in one draught. 'So here I am, home again. I just hope I don't spoil Christmas for everyone.'

'Of course you won't, silly!' Leonie yawned suddenly. 'Sorry. His nibs in here gets me up in the night a lot. Heigh-ho, the joys of pregnancy. Your turn next!'

Jess fiddled with the sash of the dressing gown. 'Sorry to keep you from your beauty sleep,' she muttered. 'But you were the one wanting answers.'

'I know.' Leonie's eyes narrowed. 'But I didn't get them all, did I? Come on, Jess, tell me what's *really* wrong. I swear I won't tell a soul if that's what you want—' She bit her lip in sudden consternation. 'Don't tell me there's someone else involved!'

'You mean another woman?' Jess shook her head. 'No. Nothing like that. Lorenzo spends every spare minute he can with me, I assure you. Night and day,' she added, smiling crookedly.

'That's a relief.' Leonie eyed her sister searchingly. 'Then it's just the matter of something to do?'

'No. It isn't.' Jess sighed heavily. 'When Lorenzo first asked me to marry him, in the flush of the first careless rapture I told him I'd be happy to have a baby right away.'

'He didn't like the idea?'

'Oh, yes. He was ecstatic at first.' Jess paid minute attention to her fingernails. 'In fact it's only by chance that it didn't happen before we got married.'

'You're so besotted with each other I can well believe it,' said Leonie, with a grin. 'So what went wrong? Lorenzo was in an almighty rush to marry you, heaven knows. He hardly gave you time to draw breath before he whisked you off to Florence.'

'True. But once the ring was on my finger my husband got cold feet.'

'About a baby?'

'Exactly. Right from our wedding night he's—he's made very sure I don't get pregnant,' said Jess, and dashed a tear away with an impatient hand.

'But why, love?'

'Lorenzo had time alone in Italy before we could tie the knot. It wasn't long, but long enough to brood, unfortunately. His first wife died in childbirth, remember. And by then he knew that Fenny was actually our little cousin, and, more to the point, that Dad's sister died soon after she was born.' Jess swiped at the tears beginning to stream down her face in earnest, and Leonie tossed a box of tissues to her. 'I pointed out that Rachel was in her forties, single, very ill, and grieving for her dead lover, and I'm young and healthy and very happily married. There's a big difference.'

'So Lorenzo is afraid to *let* you have a baby,' Leonie said thoughtfully. 'He obviously loves you to bits.'

'I know that,' said Jess indistinctly, and blew her nose hard. 'He loves me and I love him, and in every other way, in spite of differences in nationality and culture, we're very happy together. But he's adamant about a baby yet. And, human nature being what it is, that just makes me want one more. Anyway, the night before he went to Venice I—well, I tried to change his mind. I failed, as usual, lost my temper, and we had a blazing row.' She bit her lip. 'I haven't spoken to him since. I wouldn't answer the phone in the flat when he rang from Venice, kept my cellphone switched off. And to round things off I made use of my own ticket after all and flew home to punish him. But now I just feel childish and spiteful and—and—'

'You wish you'd stayed and made it up,' said Leonie with sympathy.

'Right. Nevertheless, here I am, and here I stay until after Christmas.'

'What happens then?'

'I go back to Florence and make it up with Lorenzo. If he'll have me.' Jess slid off the bed and took off the dressing gown. 'Time I left you and Baby to sleep. I'll make a dash to my room and hope I don't meet Dad on the way. Goodnight, little mother. Sleep well.'

'You get some sleep too,' said Leonie gently. 'And don't worry, Jess. When you go back to Lorenzo he'll be waiting with open arms.'

'I hope and pray you're right.'

After a hasty, silent sprint to her room Jess made quick preparations for bed, then went on tiptoe to peep in at seven-year-old Fenella, who lay breathing deeply, a nightlight illuminating her flushed face. Jess smiled lovingly, pulled the covers up higher, then went back to her room and got into the bed Lorenzo had never yet shared with her. But it felt very cold and lonely just the same. She sat up, took her cellphone from her bag and switched it on. Just in case Lorenzo rang in the night. Though if he hadn't bothered to contact her yet it seemed increasingly likely he had no intention of talking to her at all.

Desolate at the thought, Jess lay on her back in the dark, knowing that sleep would be a long time coming. Every time she closed her eyes she saw Lorenzo's face, and shivered at the thought of their last time together before he'd left for Venice. The part omitted from her account to Leo.

Lorenzo had been so triumphant that night when he'd handed her a large box emblazoned with the name of a world-famous Italian couturier.

'Before I leave I want you to have my special gift in private, *carissima*,' he said, kissing her. 'I thought you might wish to wear this to Isabella's on Christmas Day.'

Jess peeled back layers of tissue to reveal a long, creamy coat and dress knitted from finest cashmere. She gasped in delight, then whirled round and threw her arms round him, reaching up to rain kisses on his face. 'It's a gorgeous present, and much too extravagant, and you shouldn't have, but I just love it.' She narrowed her eyes at him provocatively. 'How can I show my gratitude?'

'I know a way,' said Lorenzo huskily, his arms tightening round her.

'Yes?' she prompted

'Let me see you in the dress!'

Jess laughed and slid away from him to pick up the box. 'Done. I'll take it into the guest room while you get ready for bed. Then I'll give you a fashion show.'

A few minutes later she knocked on the bedroom door. 'Are you ready?'

'Yes—also very impatient,' called Lorenzo, laughing.

Jess sauntered into their room in true catwalk style in high-heeled boots, the long coat over one shoulder, like a hussar's cloak. Lorenzo lay propped up in bed, his hands behind his head as he watched his wife glide round the room, pausing here and there, hip at an angle, her eyes holding his as she laid the coat down on a chair. Then with languorous lack of haste she took the hem of her dress in her hands and drew it little by little up her thighs and over her head until she tossed it at last to join the coat. Jess heard Lorenzo's intake of breath, then stood, hands behind her head, and revolved deliberately in silk teddy and boots and nothing else.

Lorenzo gave a stifled sound and leapt out of bed to crush her to him, and in seconds Jess lay naked beneath him on the bed, exulting as he caressed and kissed her so ravenously they were soon gasping together in a frenzy of mutual desire and she was sure victory was hers. But at the last moment Lorenzo tore himself away.

'Wait!'

'No, *please*,' she begged, and tried to hold him fast, but Lorenzo was adamant, and suddenly Jess slid off the bed and ran for the door.

Lorenzo leapt after her and caught her, holding

her fast against him. 'Where are you going?' he demanded roughly.

'To the guest room,' Jess spat at him. 'And I'm staying there until you come to your senses.'

To her horror Lorenzo's smouldering black eyes iced over, and he released her so suddenly she stumbled. 'Go, then,' he said arrogantly, and, supremely indifferent to his aroused nudity, held the door open for her.

Jess's furious pride left her with no alternative. Blazing with anger, disappointment and sheer sexual frustration she flung away to the guest room and bolted the door behind her as noisily as she could. She fell asleep eventually from sheer exhaustion after crying most of the night. And when she emerged next morning the flat was empty. Lorenzo had left to catch his plane to Venice while she was sleeping. But propped against the coffee pot was a note which said, very simply, *'Ti amo. L.'*

Alone in the dark at Friars Wood, Jess gave a deep, unsteady sigh and turned over to bury her head in the pillow. Lorenzo had no need to write notes to say he loved her. She knew very well that he did. But not enough—or in his eyes too much— to give her the one thing in the world she wanted above all others. His child.

CHAPTER TWO

JESS woke with a start next morning when a slender little figure in jeans and jersey catapulted onto her bed.

'Jess, you came for Christmas after all!' said Fenella Dysart, hugging Jess, her voice still comically gruff from the croup. 'Are you awake?'

'I am now! Hello, poppet, lovely to see you. Are you feeling better?' Jess returned the hug warmly, planted a kiss on each pallid little cheek, then raised a wrist to look at her watch. 'Glory be, Fen, it's late.'

'I know. Mummy said I must wait until you got up, but you were ages and I couldn't any more. Hurry up, I want you to see the Christmas tree. I helped to decorate it.' Fenny slid to the floor, frowning at her sister as Jess got out of bed. 'Why didn't Lorenzo come?'

'He had to work, darling.' Jess blew her nose on a tissue. 'Bother, I think I'm coming down with a cold.' She wasn't. But it was a good excuse for a tear-thickened voice when she realised Lorenzo hadn't rung in the night. 'Have there been any phone calls for me this morning, Fen?'

'Mummy didn't say. But she asked what you wanted for breakfast.'

Jess smiled brightly. 'Just toast and tea, Fen. Tell Mummy I'll have a quick bath, but I'll only be a few minutes, OK?' All of which would pass the time while she waited for Lorenzo to ring. Because after leaving all those messages she could hardly ring Italy again, in case Lorenzo's staff suspected something was wrong.

After Fenny had raced off, Jess hunted out a thick sweater and some old jeans from a drawer, then went to the window to look at the day. Situated between two major rivers, this particular corner of Gloucestershire was subject to a great deal of fog, which had been bad enough the night before for the taxi-driver to crawl from the station to Friars Wood. Today it was even worse.

'Good morning, everyone,' she said, hurrying into the kitchen later. 'Sorry to be so lazy.'

'Did you sleep?' asked her mother.

'Eventually.' Jess patted the frisking dog. 'And good morning to you, too, Marzi. How do you feel today, Leo?'

'Big,' was the terse reply.

'What time's Jonah arriving?'

'This afternoon some time. He's calling in on his parents for lunch first in Hampstead, but he'll make an early start afterwards.'

'Good move in this weather. It'll be crowded on the motorways today.' Jess sat down beside Leonie at the table. 'So what can I do to help today, Mother? I see the decorations are all up—Fen says she helped with the tree. Where is she now?'

'Watching Christmas cartoons on television in an effort to keep her quiet for a bit. She's still below par.' Frances put some fresh toast down beside Jess. 'Eat some of that while I make a fresh pot of tea. If you really want to help, do you fancy braving the fog? I could do with a few last-minute bits and pieces from the shops. Then I can get on with the mince pies.'

'No, you won't, Mother, I can do those,' said Leonie firmly. 'Otherwise you'll fall in your tracks from exhaustion before the big day.'

Frances smiled a little. 'Actually, now Jess is here to keep you company, Leo, I'm skiving off for an hour this afternoon to have tea with the Gibsons. They're staying with Elinor and Miles at Cliff Cottage.'

'Good idea,' approved Leonie. 'You must miss them now they're retired.'

'I do, professionally, too. Either Henry or Mary must have steered the four of you through every childhood complaint under the sun. The new doctors at the practice seem so young!'

'Sign of age, Mother,' teased Jess. 'Which means you can obviously do with an hour off to recharge your batteries, so I'll make dinner tonight. I trust we all like pasta? I'm quite a whizz at it these days. I'll make the sauce when I come back. Dad went into Pennington as usual today, then?' she added quickly, before anyone could ask if Lorenzo approved of her cooking.

'Yes, he did, though in my opinion Dysart's

could have functioned without him for once, even if it is Christmas Eve, but apparently not,' said Frances, bringing the tea. 'I told him to get home before dark. Or else.'

Jess drove off to Chepstow straight after breakfast, proceeding with extra care through the blanketing fog. She went round the crowded shops at top speed with her mother's list, then made a few purchases of her own, grateful for the frantic rush to help block out her worry about Lorenzo.

When she got home the kitchen at Friars Wood was full of tempting, spicy smells. Leonie, looking remarkably energetic, was rolling out pastry and supervising Fenny as the little girl carefully cut circles of it for the pies, and Frances was just finishing off enough herb stuffing to satisfy even Dysart requirements. After the first flare of hope as she went in Jess didn't even ask about a phone call. She handed over her parcels, accepted coffee with enthusiasm, then got down to work. By lunchtime there was still no phone call from Lorenzo, but the turkey was stuffed, brandy sauce made, dozens of mince pies sat cooling on racks, and Jess had made vast quantities of fragrant tomato sauce for the evening's pasta, with enough left over to freeze for another day.

After a snack lunch Frances ordered Leonie off to bed for the daily rest Jonah insisted on. 'You too, Fenny. Then you can stay up later tonight.'

'Come on, Fen,' said Leonie, holding out her hand. 'If you like you can come in my bed while

I read for a bit. And when we get up we'll decorate a little tree in the Stables and put it in Adam's window.'

'But Adam isn't coming home,' said Fenny disconsolately.

'Never mind,' said Frances. 'When he rings he'll be very pleased to hear you did a tree for him in his special place. Think how lovely it will look with all the lights twinkling on it when Daddy and Jonah come up the drive. It'll be the first thing they'll see.'

Since his eighteenth birthday Adam Dysart had occupied a separate establishment, gradually decorated and furnished to his own taste, in the converted stable block adjoining the house. Now twenty-two, with a degree under his belt, these days he was away most of the time, gaining experience in various other auction houses, both in the UK and in America, before joining Dysart's of Pennington, the auction house founded by his great-grandfather.

Later that afternoon, while Fenny and Leonie were decorating the second Christmas tree in the Stables, Jess took Marzi for a long walk round the garden in the freezing fog, shivering as she huddled into her father's sheepskin jacket. Alone, she allowed her cheerful mask to drop, and surrendered to the misery she'd been keeping hidden from the others. Why hadn't Lorenzo *rung*? She trudged on miserably with the dog, switching on her torch as they went through the wood, but at last the chill of the icy fog drove her back towards the welcoming lights of the house. As Jess drew near she saw her mother waving frantically from the kitchen window, and raced into the house with the bounding dog, buoyed up with hope.

'Phone call from Italy. The phone was ringing just as I got in,' said Frances, smiling jubilantly.

Jess grabbed the phone from the hall table, almost dropping it in her haste. 'Hello?' she said breathlessly.

'*Ciao*, Jess, how are you? Could I speak to Lorenzo, *per favore*?'

She went cold with fear. 'Roberto?' She cleared her throat. 'What—what do you mean? Lorenzo isn't here.'

'He has not arrived yet? He left hours ago.'

'Left from where, Roberto?'

'Isabella rang me to say that one of the guests at the hotel in Florence was travelling by private jet to London today. He offered a seat on his plane when Lorenzo failed to get a flight at such short notice.'

'I see.' Jess fought to keep her voice steady. 'Roberto, it's very foggy here. He—he must be delayed.'

'Of course, *cara*. Do not worry. You know Lorenzo. He will make it. When he arrives ask him to ring me. And give my love to Leonie, *per favore*. Is she well?'

'Blooming—I'll pass on your message, but I'll ring off now, Roberto, in case Lorenzo's trying to get in touch.' After a pause to pull herself together, Jess went back into the kitchen.

'Is Lorenzo all right, darling?' asked Frances quickly. 'I didn't speak to him myself, I handed the phone over before his receptionist could put him on.'

'Actually, it was Roberto, Mother.' Jess swallowed hard. 'Apparently Lorenzo got a lift to London earlier on a private jet. Roberto thought he would have arrived by now.'

'I knew he'd come after you!' said her mother with relief. 'But in this weather the plane may have been diverted to a different airfield. Don't worry, darling. That husband of yours is so anxious to see you he'll walk to get here if necessary.'

'So why hasn't he *rung* me?'

Frances Dysart smiled a little. 'If you had a major quarrel—which, reading between the lines, you obviously did—perhaps he thinks you won't talk to him if he does ring you.'

Jess thought this over, passionately wanting to believe it. 'You're probably right.'

Frances gave her daughter a swift hug. 'Give yourself a few minutes to calm down, Jess, then pop over to the Stables and bring those girls back. They've been there long enough.'

'I should say. Otherwise we'll have Jonah on our case, saying we haven't looked after his wife.' Jess attached her cellphone to the belt of her jeans, then hurried off to the stable block. And collided with a small, frantic figure hurtling towards the house.

'Hey, steady, Fen,' she said in alarm. 'What's up?'

'Come quick—something's—wrong with Leo,' gasped the child. 'She told me to fetch Mummy.'

Jess blenched. 'Good girl. You run and do that. I'll see to Leo.' She sent the little girl into the house then raced across to the Stables at top speed and burst through the front door.

'Leo,' she yelled, 'where are you?'

'Up here,' came the faint reply.

Jess took the stairs two at a time and found her sister sitting on the bathroom floor in a puddle, panting hard.

'My waters broke,' gasped Leo.

'So I see,' said Jess, swallowing. 'Can you get up?'

'I—think—so.'

Finding the strength from somewhere, Jess heaved her sister to her feet. 'Good. Now let's get you downstairs.'

'No!'

'What do you mean, no?' demanded Jess frantically. 'We have to, Leo. The baby's obviously on its way—'

'And he's going to—arrive—pretty damn soon,' managed Leo, and let out a groan as another contraction took hold of her. 'I—need to—push already,' she gasped when she could speak.

Frances Dysart shot into the bathroom out of breath, and took in the scene at a glance. 'Off with those wet clothes, Leo. Jess, rummage in Adam's drawers; there should be a nightshirt I bought him last Christmas. Leo can use that. Your father's just arrived, thank God, so he can look after Fenny.'

'Can't he just drive Leo to the hospital?' said Jess in horror as Leo let out another groan.

'No,' she panted. 'I refuse to—give birth—in the car.'

'No question of going anywhere now you've started to push, darling.' Frances unhooked the plastic shower curtain. 'Here. Strip Adam's bed and put this on it, Jess, then remake the bed and stay with Leo, while I ring the surgery.'

'Use my phone,' said Jess urgently, handing it over, then gave all her attention to her sister.

Shortly afterwards Leonie was installed on her brother's bed, wearing his nightshirt, with barely a moment's breathing space between one contraction and the next.

'I thought the pains started gradually,' said Jess, hanging on to Leonie's hand for dear life.

'You and me both!' her sister ground out. 'You shouldn't be here,' she added, sweat standing out on her forehead.

'Rubbish!' Jess mopped her sister's face with her free hand, panicking inside. But when her mother reappeared and told her to go back to the house, she flatly refused to leave her post.

'I can take over now, Jess,' argued Frances.

'Too true you can. But I'm staying too. Oops,' she added, as another pain convulsed Leonie. 'They're coming thick and fast now.'

'Tell me about it!' her sister forced through gritted teeth.

'Which doctor's coming?' asked Jess, wincing as Leonie's nails bit deep.

'Midwife, not doctor. She was out on another case, but I left a message—' Frances broke off as Leonie gave a deep, visceral groan, her face scarlet with effort as she pushed her baby on its way. 'Good girl,' added her mother encouragingly.

'What happens if the midwife doesn't get here?' said Jess, quaking inside.

'I had a brainwave and rang Mary Gibson. She's on her way—' Frances looked up. 'Though I doubt that's Mary racing up the stairs right now.'

Jonah Savage burst into the room, wild-eyed. 'Oh, my God, Leo, *darling*!' He flung himself down on his knees beside his sweating, panting wife.

'There's the doorbell. Answer it, Jonah,' ordered Frances. 'It's Dr Gibson. Bring her up.'

Jonah planted a kiss on his wife's hair, then tore out of the room, his voice raised in impassioned treaty as he brought the doctor upstairs.

Mary Gibson swept into the room briskly, smiling on everyone. 'My word, Leonie, you *are* in a hurry. Frances said you had weeks to go yet. I'll just scrub up, then I'll have a look at you.'

From then on Leonie was beyond conversation. The relentless process of birth had taken over. With her husband holding one hand, her sister the other, verbal encouragement from her mother, and the calm supervision of the doctor she'd known all her life, Leonie eventually gave birth to a yelling baby boy. Dr Gibson severed him from his mother, cleared his nose, then cocooned him in the nest of warm blankets his grandmother had ready and laid him on his mother's breast just as the midwife came dashing in, out of breath.

'I was delayed by the fog. Am I too late?'

Leonie, looking exhausted but triumphant, gave her a glorious smile. 'Just in time to do the mopping up. We managed rather well, all of us, Nurse, with Dr Gibson's help.'

Jonah, who was half-sitting, half-lying on the bed, with his arm round his wife's shoulders, dropped a kiss on her damp curls, his eyes suspiciously bright. 'Mrs Savage, you're a miracle.' He laid a gentle finger on his son's fat little face. 'So are you, young sir.'

When Jess decided it was time to make herself scarce Leonie called her back, smiling at her with gratitude. 'Thanks a million, Jess. You were wonderful. I hope I haven't scarred you for life.'

'Of course not.' Jess smiled down at the small, red-faced bundle in her sister's arms. 'And even if you have this young man's worth it—he's gorgeous. But next time, Leo, have a manicure first, please!'

Dr Gibson took hold of Jess's hand, eyeing the crescents made by Leonie's nails. She smiled in approval. 'You did well, dear. Go and bathe your hands and put some antiseptic on those cuts.'

Jonah gave Jess a grateful hug. 'We'll do the same for you some time, Signora Forli.'

'I'll keep you to that,' she said, her voice suddenly unsteady.

Frances gave her a narrowed look. 'Go on over to the house, Jess, and give Tom and Fenny the glad news. Leonie needs some privacy for a bit, so Nurse Golding will take over now.'

'Will do! See you later, everyone. Goodbye Dr Gibson.'

Jess found her knees were shaking as she went downstairs. She saw the lights twinkling on the little tree in Adam's window and caught back a sob. Now the crisis was over she longed for Lorenzo with a pain that was almost physical. After witnessing the miracle of birth first hand she desperately needed to share the joy of it with him, to reassure him that what Leonie had just achieved, with the minimum of fuss, his wife could do equally as well. Given the chance.

When she went into the house her father and Fenny came rushing to greet her.

'It's a boy!' announced Jess, and Tom Dysart enveloped her in a hug, then held out his arm to Fenny to include her in the embrace.

'Thank God,' he said unsteadily, and hugged them until both his girls cried for mercy. 'I thought Leo had a while to go yet.'

'Young Master Savage decided he wanted to join us for Christmas,' said Jess breathlessly.

'Is he lovely? What's his name? Can I see him?'

demanded Fenny in excitement. 'The doctor said I'm not catching any more.'

'I don't suppose you'll sleep tonight if you don't,' said Jess, laughing. 'But Leo needs a rest now. You can see the baby later. He hasn't got a name yet. In the meantime, I need another bath.' In answer to the anxious question in her father's eyes, Jess added, 'Leo's fine, Dad. Wonderful, in fact. Though I can't answer for Jonah. He's a bit shell-shocked.'

'As well he might be,' said Tom with feeling. He glanced down at Fenny's shiny black hair. 'I couldn't help thinking of Rachel. And worrying. Men feel so helpless at times like these.'

'You could help a lot by giving Fen some tea while I clean up,' said Jess practically.

'Can I have it in the study?' demanded Fenny.

'Wherever you like, and whatever you want,' promised Tom rashly. '*And* you can stay up for a celebration dinner later.'

Jess smiled at them, and made for the stairs, then turned back hopefully. 'I don't suppose there's been a phone call for me?'

Her father sobered. 'No, darling. If Lorenzo rings while you're in the bath—'

'Fetch me!'

Jess took a long time over her bath. Which was a mistake. By the time she was dressed and her hair dry she'd had so much time to think and agonise she was one great, aching mass of anguish little short of physical. Where on earth *was* Lorenzo?

He always carried a cellphone. He could have rung her at some stage, surely? Wherever he was? Unless... Jess stared at her reflection in dark despair, facing the fact that he might be dead. That the last words they would ever say to each other had been hurled in anger. The private jet must have crashed somewhere in the fog, and she would never know what had happened to him. She would never touch him again, make love with him, never say all the things she'd left unsaid.

It took some time to get herself in hand, but by the time her face and hair were immaculate, and she was festive, on the outside at least, in black velvet jeans and a bright pink sweater, Jess felt up to going downstairs. As she reached the hall the study door flew open, and a tall, familiar figure snatched her up in a rib-cracking hug.

'Surprise!' said her brother, and gave her a smacking kiss before setting her on her feet in the hall. 'How's the sexy *signora*?'

'Adam! You're supposed to be in Virginia.'

'*Uncle* Adam, if you please,' he corrected, laughing. 'I decided to come home after all. I rang Kate a few days ago, and she drove from Cambridge to collect me from the airport. Our plan was to sneak up on the family unawares. We should have been home hours ago, but this blasted fog slowed us down to a crawl in places. When we arrived I thought Dad had sub-let my place when we saw lights blazing from every window.'

'To welcome the new arrival. Where's Kate, then?'

'In the Stables, baby-worshipping with Fen. Dad and I aren't allowed until later. Mother says not too many at once. She's sent Dad down the road to Cliff Cottage. Apparently Elinor Gibson—well, Carew now—offered a Moses basket to Leo for the baby.' Adam pulled her into the study. 'In the meantime, let's have a drink to celebrate.'

Jess shook her head. 'I'd better do something about dinner, Adam. Good thing I made buckets of pasta sauce this morning.'

He eyed her narrowly. 'You look very tired, Jess. Big smudges under your eyes. Or is that the latest thing in eye make-up?'

'No,' she said lightly. 'Nature, not art. Plus a crash-course in midwifery! Talking of which,' she added, 'go and fetch Kate and Fenny back and make enquiries about Leo's requirements for supper.'

Jess went into the kitchen and put the radio on, tied on an apron and began taking out saucepans at top speed. She put batons of garlic bread on a baking tray, ready to heat, then, after a moment's thought, opened several cans of soup and emptied them into a pan. Though thin as a whip, Adam had an appetite that was prodigious. And if Leo didn't fancy anything solid soup would be a good idea. When she heard Fenny's voice raised in excitement in the hall Jess turned with a smile as the kitchen door opened.

'Hi, Kate—' She stopped dead, her heart in her throat. Instead of her sister, a tall, haggard man stood in the open doorway, his dark, bloodshot eyes locked with hers. Normally, even in the most casual of clothes, Lorenzo Forli achieved a certain elegance. But tonight his thick black hair was wild, he needed a shave, and the long dark coat he wore over a travel-creased suit emphasised his pallor.

'*Ciao*, Lorenzo,' said Jess, at last, when it seemed the silence might go on for ever. 'You're just in time for dinner.'

CHAPTER THREE

LORENZO started towards Jess, then halted, prevented from reaching her when Fenny came rushing to take him by the hand, bubbling with excitement.

'Lorenzo, guess what? We've got a new baby, and he was born in a stable, just like Baby Jesus! When are you coming to see him? He's so sweet.'

'Give him a chance, brat,' said Kate, dashing in to haul her away. She smiled apologetically at Lorenzo, and hurried to hug her sister. 'Hi, Jess. Great to see you. Mother will be over in a minute. You see to Lorenzo. I'll help with dinner.'

Jess held on to her sister for a moment, glad of the chance to get her pulse under control. 'My word, look at you. What a transformation!'

Kate, once the quiet, conservative one, more interested in books than looks, had crimped her long dark hair into a wild mass held out and away from her face by an expanding metal band, the style all of a piece with thick-soled trainers, khaki cargo pants, and a bright blue fleece bodywarmer zipped over a skinny cerise T-shirt. 'Student couture,' she said, grinning, and gave her sister a shove. 'Go on. Get moving. Lorenzo looks ready to drop.'

Lorenzo cleared his throat, finding his voice at

last as he tore his eyes from his wife to bend to Fenny. 'Tell me more about this wonderful baby, *piccola.*'

Fenny beamed. 'It's Leo and Jonah's baby. He arrived this afternoon. Mummy says he's a very special Christmas present. He came early and surprised us.'

'*Che meraviglia!*' said Lorenzo, looking dazed.

Fenny spun round to Jess in triumph. '*And* I know his name. He's Richard—Thomas—James—Savage,' she said carefully.

'Goodness, what a mouthful,' said Jess, and gave Lorenzo a smile so diffident Kate's eyes narrowed in surprise. 'You look very tired.'

'Lorenzo, you made it!' said Frances Dysart, hurrying in. 'Thank heavens. It's so good to see you.' She kissed him warmly in welcome. 'How did you get here in the end?'

'*Grazie*, Frances. I came by private jet. But it could not land at the usual airport because of fog.' Lorenzo threw his wife a glance. 'The pilot had to make a—a detour?'

Jess nodded. 'So what happened?'

'As he approached the airfield at Biggin Hill the pilot was informed of an occluded situation due to fog. He was switched to a frequency at Gatwick airport, and eventually succeeded in landing there.'

'Gosh, Lorenzo, that must have been a bit hairy!' said Kate, pulling a face. 'How did you get from there?'

'I waited a very long time to get on a coach,

which took an equally long time to make the journey to Chepstow, where a taxi brought me here.
After a little persuasion.' Lorenzo thrust a hand
through his hair. 'When I asked for Stavely the
driver was not happy. The fog, again.'

'So what happened?' asked Frances.

Lorenzo gave a dismissive Latin shrug. 'I paid
him a lot of money.'

'After all that you must be exhausted. Not to
mention starving and in need of a drink!'

He smiled at her. 'You are right, Frances, but
first, if it is possible, I would very much like a
shower and a change of clothes.'

'Come with me, then, Lorenzo,' said Jess, pulling herself together. 'Mother, the sauce is in the
big pan, and I've washed the salad things. I've put
some bacon out to grill, and cheese to grate. The
garlic bread is ready to put in the oven, and I've
opened some soup. Not as good as your home-
made stuff, but I thought it would fill an odd corner—'

'Darling, just go!' interrupted her mother, and,
conscious that Kate was eyeing them both with
worried speculation, Jess hurried through the door
Lorenzo held open for her.

'Is that all you've brought?' she asked, eyeing
the holdall he collected in the hall.

Lorenzo shrugged. 'It was a small plane. Also I
had much to arrange before I could leave. I had
little attention to spare for clothes.'

'Right.' Jess mounted the stairs ahead of him,

and hurried along the upper hall towards her bed-room, glad now she'd taken the trouble to tidy it before she went downstairs.

'Am I to share your room?' asked Lorenzo, standing motionless on the threshold.

'You'll have to.' Jess felt her colour rise. 'Is that a problem?'

'Not for me,' he said quietly, and came inside and closed the door. 'Is it a problem for you, Jessamy?'

'No, of course not,' she said stiffly, and looked away. Their acrimonious parting created an almost tangible barrier between them, blotting out the des-perate anxiety which had driven her frantic ever since her arrival at Friars Wood. 'Things have been very hectic here today,' she added in a rush. 'Leo was making mince pies all morning, then she in-sisted on decorating a Christmas tree in Adam's place, and for a finale went into labour suddenly late this afternoon.' Jess explained about Dr Gib-son, and Jonah's late arrival. 'The midwife was held up in fog and didn't get here until young Richard Savage had arrived. Leo was absolutely wonderful. She brought her son into the world with a minimum of fuss. I was holding her hand the entire time—look.' She held out her hand, swollen palm upwards, and Lorenzo took it in his very carefully, surveyed the marks. For a moment Jess thought he would raise it to his lips. But to her disappointment he released it gently.

'Jonah was also with her?' he asked.

'Towards the end, yes. Not that any of it took long.'

'He is a brave man.'

'No,' corrected Jess tartly. 'Leo was the brave one.'

'I meant,' said Lorenzo huskily, 'that it must be a terrible thing to watch one's wife endure such pain.'

'It wasn't *like* that.' Jess sighed. 'It's so hard to explain if you haven't witnessed the process first hand. For the first time I understand why they call it labour! And I know it isn't always so straightforward and quick for everyone, especially with a first baby. But if a woman is young and healthy there's no danger. Lorenzo—' She turned away abruptly. 'Oh, what's the use? Let's drop the subject.'

'We will talk later.' He yawned involuntarily. '*Mi scusi*. It was a very long, tiring journey.' His eyes met hers. 'At one point in the plane, when we ran into fog, it occurred to me that I might never arrive here at all. Would you have grieved for me, Jessamy?'

Sudden anger made her sarcastic. 'Grieve? Why should I do that? I look so terrific in black, for a start! What a stupid question, Lorenzo—of course I would have grieved. And, while we're on the subject, didn't it occur to you that *I* might be worried? Couldn't you have rung me at some stage?'

Lorenzo's eyes blazed with sudden anger as he switched to rapid Italian. 'Would you have answered me if I had? I rang you repeatedly from Venice with no success. So. When Isabella told me you had flown to London I swore I would try no more. I decided to confront you in person.' His black lashes dropped to curtain his expression. 'I wished to see your reaction when we came face to face.'

'And was it satisfactory?' she demanded in English.

He shrugged. 'I am not sure. You looked—' he threw out his hands in a gesture so familiar Jess felt her heart skip a beat. 'Stunned? Is that right?'

'Yes. I turned round expecting to see my sister. And found my husband instead. Thank God,' she added, with such fervour Lorenzo visibly relaxed.

'Adam insisted I go straight to you in the kitchen,' he said, smiling a little.

'I think he was being tactful, giving us time alone. But Fenny put paid to that.' Jess returned the smile, her eyes softening. 'Look, I must go downstairs and help with dinner. Have your shower, then join us. The Dysarts are in celebration mood tonight.'

'Then the Forlis will celebrate with them,' he said very deliberately, and this time when he took her swollen hand in his he raised it to his lips and kissed the palm, the tip of his tongue lingering on her swollen flesh. 'I will hurry.'

'I'll go on down, then,' said Jess, her voice gruff because she wanted him to sweep her into his arms and kiss a great deal more than her hand. 'See you later.'

'Jessamy.' He barred her way as she moved towards the door, and looked deep into her eyes. 'Tell me you are glad I came.'

She nodded, flushing a little under the searching black scrutiny. 'Of course I'm glad. *Very* glad.'

Lorenzo opened the door for her, his weariness suddenly vanished. 'Tell your mother I shall be ten minutes only.'

'Good,' echoed Jess lightly, turning away. 'I'm starving.' She turned back suddenly. 'Lorenzo—'

'*Si?*' he said expectantly.

'You need to contact Roberto. He rang earlier, asking to speak to you.'

The light in his eyes dimmed a little. '*Va bene.* I will ring him at once, and ask him to call Isabella and say I have arrived safely.' He raised an eyebrow. 'So you knew I was on my way.'

'Yes.' Jess looked at him steadily. 'Hours ago. Endless, worrying hours, Lorenzo.'

His mouth twisted. 'Forgive me, Jessamy. I would have rung while I was waiting so long for a coach at Gatwick. But the battery on my cellphone was dead by this time, and I was sure that if I left to find a telephone I would miss the coach.'

'You're here now. That's all that matters. But Roberto will be anxious, so I'll take you into my parents' bedroom. You can use the telephone there.'

*   *   *

Downstairs Jess found everyone gathered in the kitchen, including Jonah, who swept her into a convulsive hug the moment she went through the door.

'My wife ordered me to say thank you again. Where's Lorenzo?' he demanded. 'I'm very glad he finally made it. Leo was so relieved she promptly went to sleep.'

'Lorenzo's in the shower; he won't be long.' Jess smiled warmly at the elated father. 'I trust the heir apparent is sleeping, too?'

'For the moment.' Jonah gave a great, luxurious stretch and grinned at Adam. 'Sorry to commandeer your place, old chum. But Leo thinks it best we stay over there so you can all sleep in peace when my son bawls in the night. My son,' he repeated in wonder, and Tom Dysart laughed and clapped him on the back.

'Have you rung your parents with the news?'

James and Flora Savage, it seemed, were astonished but ecstatic, and were bringing Helen, their sister-in-law, with them next day to Christmas dinner.

'And to drool over the baby,' said Adam with a grin. 'I haven't even seen him yet. Who does he look like?'

'Himself,' said Frances, stirring soup in a saucepan.

'He's cute. Aunt Helen will love him,' said Fenny happily, and leaned down to stroke the dog. 'You'll like him, too, Marzi.'

'Are you eating with us, Jonah?' asked Kate, as she began laying the table.

'No, sweetheart. I've just come to wet the baby's head with some of your father's champagne, then I'll take some supper over to Leo and share it with her.' Jonah chuckled. 'I'd better warn you, Frances. She's determined to get up tomorrow and bring the son and heir to join in at Christmas dinner.'

'Of course,' said the new grandmother promptly. 'If he yells we can all take turns to cuddle him.'

'I'll just wait to say hello to Lorenzo, then I'll get back,' said Jonah, draining his glass. 'Has he recovered from his journey, Jess?'

'He's fine. He'll be down soon.' Jess joined her mother and sister at the central island. 'What can I do to help?'

'Put some soup in a Thermos for Jonah. Kate's packed a basket with some basic provisions.' Frances smiled happily. 'I've put in a container of your sauce, and Jonah can cook the pasta in Adam's kitchen.'

'How about the baby?' asked Jess in an undertone. 'Is Leo feeding him herself?'

'Yes. She's already put him to the breast, but he just went to sleep. I hope he goes on sleeping too, for a while at least, to give Leo a rest.'

'Don't worry, Frances,' said Jonah, coming to join them. 'I'll happily walk the floor with him if he cries in the night. My wife has done quite enough for one day.'

'You can say that again,' said Kate, laughing. 'You should see all the mince pies she made this morning! I've put some in the basket for you.'

Jess turned, knowing instantly, as she always did, that Lorenzo had come into the room. Jonah smiled broadly and went to him, hand outstretched.

'Glad you made it. I've been hearing tall tales about your trip.'

'It was most tedious,' said Lorenzo, hesitated a moment, then embraced Jonah as he would have done his own brother. 'I congratulate you on the birth of your son. Please give Leonie my good wishes.'

'You can give them to her yourself, if you like,' said Jonah, looking enormously pleased. 'She expects everyone to come and inspect the new arrival at some time.'

Lorenzo gave Jess a questioning look. 'We shall do this later, perhaps?'

'Yes, of course.'

'After dinner,' said Frances firmly. 'Off you go, Jonah. If you want anything else just ring, and someone will bring it over.'

Because the dining room was already prepared in splendour for Christmas dinner next day, the seven of them crowded round the kitchen table for supper. This put Jess in such close proximity to her husband they were in close physical contact throughout the meal, a circumstance which Lorenzo so openly relished she began to relax at last, filled with joyful relief that they were together again.

Tom opened another bottle of champagne after they finished the soup, and before they began on the pasta he held up his glass in toast. 'To all the safe arrivals today.'

'Amen to that,' said his wife, and raised her glass to Lorenzo.

'Tante grazie,' he replied. 'Now let us drink to your grandson.'

'To Richard,' everyone echoed, then fell to with enthusiasm, praising Jess lavishly for the sauce.

'It is my favourite,' declared Lorenzo. 'Not even Carla, my housekeeper at Villa Fortuna, does better than this.'

Jess looked startled. 'You mean that?'

'I always mean what I say, Jessamy.' Lorenzo smiled down into her eyes, then turned back to Kate. 'Tell me, cara. How was your first term at the university?'

CHAPTER FOUR

'IN SOME ways it was the most tiring, and in other ways the happiest Christmas Eve Jess had ever spent: a day of experiences which had taught her a lesson in true values. After being part of the miracle of birth with Leonie, Jess felt she had been granted a miracle herself in having Lorenzo arrive safe and sound after the horror of thinking she would never see him again. Now he was with her nothing else mattered. It was enough just to be here together, in the midst of her elated, animated family, his hand openly holding hers while they listened to Kate's tales of student life.

'How are you coping with the male population?' demanded Adam, beginning on his fourth mince pie. 'Be careful, half-pint. Some of those guys straight out of single sex schools are like kids let loose in the candy store when they get to university.'

'Speaking from experience, no doubt?' laughed Kate. 'Don't worry. I've got a minder. He's six foot three, plays rugby, weighs a ton, and keeps unwanted wolves from my door.'

'You're sure "minder" is the right word?' said her father dryly. 'No aspirations himself where you're concerned?'

179

'None,' she assured him airily. 'Not,' she added honestly, 'that I'm in much danger from the rest of the pack, really.'

'Why do you think that, *cara*?' said Lorenzo curiously, and smiled at her, his eyes gleaming as his fingers tightened on his wife's hand. 'Like all the Dysart ladies, you are most attractive, Kate.'

She smiled back demurely. 'Thank you, kind sir. Unfortunately I also have a brain. It puts most blokes off. Worse still, I work hard. The ultimate turn-off for some. So Alasdair and I sort of stick together. He works hard, too.'

'Surely you play sometimes, too?' said Frances.

'Of course I do. I watch Alasdair's matches sometimes, then go out to the pub with him and the rest of the rugby crowd afterwards. Everyone sort of takes it for granted we're a couple. I don't mind. It saves a lot of trouble.'

'This Alasdair's got it made,' said Jess slyly. 'Does he appreciate having such a gorgeous little pal on hand?'

'I work with him, not play,' retorted Kate, unmoved. 'And I'd hardly describe myself as gorgeous.'

'I would,' said Lorenzo promptly, smiling at her.

Adam eyed his young sister objectively, obviously seeing her in a new, different light. 'Look, make sure you don't send out any wrong signals to this hunk, Kate. Rugby locker rooms tend to nurture certain basic instincts in the male—'

'It's time Fenny was off to bed,' interrupted Frances hastily.

'I'll take her,' volunteered Jess, and caught Lorenzo's eye. 'She's very tired. Perhaps you'd like to carry her upstairs?'

He jumped up with alacrity and held out his arms to the drooping child. 'Come, *principessa*. Soon it will be time for Babbo Natale to arrive, no?'

'Who's that?' said Fenny sleepily, putting her arms round his neck.

'Father Christmas, of course,' said Jess, as Lorenzo carried the child round to receive good-night kisses from the others.

'I'm too tired to read for myself tonight. Will you read to me, Jess?' pleaded the little girl when she was finally tucked in bed.

'You bet.' Jess turned to smile at Lorenzo. 'You can go down if you like. I won't be long.'

He shook his head. *'Permesso,'* he said to Fenny, and sat at the foot of her bed. 'I shall stay to listen.'

Fenny wriggled down in the bed with pleasure, but before Jess was even halfway through the story the child had fallen deeply asleep.

Silently Jess tiptoed from the room with Lorenzo, but when they passed the open door of her room he drew her inside and took her in his arms.

'Ti amo,' he whispered, and kissed her fleetingly, but let her go before she could respond.

Jess looked up into his eyes for a long moment, telling him without words that she reciprocated in full, then went downstairs with him to join the others, who were still at the kitchen table, drinking coffee.

'I need some wrapping paper for all the millions of presents I brought,' announced Adam. 'You can help me, Kate.'

'Suppose Mother doesn't have enough paper?' she demanded.

'Mother always has enough,' said her son, with such confidence everyone laughed.

'Jonah just rang,' said Frances. 'If you'd like to go over now with Lorenzo, Jess, apparently it's a good time.'

'We'll have coffee when we get back, then,' said Jess, and smiled up at her husband. 'Ready?'

Jonah was waiting for them at the door to the Stables. 'Come in. Fancy a drink, Lorenzo?'

'I have already toasted your son in champagne, so perhaps some coffee would be better.' Lorenzo smiled. 'Otherwise I might fall asleep before I can pay proper homage to the new arrival.'

'Coffee coming up, then,' said Jonah promptly. 'Jess, you go up first while I make it. I'll bring Lorenzo after you've had a chat with Leo.'

Adam's bedroom had undergone a transformation since Jess had last seen it. All traces of the momentous happenings earlier were gone. There were fresh covers on the bed, Leonie was propped up against snowy pillows, and she looked so serene it was hard for Jess to believe that earlier her sister's face had been sweating and crimson with effort. The result of her labours lay in a securely wrapped bundle beneath the hood of a Moses basket covered in blue-striped white cotton.

'No need to tiptoe around,' said Leonie cheerfully. 'He may as well get used to the big noisy world. Are you over the shock I gave you, Jess?'

'Just about. It was all so sudden.'

'Just between you and me, it wasn't. I had quite a backache all morning, but I put that down to standing about with the mince pies. And when I started getting the odd stomach cramp while I was doing the tree with Fenny I just put it down to indigestion.'

'For heaven's sake, why didn't you say?'

'It never occurred to me I was shaping up for labour or I would have, believe me. Anyway,' added Leonie contentedly, 'you must admit that the end result is pretty terrific.'

'I'll say! But if he's sleeping like that now, will he sleep tonight, do you think?' said Jess, peering down at her nephew.

'Probably not. Though I am assured that Daddy will leap out of bed if he doesn't.' Leonie giggled. 'Jonah's already had a go at changing a nappy.'

'Lorenzo said he was brave,' said Jess, impressed.

'Talking of which, how are things? Lord, Jess, I was so relieved to hear he made it.'

'We haven't had much time alone together

yet—' began Jess, then jumped as young Richard Savage opened his mouth and let out as big a roar as he could manage. 'Whoa, there. Can I pick him up?'

'Help yourself. Cut him off before he gets to full throttle,' begged his mother.

Jess turned back the blanket, gingerly picked up the small bundle and held the baby up against her shoulder. When the crying stopped abruptly she smiled in delight. 'Who's a good boy for his auntie, then?' she crooned, smiling down into the small, crumpled face, then looked up in surprise when Leonie went off into gales of laughter. 'What?' she demanded.

'Mother, Kate and even Fenny were all the same. Why do women suddenly go ga-ga when they get their hands on a baby?'

'Search me.' Jess smiled apologetically into the baby's blue, unfocused eyes. 'Sorry, Richard Thomas James. Mummy says no baby-talk.' She looked up at her sister. 'Why did you use up all the family names in one go, Leo?'

'Jonah's idea.' Leonie shook her head pityingly. 'According to him, that's it. No more babies. He swears he won't put me through that again. All the antenatal classes and reading up on the subject were no preparation for the actual experience of childbirth, apparently. It scared him silly.'

'Did it scare you silly, too?'

'Not in the least. I can't say I enjoyed it, exactly, but it didn't put me off doing it again.' Leonie smiled a little. 'I dare say I'll find a way to change his mind.'

'I hope you have more success than me.' Jess sighed, then smiled as the baby stretched a little in her arms. 'By the way, harking back to nappies, where did you get all the gear?'

'I've been taking the basics everywhere lately, just in case. And Eleanor Gibson sent up a few more things in the Moses basket.'

'I was rather envious when she married Miles Carew, you know,' said Jess, rocking her nephew. 'He came to give a talk at our school while he was still in the army. I was madly in love with the dashing major for weeks afterwards.'

'All the nice girls love a soldier,' said Jonah, ushering in Lorenzo, who stopped dead when he saw Jess with the baby in her arms.

'Come and meet our nephew,' said Jess, with slight emphasis on the pronoun.

Lorenzo's face relaxed, and with a smile, and a swift greeting to the new mother, joined his wife in contemplation of young Richard Savage. 'He is a fine boy. I congratulate you, Leonie.'

'Want to hold him?' said Jess, and handed the baby to him.

Lorenzo received the little body without turning a hair, and with practised skill held him up against his shoulder, steadying the small head with a firm hand.

'Hey,' said Jonah with respect. 'You're an expert.'

'I have experience with my nephews,' Lorenzo informed him, then addressed the baby softly in Italian, to Jess's amusement.

'Same baby-talk, different language,' she told her sister.

Suddenly the baby gave a yawn, and dribbled on Lorenzo's dark blue sweater. Leonie collapsed against the pillows, laughing.

'Honestly, young Savage,' said his father, removing him. 'That's not the way to treat guests.'

'Come with me. I'll sponge it off,' said Jess, and led Lorenzo to Adam's bathroom, where he promptly closed the door and seized her in his arms.

'Kiss me!' he commanded.

Jess obeyed, every last trace of constraint between them vanishing as their lips met and their bodies curved together like two halves of a whole.

When Lorenzo raised his head at last he was breathing raggedly. 'We must not linger.'

'No,' she said breathlessly, and turned away to pick up a sponge. 'Here. Let me clean you up.'

By the time they rejoined the new parents, both Jess and Lorenzo had themselves in hand, but something in their altered body language brought a knowing gleam to Leonie's eyes. She smiled over the head of the baby snuggled against her breast. 'Better now?' she asked softly.

'Much better,' said Lorenzo with emphasis. 'But it is time we leave you to rest.'

Jess took a small parcel from her jacket and

handed it to Jonah. 'Kate and I put this together after dinner before I came across. Richard's first Christmas stocking.'

Jonah swallowed hard as he opened the little parcel, plainly so emotional for a moment he couldn't speak. Kate had decorated one of Fenny's red socks with a big tinsel bow. Inside was a tiny rubber duck for the bath, a packet of dummies, and a box containing a gold St Christopher medallion.

'Jess!' said Leonie, touched. 'What a lovely thought. Tell Kate I love it.'

'Kate transferred the duck from Fenny's stocking, I bought the dummies this morning as a nonsense present for you, and the medal is from Lorenzo and me. We bought the St Christopher a while ago, on the Ponte Vecchio, but I didn't want to send it in a parcel with the other things in case it got lost.' Jess bent to touch a finger to the baby's cheek, then kissed her sister and gave Jonah a hug. She put her hand in Lorenzo's and smiled on the tableau made by the new parents with their baby son. 'Goodnight, you three. Merry Christmas.'

CHAPTER FIVE

LORENZO slid his arm round Jess and held her close as they walked slowly through fog which wrapped them in a private, white world of their own.

'Am I forgiven, *carissima*?' said Lorenzo, as they paused before mounting the steep path to the front door of Friars Wood.

'Lorenzo, don't!' Jess turned and buried her head against his shoulder. '*I* need forgiveness, not you. I behaved like a spoilt child. I know your work must come first. But it wasn't just about work and responsibility. You know that. After—after we quarrelled, I felt so miserable I needed to come back to Friars Wood.'

'You mean you wanted to come home,' he said heavily.

Jess tipped her head back to look up into his face. 'No. I didn't say that. Now we're married, home for me is where you are, Lorenzo. But you were in Venice and I was in Florence alone. And after what happened between us, suddenly I couldn't bear it. I should have told you I was going, I know—'

'But you did, *carissima*.' He laughed a little, then bent his head to rub his cheek against hers.

'You told Isabella. You knew she would ring me the moment you had left for the airport.'

'Yes, I did.' Jess smiled guiltily. 'I was still too angry and hurt to ring *you*—'

'So you chose the best way to inform me.' Lorenzo kissed her swiftly. 'You knew I would follow as soon as I could.'

'No. I wasn't at all sure of that. But I hoped. Lord, how I hoped.' Jess was suddenly stabbed with remorse. 'Did it make things very difficult for you in Venice, Lorenzo?'

'This is of no consequence.' He held her away a little, his hands urgent on her arms. 'You must know that you are the most important thing in my life, Jessamy. I was forced to go to Venice because my uncle, also some of the hotel staff, had caught influenza. But by the time Isabella rang to tell me you had gone I had already taken on more temporary staff. So I simply ordered Gian Domenico to take over until his father recovered. It will do young cousin Giando good. And I asked Roberto to return early from his skiing holiday. He will look after both Florence hotels in my absence. Never again will my work make you unhappy, *amore*, I swear.'

Jess decided that this wasn't the moment to mention the other bone of contention between them. Instead she reached up and kissed her husband's mouth in passionate gratitude. Then she shivered a little. 'I'm cold,' she said huskily. 'Let's go inside. It's an early start in this house on Christmas Day, so we'd better go to bed soon.'

'Your words are music to my ears,' he assured her fervently, and ran with her to the door, where Jess stayed his hand before he could tap on the glass below the holly garland on the door.

'Wait.' She cleared her throat a little, then smiled up at him mischievously, and very softly began to sing the first verse of 'Away in a Manger' in a true, clear soprano. She knocked gently, then began on the second verse, by which time all the remaining Dysarts, bar Fenny, had gathered in the hall to listen. Lorenzo gazed down at her with something like awe in his eyes, and as the last plangent note died away Tom Dysart threw open the door and gave his daughter a hug.

'It's a long time since you've done that, Jess. That was beautiful.'

'And a very appropriate choice of carol in the circumstances,' said Frances, blinking away a tear.

'You did not tell me you could sing, Jessamy,' said Lorenzo, looking dazed at the discovery.

'You never asked!' She laughed up at him as he took her jacket. 'I couldn't go on as Tosca, but I used to sing solos with the school choir.'

'A woman of many parts, my sister,' said Adam, and fished in his pocket for a penny. 'Here you are.'

'She deserves a lot more than that,' said Kate, and took Jess's arm. 'Come in the kitchen. Dad's mulled some wine. We're drinking it round the kitchen table now Adam's finished his parcelling. I did mine before I came.'

'Tomorrow, Lorenzo,' said Frances wryly, 'I promise faithfully you shall have some proper comfort, with a fire in the drawing room and a meal eaten formally at the dining room table.'

'A warm welcome is much better than formality, Frances,' he assured her, and looked at Jess. 'I am so very happy to be here.'

After all the presents were stacked under the great tree in the drawing room, Jess volunteered to deliver Fenny's Christmas stocking on her way to bed.

'Thank you, darling,' said Tom Dysart. 'You must be exhausted, Lorenzo. Sleep well.'

After a round of goodnights and Christmas wishes Jess and Lorenzo went quietly up the stairs together and on into Fenny's room at the end of the upper landing. Jess bent and very carefully laid the stocking at the foot of the bed, then in silence they turned away and crossed the landing to the room Jess had slept in most of her life.

'We share a bathroom with Adam and Kate,' she said a little awkwardly, 'so we'll have to take turns. Shall I go first?'

'Whatever you wish, *carissima*. You are shy, no?' he teased.

'Yes. Ridiculous, isn't it?'

When Jess got back Lorenzo dropped a kiss on her hair and said very deliberately, 'I shall be five minutes, no more. I am cold.'

After he went Jess undressed at top speed, and pulled on a nightgown bought for her trousseau and never worn. She slid into bed, and by the time she'd settled herself against the pillows Lorenzo was back. Untroubled by the shyness his wife was suffering, he stripped off his clothes and dived into bed.

'Turn off the light, *tesoro*,' he said, shivering.

'Listen,' she whispered, 'the church bells are ringing. It's Christmas Day.'

'Our first Christmas Day together. *Buon Natale*, Jessamy,' he said, and drew her into his arms in the warm, welcoming dark.

'Merry Christmas, Lorenzo,' she said breathlessly, then laughed as he gave a sudden, unromantic yawn.

'*Mi scusi,*' he muttered against her hair. 'Sleeping has been a problem for me since our parting.'

'For me too,' she said with feeling.

'I know. You have dark rings under your beautiful eyes.'

'So have you.'

He turned her face up to his and kissed her tenderly. 'Then, *diletta mia*, let us sleep now. It is joy enough just to be together. There will be other times for love.'

Soon Lorenzo was sleeping deeply, but Jess lay awake for a while, curled against him in complete content. Passionate though their relationship was, at this moment all she needed in life was just to lie close to her husband in the dark, savouring the

pleasure of his warm body against hers. She offered up silent, fervent thanks for his safe arrival,
then slid into sleep as deep as Lorenzo's. So deep
Jess felt as though only a few minutes had passed
when she woke to a faint tapping on the door.

'Can I come in?' whispered Fenny.

Jess gave Lorenzo a little dig in the ribs to wake
him, made sure he was respectable enough to receive visitors, then switched on the light and turned
the bedclothes back on her side a little to make
space for the child while Lorenzo came yawning
to life. 'Come on then, poppet, only be as quiet as
you can. Let Mummy and Daddy sleep for a bit.'
Jess felt Lorenzo vibrating with silent laughter as
Fenny settled herself with her Christmas stocking.

'I brought this to open with you,' said Fenny,
beaming on them both.

'But of course, *piccola*,' said Lorenzo promptly.
'It is more fun when others can share, no?'

Soon the bed was awash with puzzles and
games, a glove puppet, a flotilla of ducks, a mock
leopardskin purse, a little silver heart on a chain,
pink sugar mice, nuts, a tangerine, chocolate
money, and a shiny pound coin. Jess and Lorenzo
made the necessary noises of approval as Fenny
took out each item, but when the last one was examined and admired the child put everything carefully back and looked up at Jess, her hazel-green
eyes troubled.

'What's the matter, darling?' asked Jess.

The little girl sighed heavily. 'One of the girls

in school said Father Christmas isn't a real person at all. Her father puts the stocking in her room.'

'Well, Dad didn't put the stocking in your room, Fenny,' said Jess with perfect truth.

'I think,' said Lorenzo carefully, 'that Father Christmas is real to all boys and girls who believe he is real. And you must go on believing, Fenny, because of baby Richard, so that he can enjoy waiting for Babbo Natale just as you do.'

Fenny's face cleared like magic, then she looked round guiltily as someone knocked on the door. 'Oh, *no*! I woke Mummy after all.'

'Come in,' said Jess, chuckling, but it was Kate who put a sleepy face round the door, her hair hanging in a wild, tangled mass round her shoulders.

'Honestly, Fen,' she said yawning. 'What are you doing in here?'

'Sharing her stocking with us,' said Lorenzo, his eyes dancing. 'Would you care to join us?'

She grinned. 'Looks a bit crowded already. I thought you were going to open your stocking with me, Fen.'

'I was. But you were asleep. But I can come and do it again now if you like,' said Fenny, scrambling out of bed.

'Good idea. Come and get your dressing gown.' Kate smiled, and fluttered her eyelashes at Lorenzo. 'You two can go back to sleep for a bit.'

When they were alone Jess slid down into her

husband's waiting arms. 'I bet Christmas is normally more peaceful for you,' she said, yawning.

'You joke, *carissima*. When I spend Christmas with Isabella and Andrea my nephews usually join me long before this.' He stroked the head she snuggled into his shoulder. 'Ah, Jessamy, if someone had told me last year that I would be holding my beautiful new bride in my arms next Christmas morning I would not have believed it.'

'Me too. It's like a dream come true.' Jess shivered. 'Whereas yesterday it was beginning to be a nightmare. I was utterly frantic with worry after Roberto rang.'

He gave a deep, contented sigh. 'I am sorry you were so distressed, *amore*. Yet glad, too, to know you care so much.'

'Surely you know that by now,' she retorted, and twisted in his arms to look up into his face.

Lorenzo's eyes gazed deep into hers, then he nodded slowly. 'Yes. Now, at last, I truly believe I do.'

'I should hope so.' Jess kissed him to emphasise her point.

He returned the kiss with interest, his arms tightening to hold her close. Jess felt his body grow taut, and her own respond, and smiled ruefully into his gleaming, half-closed eyes.

'I'd better get dressed,' she said with open reluctance.

Lorenzo sighed regretfully. 'Yes,' he agreed. 'Otherwise who knows who may come in next?

Adam would be shocked, I think, if he found me making passionate love to his sister.'

'In the unlikely event that he's awake, I doubt it would shock him. But, Christmas or no Christmas, Adam will have to be hauled forcibly out of bed unless he's changed lately.' Jess smoothed Lorenzo's black hair from his forehead. 'I wonder if young Richard Savage let his parents sleep at all last night?'

He smiled and caught her hand in his to kiss the sore palm. 'No doubt the proud father coped well if he did. Leonie has taken to motherhood with great ease, no?'

'She certainly has.' Jess hesitated. 'Lorenzo.'

'*Si?*'

'Has Leo's experience made you any happier about childbirth?'

'Not happier, *carissima*,' he said honestly, and thought for a moment. 'I think the word is re-signed.'

Jess held her breath, her eyes questioning on his.

'I can deny you nothing when you look at me so.' Lorenzo drew in a deep breath, then smiled at her. '*Va bene*, I promise that from now on we shall allow nature to take its course.'

Jess threw her arms round him and kissed him in passionate gratitude. 'Darling, just to hear you say that is the best Christmas present of all.'

'How I wish we could begin on such a course of nature at this very moment, *carissima*,' he said huskily, and smoothed a hand over the satin covering her breasts. 'Is Leonie nursing her son herself?'

'Yes. Though she won't have any real milk yet.'

'But to suck at his mother's breast will be of comfort,' said Lorenzo absently, his eyes on the curves half visible above his wife's nightgown. He slid it from one shoulder and took a nipple into his mouth, pulling on it in a way which turned Jess's heart over.

'*Mi amore,*' he said thickly after a throbbing moment, and buried his face against her breasts.

They lay still together for a while, but at last Jess forced herself to move away a little, and smiled ruefully into Lorenzo's eyes. 'I'm going to have a bath. I won't be long.'

'If we were at home I would join you,' he said, releasing her unwillingly.

'Which would make us *very* late for breakfast.' Jess slid out of bed and sat on the edge, looking at him. Dishevelled, heavy-eyed and in need of a shave, her husband nevertheless looked years younger than the haggard man who'd taken so terrifyingly long to arrive the day before.

'Why do you look at me like that?' Lorenzo enquired.

'I'm just so thankful you're here with me,' she said huskily.

'I, also.' He reached out a hand for hers. 'When the plane ran into fog I prayed very hard, Jessamy.'

'I prayed, too. And my prayer was answered, thank God.' She leaned down and kissed him, her lashes wet. 'Come on, lazybones, hurry up. I'm hungry.'

CHAPTER SIX

CHRISTMAS morning was invariably busy at Friars Wood, but on this occasion it was a frenzy of activity from very early on. When Jess and Lorenzo went into the kitchen to a chorus of greetings from Tom, Frances and Kate, the scent of roasting turkey was already mouthwatering in the air, and a pudding was simmering on the hob.

'How are things over at the maternity ward, Mother?' asked Jess, as she provided Lorenzo with toast and preserves.

'Nurse Golding's just arrived to check on Leo and the baby.' Frances chuckled. 'I gather Jonah did have to walk the floor a bit, until in desperation he eventually raided young Richard's stocking and offered him one of the dummies you bought, Jess.'

'Dummy?' said Lorenzo, mystified.

'*Tettarella,*' explained Jess, after some thought. 'Comforter, pacifier, Mother's salvation. Whatever you like to call it. I saw them when I was in town yesterday morning. Orthodontically approved, of course! They were meant as a joke for Leo, but I'm glad they came in handy. I suppose Adam's still sleeping, but where's Fenny?'

Tom grinned as he helped Lorenzo to coffee. 'She's watching the baby take his first bath.'

Kate chuckled. 'None of the presents she gets will be as fascinating as the new baby.'

'And how is Leonie feeling today?' asked Lorenzo.

'She's a bit tired,' said Frances, 'but that's only natural. When she's nursed the baby for a while Jonah's going to bring him over here and let her get some rest, so she'll be able to enjoy the rest of the day.'

'We'll take turns keeping him quiet,' said Jess, and grinned at Lorenzo. 'Are you up for that, darling?'

Lorenzo, who this morning was very obviously ready to agree to anything his wife or anyone else desired, nodded vigorously. 'I shall be most happy.'

Kate got up to clear away. 'Uncle Adam can take a turn, too,' she said chuckling. 'If he ever gets up, that is.'

'If babysitting is the order of the day we'd better get cracking,' said Tom. 'Time I lit the fire in the drawing room. Kate, can you take the dog out?'

'I can do that,' offered Lorenzo. 'I feel the need for fresh air after my journey yesterday.' He gave Jess a kiss, took advantage of the sheepskin jacket Tom offered, clipped a lead on the frisking dog and went out into the bright morning, blowing a kiss to his wife as he passed the kitchen window.

'It's obvious that everything's all right between you now,' said Frances in an undertone, when Kate went to answer the phone.

'Yes.' Jess looked sober. 'The possibility of never seeing Lorenzo again put my priorities in order very rapidly, believe me.'

Kate came back, chuckling. 'That was Mrs Briggs, wishing us a Happy Christmas. When she heard the baby had arrived she was frothing at the mouth. She can't leave the turkey to come herself, so one of us must spare a moment to pop down there to fetch the present she's got ready for the baby.'

'Adam can do it,' said his mother firmly. 'Go and wake him. Good old Mrs Briggs,' she added affectionately. 'I had a job to make her stay away yesterday, but I couldn't let her clean and polish on Christmas Eve. I'll be in more need of her services afterwards.'

Kate decided to be noble and take a coffee up to Adam. 'As it's Christmas,' she added sheepishly, as she went out.

'Those two are still thick as thieves, I see,' commented Jess. 'But Kate's changed a lot. She's less shy—more certain of herself. Do you think this Alasdair she talks of is responsible for that?'

'Possibly.' Frances smiled. 'To be honest I was worried before she went to Cambridge. Life there was bound to be so different from anything she'd known before; I wondered how she'd cope. But she has. And if the mysterious Alasdair has made it easier for her I'm grateful.'

Shortly afterwards the kitchen was alive with noise and bustle again when Adam came in demanding breakfast. Kate flatly refused to cook for him. Lorenzo came back with the dog, and Tom returned to report that the fire was drawing well and was not, as his wife had commanded, smoking in the slightest, due to the seasoned cherrywood faithfully saved for it.

'Why can't I have bacon and eggs?' demanded Adam, eyeing his toast with disfavour.

'No one has that sort of thing on Christmas morning,' Kate said firmly.

'But I've been away from the bosom of my family for ages; you'd think you'd be happy to feed me,' he said, looking martyred. 'I'm a growing lad—'

'Lord, I hope not,' said his mother fervently. 'Toast and marmalade is the only thing on offer, so eat it, then drive down to Mrs Briggs, please, Adam. She's got something for the baby.'

Fenny came running in to announce that the nurse had just left. 'Jonah says can someone help with the baby stuff,' she said breathlessly. 'He's going to bring Richard over now, so Leo can rest.'

'I will,' said Adam, gulping down the last of his coffee. 'I can go down to Maison Briggs later.'

The small procession arrived shortly afterwards, with Jonah bearing a tightly wrapped bundle, Adam bringing up the rear with the Moses basket and a holdall, and Fenny running alongside like a small tug bringing a liner into port. The moment Jonah was through the door he handed his son to Frances.

'There you are, Grandma. All yours.'

'Thank you, Jonah. I'd better make the most of this before your mother arrives,' she said, smiling as she received her grandson. And because young Richard Savage was perfectly happy to lie in his grandmother's arms, but vociferous with his objections when laid in the Moses basket, Frances Dysart was obliged to sit enthroned with him, and delegate her usual tasks to whichever of her family volunteered to take them on.

'Because no way am I handing you back to your daddy yet,' she declared, smiling lovingly at the baby.

'I could hold him,' said Fenny eagerly.

'And so you shall later,' promised Frances. 'When we're all in the drawing room, and you're comfortable on the sofa, I'm sure Jonah will let you cuddle him.'

'Of course you can, Fen,' said Jonah promptly. 'I could have done with some help in that area in the night, believe me!'

Lorenzo was only too happy to take on any task Frances desired, and threw himself into the spirit of the things with an enthusiasm which both amused and touched his wife. He helped Fenny set out Christmas crackers on the dining room table, then insisted he help Jess peel potatoes, and even made a start on the brussels sprouts, declaring he was perfectly happy to prepare them as long as he wasn't obliged to eat them.

'Barbarian,' said Jess, laughing, and rubbed her cheek against his arm as they worked.

Tom, viewing their loving rapport with relief, took the turkey from the oven, as Frances instructed, then firmly took charge of his grandson. 'Your job to see if it's done, Chef,' he told his wife.

By the time Adam returned with a gaily wrapped package from Mrs Briggs, the meal was well in hand, but young Richard Savage was protesting.

'He's wet,' said Frances, investigating. 'Fancy changing his nappy, Jonah?'

'Not enormously, no,' he admitted warily. 'He's so small, and he wriggles so much. It's a terrifying job.'

To the riveted audience it was obvious that the new father, so proficient at most other things, was all fingers and thumbs as he laid his son on a towel on the table and removed the offending garment.

'You put the wet nappy in this little bag and tie it up,' said Fenny, demonstrating efficiently. 'Then you put it in the bin.'

'Wow, Fen,' said Adam, impressed. 'You're a quick study.'

'Easy-peasy,' she said airily. 'My friend Laura's got a baby sister.'

'Laura, the fount of all knowledge,' he teased.

Young Master Savage strongly objected to the process of nappy-changing, and made no bones about his disapproval. Soon afterwards, when it became obvious that no amount of cuddling was going to quieten him, Jonah wrapped him up and took him off to seek comfort from his mother.

'We should be with you in an hour. Perhaps someone could come over and give us a hand then,' he said, as he took his wailing son away.

After Jess had joined Lorenzo in a call to Lucca, to wish his sister and her family a Happy Christmas, they returned to the kitchen to drink coffee with the others, then Jess got up and beckoned to Lorenzo. 'I'd like to see Leo myself, ask if there's anything she needs. We can supply any help required.'

Kate grinned as she looked up from the gravy she was stirring. 'If the baby carries on airing his views like that perhaps you should try a lullaby, Jess!'

On the way to the Stables Lorenzo swung his wife's hand in his, breathing deeply in the still, cold air. 'Isabella was deeply relieved that all is now well with us, Jessamy. But even though I regret our quarrel very much, *carissima*, because it has brought us here together, like this, I am also glad of it.'

'You're enjoying Christmas at Friars Wood?'

'Very much.' He smiled down at her, then paused as they reached the door of the Stables and bent to give her what was meant to be a fleeting kiss, but changed into something so much more that when the door opened they were still locked in each other's arms, lost to the world.

'Ahem,' said Jonah, grinning from ear to ear.

With an impenitent shrug Lorenzo released his scarlet-cheeked wife. 'It is no sin to kiss one's wife,' he said, laughing.

'Better than kissing someone else's,' agreed Jonah. 'Come with me, Lorenzo. I'll give you a glass of something while Jess goes up to Leo.'

Leonie sat propped up against the pillows on Adam's bed, fully dressed, but with her shirt unbuttoned to allow her son access to her breast.

'Hi!' said Jess, taking the chair beside her. 'How's little mother?'

'Fine. But not so little any more. It took some time to find something reasonably festive which fitted.' Leonie pulled a face. 'I thought I'd be back to normal once I'd parted with his nibs here, but not so, alas.'

'You may be a touch on the voluptuous side, Leo, but you look wonderful!'

'I feel amazingly good, actually. A bit sore here and there, but nothing untoward. No stitches, thank goodness.' Leonie looked steadily at her sister. 'And how are things with you two?'

Jess met the look head-on. 'Better than I deserve. I can't believe, now, that I behaved like that. Running back here because I couldn't get my own way. Things will be different from now on.'

'The first year of marriage is always difficult, remember. And you and Lorenzo didn't live together first, like most people these days. You need time to adjust to each other.'

Jess shivered. 'Yesterday I thought our time together had run out. If Lorenzo's plane had crashed—'

'No point in thinking like that,' said Leonie swiftly, and shifted the baby to the other breast.

'Does that hurt?' said Jess curiously as she watched the small mouth fasten avidly.

'A little bit. But once the milk really comes in I'll be fine. And so will he.' Leonie smiled at the drowsy little head. 'Funny to think that this time yesterday he hadn't arrived.'

'You gave me a terrific shock,' said Jess ruefully. 'When I saw you sitting there in the bathroom my life passed before my eyes!'

'You were wonderful. No panicking—'

'I was a jelly inside.'

'But you didn't show it. *And* you had the bottle to hang on through the whole performance.' Leonie smiled. 'I wouldn't have blamed you if the overture had sent you running for cover.'

'Wild horses wouldn't have dragged me away.' Jess smiled as the baby's mouth parted and the little head lolled. 'Is that it?'

'For now. He's tired. All that sucking takes effort.' Leonie wrapped her son securely, then smiled at Jess. 'Could you pat him against your shoulder to get his wind up? Time we were making a move.'

Jess handled her nephew as though he were a stick of dynamite, but Richard Savage settled contentedly against her shoulder as she straightened.

'Brilliantly done,' said her sister, getting off the bed. 'I'm looking forward to the little walk. Jonah was all for carrying me over to the house, would you believe?'

'I do believe. Not much wrong with *your* first year of marriage so far,' said Jess soberly.

'Ah, but this should have been our eighth year, not our first, remember? We had all those years in the wilderness without each other.' Leonie smiled. 'It tends to make us appreciate what we have.'

Jess nodded. 'Point taken. Can I carry the baby downstairs?'

'Carry him all the way to the house if you want.' Leonie gave her abundant bronze locks a final flick with the brush, added a touch of lipstick, then waved her sister on. 'You go first. I'm not up to speed yet.'

Jess went down the stairs with great care, her eyes on her sleeping burden. When she reached the ground floor she looked up to see her husband watching her in a way which made her heart leap.

'Shall I take him?' asked Jonah.

'No, darling,' said his wife, joining them. 'Lorenzo can go on with Jess and the baby. You and I will make stately progress behind them.'

'I could easily carry you—' he began, but Leonie shook her head, laughing.

'No, you couldn't. I'm not the sylph I was, believe me. Anyway, I don't need to be carried. The exercise will give me a good appetite for the turkey.'

'If you wish, Jessamy, I could take the baby,' offered Lorenzo, hovering.

She shook her head firmly. 'Jonah's mother will be arriving with his aunt Helen any time now. This is my last chance to cuddle Richard for the rest of the day.'

Lorenzo laughed indulgently as they walked back to the house, leaving the new parents to follow slowly behind out of earshot. 'Take care,' he warned, as he took her elbow to guide her up the steps towards the door.

'I have done this before, you know,' she informed him. 'I'm not a total amateur.'

Lorenzo frowned. 'You have friends with children?'

'No. But Fenny's only seven, darling. I used to look after her a lot when she was a baby.'

'I had forgotten that,' he said, sobering, and Jess bit her lip, annoyed with herself for reminding him of the tragic circumstances of Fenny's birth.

Tom ushered them straight into the drawing room. 'Come and join us, Lorenzo. Adam and I are taking five in here while Kate and Frances put the finishing touches to the meal. Jonah's people should be here any minute.'

'Can I trust you men to take care of the baby?' demanded Jess. 'I need to run up and change.'

'I'm quite capable of dealing with my nephew,' said Adam loftily, looking on while Jess settled the baby down in the Moses basket.

'No poking him awake, mind!'

'As if,' said her brother aggrieved.

Jess squeezed Lorenzo's hand as she went from the room, then took a look in the kitchen.

'Everything's in hand,' said Frances, who was now wearing a red wool dress more in keeping with the occasion. 'Kate's taken Fenny up to change, so you dash off and do the same. How's young Master Savage?'

'He's in with the men, but Leo's on her way, so I'll leave you to settle her on a sofa.' Jess tore from the room and raced upstairs. In her room she stripped off sneakers, jeans and sweater, and put on her supple suede boots. She took the creamy cashmere dress from the wardrobe and pulled it over her head, wriggling until it fitted snugly round her hips. She added at touch or two of make-up, brushed her hair into place, then hurried from the room, almost colliding with Kate in the doorway.

'Wow,' said her sister, eyeing the dress. She reached behind Jess to examine the label, and whistled softly. 'Did Father Christmas bring you this?'

'It's Lorenzo's present to me,' said Jess happily. 'There's a matching coat to go with it.'

'Greater love hath no man!' Kate pushed back hair which had been washed and de-crimped, and now fell in a gleaming mane down her back. 'I won't ask what went wrong between you and Lorenzo, because it's obviously been put right. But I'm glad you're home, Jess. Christmas wouldn't have been the same without you. Now let's go down before I go all mushy,' she added briskly.

'There's the doorbell,' said Jess, as they hurried along the landing. 'Jonah's family, no doubt. Perfect timing.'

CHAPTER SEVEN

THE moment Flora and James Savage arrived, with their sister-in-law Helen in her wheelchair, the day's festivities shifted up another gear. After joining in the hubbub of kissing and congratulations Jess left Lorenzo to Adam and Jonah, and insisted Frances stay with everyone in the drawing room while she helped Kate with the vegetables their mother liked to leave to the last minute.

The two girls worked together at speed, enjoying the respite before the festivities. They chatted happily together, bringing each other up to date with their news while they drained and decanted vegetables, filled sauceboats, and finally loaded everything on to the familiar old trolley where the turkey waited in all its savoury fragrance.

'You push and I'll pull,' said Kate, as they trundled towards the dining room. 'Do you think the baby will let Leo have some lunch?'

'With two grandmas and a selection of aunties all ready to entertain him I think it's a fairly safe bet!'

They went to the drawing room door, caught their mother's eye, and Frances stood up and clapped her hands.

'Lunch is served, everyone.'

There was an instant burst of activity. Jonah pulled his wife to her feet, Adam took the handles of the Moses basket, Lorenzo took the base, Jess pushed Helen's wheelchair, and Tom hurried off to open the wine while Kate took Fenny ahead to show everyone to their places round the long, festive table.

Before he began carving the turkey Jess set in front of him Tom Dysart paused, and demanded everyone's attention.

'Before we eat let's take a little time to give thanks for the surprise appearance of young Richard Savage yesterday, also for the safe arrival of Lorenzo and of everyone else who travelled, both yesterday and today, to join us for this extra-special occasion. And, last but not least, let us be truly thankful not only for the food, but to those who prepared it.'

'Hear, hear,' said James Savage with enthusiasm, and got to his feet. 'I'd like to propose a toast myself. To Leonie, with my grateful thanks for giving Flora and me the best Christmas present we could possibly have.'

The toasts were drunk, then Tom began carving and Frances and Kate handed round plates while Jess rushed back to the kitchen to take the roast potatoes from the oven and transfer them to a hot platter. As the meal progressed the baby made no objection to the noise when cracker-pulling was followed by bursts of laughter at the corny jokes inside.

'Obviously a party animal, our son,' said Leonie, looking into the cot as she began to eat. 'He's not asleep, you know.'

Jonah leaned over to investigate, grinning as he saw two tiny flailing fists. 'I should get on with your lunch, darling. I think he may be shaping up for a protest.'

'No need to interrupt your meal, Leo dear, even if he does,' said Flora Savage swiftly. 'Plenty of willing hands to take him until you've finished.'

'Jonah says *I* can cuddle him later,' said Fenny, putting in her claim first, and Helen laughed affectionately and patted her hand.

'I hear you watched his bath this morning. Was that fun?'

While Fenny launched into a full, unabridged account of the entire process, Jess turned to Lorenzo with a smile. 'By this time Fenny's usually had all her presents and the rest of the day is a bit of an anticlimax.'

He laughed softly. 'This Christmas all she can think of is the baby.'

Something in his voice sent Jess's spirits soaring. She smiled up into his eyes. 'More champagne?'

Lorenzo shook his head. 'As you know well, I need very little wine when I am with you, *tesoro*.'

Jess flushed as she found several pairs of indulgent eyes watching them, but right on cue the baby raised his voice in furious protest. Flora Savage put down her knife and fork so promptly everyone laughed, and Jonah removed his son from the cradle to hand him over.

'There you are, Granny. The moment you've been waiting for!'

Leonie watched in amusement as her mother-in-law began addressing her grandson with the usual stream of baby-talk. 'Not that I've any objection,' she whispered to Jonah, 'if it produces the right result.'

By the time Christmas pudding and brandy sauce had been consumed, and everyone was replete, it became obvious that no amount of cuddling and baby-talk would pacify the miniature tyrant any longer.

'I'll retire to the study sofa,' said Leonie, taking her husband's hand to get up. 'There are times when a son needs his mother, I'm afraid, Granny.'

Flora Savage handed over the squalling bundle and gave Leonie a kiss. 'You look tired, dear. Which is hardly surprising. Have a good rest away from all the noise. Jonah, you go with her and see she stays quiet for a while.'

Leonie fixed everyone with an admonishing eye over her son's head. 'But listen, no present-opening until I get back to you, OK?'

The older generation were banished to rest in the drawing room, and Lorenzo and Adam, with some enthusiastic assistance from Fenny, helped Kate and Jess as everything was cleared away, the dishwasher loaded, and coffee and tea made to send into the drawing room.

'All right, Marzi, hold your horses,' said Jess, as she put some turkey bits and pieces into his bowl. 'After that,' she added, as the dog began wolfing down his treat, 'he'll need a good long run. And by the time we get back maybe Leo and Jonah will be ready to join us.'

'And Richard too,' said Fenny eagerly.

'And Richard too.' Kate ruffled her hair. 'Go on, get your fleece on; we're all going for a walk. Unless,' she said demurely, turning to Jess and Lorenzo, 'you two have other plans?'

'A walk would be delightful,' Lorenzo assured her, grinning.

'Only I must be back by five,' said Kate, glancing at her watch.

'What happens at five? It's dark by then,' said Adam, rejoining them.

'Never you mind,' muttered Kate.

The light was fading fast in the still, silent afternoon as they went outside. Lawns, orchard and woodland surrounded Friars Wood on three sides, but the fourth was bounded by the cliff path, which gave a view of the six-hundred-foot drop to the River Wye below. The retriever, deliriously happy with so much company, rushed all over the place to investigate smells and sounds, his herding instincts sending him back at regular intervals to the group of walkers.

'You are happy, *carissima*?' asked Lorenzo, holding Jess's hand in his inside the pocket of Tom Dysart's sheepskin jacket.

'More than I ever hoped to be,' she assured him, and reached up to kiss his cheek, losing her footing in the process. Lorenzo snatched her up into his arms.

Adam grinned. 'Honestly, Jess, look at the heels on those boots! You never learn, do you?'

Lorenzo set his burden down carefully. 'I think my wife is perfect as she is.'

Kate roared with laughter as Adam looked lost for words for once. 'Well said, Lorenzo. Come on, big brother, I'll race you across the bowling green.'

The wide stretch of lawn was the only flat place of any size throughout the tiered garden, and with a roar Adam set off after Kate, his long legs covering the ground at a rate that should have defeated his sister, but to his astonishment she was at the far hedge long before he reached it, winning loud applause from the others on the terrace.

'You might—have—warned me,' panted Adam as he caught up with his sister, who, to add insult to injury, wasn't even breathing very hard. 'What happened? Are you training for the London Marathon or something?'

'No. I just run a bit with Alasdair now and then.' Kate grinned at him as she skipped up the steps to the terrace. 'You're out of shape, Adam Dysart. Too much soft living.'

'I'll give you soft living,' he growled, and picked her up and slung her over his shoulder like a sack of potatoes as they joined the others. 'No screaming, Auntie,' he reminded her, as she beat furious fists on his shoulders. 'You'll disturb the baby.'

'I do so hate a poor loser,' giggled Jess. 'Put her down, for goodness' sake, Adam.'

Adam dumped Kate down and advanced on his sister, grinning. 'Fancy the same treatment your-self, by any chance?' He laughed, holding up his hands in mock surrender when Lorenzo raised a warning eyebrow. 'All right, all right, I didn't mean it.' He heaved a sigh. 'Would you believe it? Fancy being trounced by a half-pint female like Kate. I must be losing my touch.'

Fenny slipped a consoling little hand into his. 'I think you run very fast, Adam.'

He smiled down at her. 'Then who cares what the others think? Come on, Fen, time to open those presents. Only quiet as we go in. We don't want to disturb young Savage.'

When they arrived in the drawing room they found Leonie there before them, installed on one of the sofas with Jonah, and the baby, dummy firmly in mouth, fast asleep in the Moses basket beside her. In contrast to the deepening twilight outside, the room appeared even more welcoming than usual, with rose-shaded lamps lit and lights twinkling on the mammoth Christmas tree in the window.

'About time, you lot,' said Tom, 'otherwise it'll be Boxing Day before we open the presents.'

Jess ordered Adam and Lorenzo to deliver the parcels she was sorting out with Kate, and soon everyone was exclaiming in pleasure over their spoils. Fenny almost disappeared beneath a pile of wrapping paper as she unwrapped books, games and CDs, and the latest incarnation of Barbie. But she gave a cry of pure ecstasy when she came to the suede jacket Lorenzo and Jess had bought for her in Florence.

'It's so *cool*!' she cried, scarlet-faced with excitement as she gave them both an ecstatic hug.

Cries of appreciation and thanks came from all sides, not least from Leonie when she found that Mrs Briggs's parcel contained several beautifully knitted woollies for the baby. But there were tears in her eyes, and in a few of the other eyes looking on, when Jonah presented her with a double string of pearls to celebrate the birth of their son.

Jess had expected nothing from Lorenzo, and had taken care to let everyone know that the dress she was wearing was his gift, along with its matching coat, either of which alone would have been enough to delight her. But when he produced a parcel which contained a handbag from the same source as her new boots Jess gave him a hug, and a look which said everything she had no intention of putting into words in public.

'*Cara,*' he whispered. 'I have another gift for you but I wish to present it later. In private.'

Jess smiled, surprised. 'I thought you'd given me more than enough already, Lorenzo.' She reached behind the tree and brought out the remaining parcel, a flat, square box wrapped in heavy gilt paper. 'I hope you're pleased with this.'

By this time everyone else had finished exclaiming and thanking each other, and great interest was taken in the parcel Lorenzo was opening with such unusually clumsy fingers Adam handed him the scissors provided for when Fenny grew impatient with knots and bows. Lorenzo cut the gold ribbon, removed the paper from a white cardboard box, then took out an object swathed in tissue.

Jess felt tense as Lorenzo removed the last wrapping to reveal a pencil study of her own head and shoulders, with the faintest suggestion of the Arno and Ponte Vecchio in the background. His teeth sank into his bottom lip as he stared down at it.

'What is it, Lorenzo?' demanded Fenny, leaning over his shoulder as he knelt beside his wife. 'It's you, Jess—and it's *lovely*!'

Lorenzo got to his feet, pulling Jess with him, and very deliberately kissed his wife's mouth. *'Tante grazie, carissima,'* he said huskily. 'It is exquisite.'

'Let's all have a look,' called Leonie, and with pride Lorenzo took the portrait on a tour of the room.

'I wanted Jessamy to sit for her portrait but she would not,' he informed Frances, directing a smile at his wife. 'Now I see why.'

'I didn't want anything formal in oil. And, having a lot of time on my hands these days,' Jess added, making a face at him, 'I wandered around

Florence, watching the artists you see working everywhere. Inspiration struck when I found this one.'

'So. You gazed at him with this particular look in your eye,' said Lorenzo, eyeing the portrait, 'and he agreed at once, this artist?'

'*She* agreed,' corrected Jess. 'I saw this girl near the Ponte Vecchio one day, sketching a pair of scruffy young students—'

'Hey,' said Kate indignantly.

'Nothing personal,' Jess assured her, grinning. 'Anyway, the artist had caught the essence of their youth, their sheer enjoyment of life, somehow. I was impressed. But when I asked her to draw me she wasn't at all keen at first. She said I looked too glossy, not challenging enough. I promised to return unadorned, dress down, do whatever she fancied. I managed to persuade her eventually, and the result is as you see.'

'Damn clever,' said Adam, eyeing the drawing with a professional eye. 'She's very good at her craft. The eyes are amazing—I can almost tell what you're thinking, Jess.'

'I hope not,' she said flippantly. Her mind had been on her husband while she posed. The look the artist had caught so skilfully was meant for Lorenzo alone.

'Right, talking of portraits,' said James Savage briskly, 'time for a photo session, everyone, before young Richard wakes up.'

It was the signal for several amateur photographers to take shots of the happy scene. Richard Savage was photographed in cherubic sleep, and when the various flashbulbs woke him Leonie picked him up and sat with Jonah's arm round her. Then came shots with each grandmother, followed by a poignant study of Helen smiling down tenderly on the child named for her dead husband. At last Fenny was arranged comfortably on the sofa, the baby given into her careful embrace, and she beamed at the camera in delight.

Leonie then declared the session over. 'The next photo opportunity can wait until tomorrow, I think. Right now my son and I both need a little peace and quiet, if you'll all excuse us for a while.'

'Why not go up and have an hour on your own bed upstairs with Richard?' suggested Frances. 'Then you and Jonah can join us for some kind of snack later. Flora says they don't want to be late getting back this evening.'

'We're only going to the flat in Pennington overnight, not back to London,' said James, yawning. 'But after all the excitement you'll be glad of a peaceful evening later.'

After Jonah had borne his wife and son away the senior members chatted comfortably together. Adam took Fenny off to the study to settle her in front of one of her new videos, Lorenzo helped Jess clear up all the discarded wrapping paper, and Kate, who kept sending surreptitious glances towards the clock, offered to make tea, but was refused. No one, it seemed, had room for anything at all.

'I'll just wash the cups, then,' she said quietly, and Lorenzo got up to carry the tray for her.

Jess followed them into the kitchen, yawning. 'Fancy another walk with the dog, darling?' she asked her husband.

'Of course,' he said promptly. 'Will you come too, Kate?'

She grinned lasciviously. 'Play gooseberry? *Moi?* No fear. I'd rather do the dishes.'

Wrapped in borrowed coats and scarves, with Tom Dysart's powerful torch to light the way, Jess and Lorenzo walked briskly along the cliff path, Lorenzo holding firmly to the leash.

'He wants to run,' he said, laughing.

'In the daytime we let him. But since he got lost this year we keep a firm hold in the dark.' Jess tightened her fingers around Lorenzo's. 'Rein him in. Show him who's boss.'

'I hope he likes the idea better than you do,' said Lorenzo slyly. 'At least the dog is unable to run away at the moment, unlike my wife, who left me the moment I exerted a touch of authority.'

'A touch!' she said wrathfully. 'You said go, remember. So I did.'

'I shall never let the word past my lips again,' he said, half joking, as they began descending the slope of the walled garden.

'I won't run away again, either,' she promised, not joking at all.

Lorenzo came to an abrupt halt, ignoring the dog who frisked round them in impatience to keep moving. 'It would be easy to say that I shall never hurt you, or give you cause to be unhappy. But I am human, *carissima*, and I am a man, and therefore fallible. But one thing I can swear with certainty. *Ti amo*, Jessamy. And while there is breath in my body I will always love you.'

Jess hugged him close, too full of emotion to speak, until the dog leapt up at them in demand, and they both laughed and continued their walk through the wood, letting the dog rootle and sniff to his heart's content before they retraced their steps back to the house. They were taking their coats off in the kitchen when the telephone rang, and smiled at each other when Kate shot off to answer it before anyone could beat her to it.

'She's been on edge this past hour, so she was obviously expecting fhat,' said Jess. 'No wonder she didn't come for a walk.'

'A lover, perhaps?' asked Lorenzo, then smiled as Jess looked stunned. 'She is a most desirable young woman, *tesoro*. Is the idea so astonishing?'

'I suppose not,' said Jess blankly. 'It's just that I think of her as my kid sister, I suppose—and want to fight anyone who even thinks of hurting her.'

'Adam also,' said Lorenzo dryly, and kissed her cheek. 'Do not worry, *carissima*, it is only a phone call.'

Jess nodded. 'Yes, of course. I'm being silly.'

She looked up with a smile as Kate came back into the kitchen. 'Want some coffee?'

'That's shorthand for ''who was on the phone?'' I assume,' said Kate, looking flushed. She thrust a hand through her hair. 'Jess, do you think Mother will mind if I ask someone to supper tonight?'

Lorenzo bent swiftly to stroke the dog's head, avoiding his wife's eye.

'There's no shortage of food, certainly,' said Jess non-committally. 'Who did you have in mind?'

'Alasdair.'

CHAPTER EIGHT

JESS went to fetch Frances from the drawing room, deciding that this was a request best put to a higher authority.

'What is it, darling?' said Frances anxiously, as Jess hurried her back to the kitchen. 'Nothing wrong with the baby, is there?'

'No. Kate has something to ask you, that's all.'

'I know it's Christmas Day, family day and all that,' began Kate as her mother came in. She began twisting a lock of hair round and round her finger as she always did in times of stress. 'But would you mind if I asked someone to supper tonight?'

'Is that all?' said Frances, relieved. 'Of course I don't mind. One of your friends from school at a loose end?'

'College, not school. Alasdair Drummond—my friend at Trinity—the one I told you about—' Kate flushed bright red, and Jess took pity on her.

'Kate would like Alasdair to come to supper.'

'Does he live in the locality, then, Kate?' said Frances, surprised.

'No, he's from Edinburgh. But his parents are in Australia, visiting his sister, and his grandparents insisted he spend Christmas with them. They live in Gloucester, but they're going out to friends this evening, and he'll be on his own. So I thought you wouldn't mind if he came here for an hour,' finished Kate in a rush.

'No, I don't mind at all,' said her mother, so promptly Jess gave her a surprised glance. 'Give him a ring right now. But let me have an hour's grace to get things ready.'

Kate smiled guiltily. 'Actually, I was so sure you'd say yes I've already invited him.'

'Have you now?' said Frances dryly. 'Think I'm a soft touch, do you?'

'Of course not, Mother, you're an absolute star.' Kate hugged her gratefully. 'Thanks a million. I'll go up and have a shower in Fenny's bathroom so I don't wake the baby.'

After her flushed, excited sister had rushed from the room, Jess gave Frances an amused look. 'You fielded all that with amazing equanimity, Mother dear. The rest of us were never allowed to invite anyone here on Christmas Day.'

'Ah, but I think Frances feels it is wise for this young man to see Kate against the background of her family,' said Lorenzo, and smiled at his mother-in-law. 'Should he have any mistaken intentions towards Kate, the thought of a large father, brother, even the presence of Jonah and myself, might act as deterrent, no?'

'Precisely,' agreed Frances, returning the smile warmly.

'How did *you* feel when you first came here, Lorenzo?' asked Jess curiously.

'I was determined that my intentions towards you should be plain for all to see from the moment I met you,' he said, putting his arm round her.

'They certainly were,' agreed Frances, then frowned thoughtfully. 'I think we'll persuade James and Flora to stay on for a while if Helen's up to it—make it more like a party and less like a family inquisition for the poor lad. I'll do the kind of meal we can eat on our laps, keep it informal. I'd better broadcast the news, and get everyone up to speed.'

Jonah's family were only too pleased to accept the extension to the day. And Tom Dysart was in full agreement with Lorenzo that it was a good thing for the mysterious Alasdair to see Kate in her own environment. Adam, however, when he was finally roused from his prolonged nap, was anything but pleased.

'I knew it,' he said bitterly, storming into the kitchen. '*Minder?* Who did Kate think she was kidding? So instead of playing games or dozing in front of the Christmas film on television, like everyone else in the known world, now we've got to be polite to this muscle-bound idiot instead.'

'If he's at Cambridge he can hardly be an idiot. Especially if Kate likes him. What's eating you?' said Jess, surprised.

'I warned you,' he said, scowling. 'He's probably from some Scottish male academy where girls never set foot. One look at Kate and—'

'Oh, shut up, Adam,' said Jess, beginning to assemble napkins and knives and forks. 'Lorenzo, would you carve the ham, please? We might as well get everything ready.'

'Bring out the fatted calf while you're at it,' jeered Adam.

'Enough!' said Jess irritably.

'Your brother is in shock. Until now he has not thought of his little sister as having a lover,' said Lorenzo, honing a carving knife with expertise.

Adam stared at him in utter horror. 'Lover?' he said faintly.

'Isn't that what you're making all the fuss about?' demanded Jess.

Adam thrust a hand through his curly dark hair, looking horribly embarrassed. 'Yes, no—I don't know. Oh, hell, I hate sleeping in the day. I need a shower.'

'Use the one downstairs so you don't disturb the baby,' ordered Jess, and let out a gurgle of laughter at the look of dismay on Adam's face.

'But it's like an igloo in there!'

'Cold showers are very good for you,' said Jess without sympathy.

'Maybe we should offer one to lover-boy when he comes, then,' snapped Adam, and stormed out again.

'Poor Adam,' said Lorenzo, laughing. 'This is how Roberto behaved when Isabella first met Andrea. He, also, could not bear to think of his sister as the object of some man's desire.'

'Did you feel like that?'

'No. I liked Andrea. And I already knew him well. Besides, it was not Andrea himself that Roberto objected to. Merely the idea of Isabella with a lover. Just like Adam and Kate.'

'Put the knife down, darling,' said Jess suddenly.

'Perche?' said Lorenzo, obeying.

'Because I have a sudden need to be kissed. By you.'

'At once,' he said promptly, and took her in his arms, his mouth meeting hers with relish as she locked her hands round his neck. They broke apart, laughing, when they realised Fenny was watching them from the door, her nose wrinkled in distaste.

'Yuck. I hate kissing.'

'Forgive me, *piccola*, but I like kissing Jessamy very much,' said Lorenzo apologetically, eyes gleaming. 'She is my wife, you see.'

Fenny nodded glumly. 'Jonah kisses Leo a lot, too.' Her eyes lit up. 'Where's the baby? I fell asleep watching the video.'

'He's upstairs with his mummy and daddy,' said Jess. 'We'll leave them in peace until they come down. You can pass the time by showing all your presents to Aunt Helen.'

By the time the surprise guest was due to arrive Kate was very obviously on edge. When she rejoined everyone in the drawing room she had changed back into the cargo pants, worn this time with a canary-yellow T-shirt and a long black cardigan, but time hadn't allowed for any hair-crimping. As a result, despite a new layer of eye make-up, she looked very pretty but also very young, with her hair hanging down her back.

'You look quite delicious, Miss Kate,' said James Savage, and held out his hand. 'Come and sit by me and tell me what mischief you've been getting up to at Cambridge.'

Kate's air of tension gradually evaporated as she chatted about her course and her job at the restaurant to Jonah's parents, and firmly ignored her brother's air of cold disapproval.

Much to Fenny's disappointment, the baby had been settled down in Leonie's room, with Fenny's old baby-listener beside him.

'It's his bedtime, poppet,' explained Leonie. 'We really must establish a routine if we can. And we'll hear him through this the moment he cries.'

'I'll do the sprinting if necessary,' Jonah said, sitting down by his wife. He grinned at Kate. 'So when is this pal of yours arriving, sweetheart?'

'Any minute now,' she said tensely, eyeing her watch.

'Right,' said Tom, jumping up. 'Time for a round of Christmas cheer, I think. Adam, throw a couple of logs on the fire and give me a hand.'

Jess was in the dining room, collecting supplies of nibbles to consume with the drinks, when she saw a car draw up outside. She hurried to the front door and threw it open before the visitor could ring the bell, smiling warmly as a tall, athletic young man came up the steps towards her.

'Hello. I'm Jess Forli, Kate's sister. Welcome to Friars Wood.'

'Hi. Alasdair Drummond.' He took her hand in a bruising grip. 'Kate talks about you a lot. It's very kind of your family to put up with a stranger on Christmas Day.'

Kate's fellow student was built on heroic scale, with the shoulders of a rugby forward, exactly as she'd described him. He had piercing light grey eyes and close-cut brown hair that would wave if left to grow longer, and, Jess realised with a pang, he was very attractive indeed in an intellectual kind of way. But Kate had left one important detail out of her description. This was no lad straight out of school—Scottish academy or any other kind. At a guess Jess decided he was at least her own age, which meant several years older than Kate.

'No problem with the catering at this time of the year,' she assured him. 'Come in and meet the rest of us. It's just a family party.'

'All the more reason for my thanks.' He smiled wryly. 'It really wasn't my idea to gatecrash, but Kate insisted. Apparently she's got some problem with her work she'd like me to look at while I'm here.'

Jess felt very thoughtful as she led Alasdair Drummond along the hall towards the hubbub coming from the drawing room at the far end. She threw open the door and went in ahead of him, beckoning him inside, her heart contracting as she saw the look of unguarded delight on Kate's face

before her sister schooled her expression to one of
friendly welcome.

'Hi, Alasdair,' said Kate, jumping up to greet
him. 'You made it, then. Come and meet everyone.'

Within seconds the newcomer was absorbed into
the family gathering, fitting in with the ease of a
man used to most kinds of social occasions, as
comfortable with James Savage and Tom Dysart
as with Adam, whose attitude took a visible U-turn
from the moment he set eyes on the unexpected
guest.

'Kate was pretty cagey about her pal, wasn't she?'
said Adam in an undertone to Jess, as he helped
her transfer platters of food from the kitchen to
the dining room table. 'Four years in Edinburgh,
another at Harvard, now research at Trinity.
I pictured some randy teenager, but I was wrong.'
He gave Jess a mocking bow. 'And I admit it
freely.'

'So you're not worried any more?'

'Not a bit. It's obvious he doesn't think of Kate
in that way. He treats her like a kid sister.'

But watching Kate and Alasdair together, when
everyone crowded into the dining room to help
themselves to the meal, Jess wished she could
share Adam's relief.

'A bit of a surprise, this Alasdair,' murmured
Leonie, after Kate had taken her guest back to the
drawing room to eat.

'Yes. Adam, you'll be pleased to know, is relieved.'

'Poor misguided youth. Is he blind?'

'You can see it too, then? Kate's madly in love.'

'But Alasdair isn't,' said Leonie flatly.

'Not with Kate, anyway.' Jess sighed and buttered a piece of bread. 'Oh, well, it had to happen for her some time. And I don't think she'll come to any real harm with this man, at least.'

'Not physically, no.' Leonie smiled up at Jonah as he came in. 'Is all well upstairs?'

'Sleeping like a baby,' he chuckled, brandishing the monitor.

'Marvellous. I'll wolf this down while I can, then.'

'What is wrong, Jessamy?' said Lorenzo, joining them. 'You look troubled.'

'Do I?' she said in dismay. 'And I thought I was hiding it so well.'

'She's worried about Kate's friend,' said Leonie bluntly.

Lorenzo nodded. 'Not a lover, as Adam feared, after all. But just as dangerous to Kate in a different way. She is in love, no?'

Jonah nodded soberly. 'Poor kid. He doesn't see her that way at all, does he? If anything he's more brotherly towards her than Adam.'

Lorenzo put his arm round Jess. 'Do not upset yourself, *carissima*. You cannot live Kate's life for her.'

'I know.' She smiled brightly. 'Come on, then, let's go and join the fray.'

The evening was a very pleasant rounding off to a happy day, but shortly after supper Leonie grew visibly tired, and was advised to get to bed by her anxious parents. Jonah went up to fetch the baby, and, because Adam was deep in hot discussion of the coming six-nation rugby season with Alasdair and Kate, Lorenzo went off with Tom Dysart to carry Leonie's belongings back to the Stables.

Before Jonah took Leonie away Alasdair Drummond expressed his pleasure at meeting them, inspected the small face in the Moses basket with due reverence and offered his congratulations.

Shortly afterwards Fenny was taken to bed, then Flora and James Savage left with Helen, and Alasdair announced it was time that he, too, was on his way. After a round of polished thanks he said his goodbyes and Kate saw him out to his car.

'Nice chap,' said Tom thoughtfully.

'Very,' agreed his wife.

'Kate won't come to any harm there,' said Adam with satisfaction.

Jess sat down beside Lorenzo on a sofa, exchanging a troubled glance with him as he put his arm round her.

'Don't worry, love,' said Frances. 'Kate's a big girl now.'

Jess smiled. 'I know.'

'Nothing to worry about,' Adam assured her, then looked up with a grin as Kate came back in, her eyes like stars. 'You never said your friend was a lot older than you, half-pint.'

'You never asked,' she said carelessly, and turned to her mother. 'Nothing happening tomorrow, is there?'

'Not here. Your father and I are invited to drinks before lunch with the Andersons. The rest of you can forage for yourselves. Why, darling?'

'I'm meeting Alasdair in a pub at lunchtime. He's going to look over a project I'm doing for next term,' said Kate with satisfaction.

'Can I come?' demanded Adam.

'No you can *not*,' she said indignantly, then gave him a sisterly shove when she realised he was teasing.

Jess got up, holding out her hand to Lorenzo. 'Well, everybody, if you don't mind we'll call it a day. Fenny had us up bright and early this morning. I'm a bit tired.'

'You've been an enormous help, darling,' said Frances, embracing her. 'It's been a lovely day.'

After a round of goodnights, Jess and Lorenzo collected their share of the Christmas spoils, then went upstairs, hand in hand.

'Are you very tired?' asked Lorenzo, when they reached their room.

Jess smiled at him. 'No. But, much as I love my family, I feel a sudden, desperate need to be alone with my husband.'

He returned the smile, rubbing his cheek against hers. '*Grazie, mi amore.* I am fond of your family too, but there are times when a man needs only the company of his wife.'

Unlike the night before, Jess felt no shyness of any kind, only eagerness to get through the bathtime ritual at top speed. When Lorenzo rejoined her after his own session she was propped up in bed, wearing the apricot satin nightgown of the night before.

Lorenzo sat on the bed, looking at her. 'You look good enough to eat, Jessamy.'

'Like a ripe fruit! Are you hungry, then?'

'Only for you.' He smiled. 'But, even now, if all you wish to do is sleep, *innamorata*, I shall be very happy to hold you in my arms all night and let you do so.'

'Happy?' she teased.

He shrugged ruefully. 'Willing, then. *Allora*, let us just talk for a while, because there are things I must say to you.'

Jess patted the place beside her. 'Let's do our talking in here.'

'But when I hold you in my arms I find it impossible to concentrate,' he informed her.

She held his eyes. 'I very much *want* you to hold me in your arms.'

'Then I shall.' Lorenzo leapt to his feet and undressed, then slid into bed. 'Is this nightgown giving me a message?' he asked huskily, as she reached to switch off the light.

'I hope so.'

'What is the message, *amore*?'

'It's supposed to make me tempting enough to make you forget about talking,' she said bluntly.

'Ah!' He kissed her fleetingly. 'I thought perhaps it was saying you do not wish to be touched.'

'Wrong,' she said breathlessly, and took his hand in hers to smooth it over the satin covering the full curves of her breasts. 'Surely you can tell that I'm desperate for your touch, Lorenzo. I long for your mouth on mine, your hands on my body—'

His mouth stifled the rest of her words as he slid the nightgown from her shoulders, just as he'd done early in the morning, but this time when his mouth closed over a taut, pointing nipple his hands moved downwards, taking the slippery fabric with them as he skimmed the nightgown from her body and discarded it. Jess shivered with delight as Lorenzo drew her against him, whispering in his own language as he told her how beautiful and alluring she was, and how much he had missed her and longed for her. Jess replied in kind, haltingly at first, then suddenly fluent as his caresses set her on fire.

'This is the time for love, then?' she whispered, as she felt him aroused and ready against her. 'Not talking?'

'With you in my arms it is always the time for love,' he said hoarsely, and kissed her with such explicit emphasis to his words there was no more talk of any kind other than the choked endearments which stoked their mutual flame higher.

Jess responded fiercely, her mouth as urgent as

his, but soon his lips left hers to travel down her body in the hot darkness of their bed, seeking the place which throbbed in hot, moist welcome to his seeking tongue. She gasped, her thighs opening in helpless abandon to his caresses, and Lorenzo slid up her body and entered it with a swift, sure thrust, and kissed her hard to smother their mingled gasps of ecstasy at the contact. His hands slid beneath her hips to hold her closer, and her legs locked around him, their bodies joined in a driving urgency which brought them rapidly to fulfilment.

Still locked in each other's arms, they fell almost instantly asleep, but at some time in the night Jess opened her eyes in the darkness, her mouth curving in a smile as old as Eve. She kept very still, not caring that Lorenzo was making it difficult for her to breathe. This was where she was meant to be; she knew beyond all doubt. Not here in Friars Wood, nor in their apartment in Florence, nor even in the countryside in Tuscany at Lorenzo's family villa there. The location was immaterial. Her flight from Italy had taught her a vitally important lesson. Without Lorenzo her life had no meaning.

She stretched experimentally, and Lorenzo gave a deep sigh and loosed his hold a little. Able to breathe more freely, Jess smiled again in the darkness. Unknown to Lorenzo he had given her quite the best Christmas present possible. Tonight there had been no hiatus while Lorenzo protected her against the possibility of a child. And, knowing Lorenzo as she did, she was certain he had neither been careless, nor the victim of his own passion. The omission had been deliberate.

'*Carissima?*' said Lorenzo sleepily. 'You are awake?'

'Yes.'

He turned on his back, drawing her close to smooth her head against his shoulder. 'It seems I could not let you go, even in sleep.'

'I liked that a lot.' She sighed deeply. 'My bed was very cold and lonely before you came, Lorenzo.'

'I am glad,' he said fiercely. 'I did not sleep well in my room in Venice, either.'

'You know why I ran away?'

He turned her face up to his and kissed her. 'To bring me to my senses, you said, no? And you were successful.'

'Lorenzo.'

'*Si?*'

'Downstairs you said you had something to give me in private.' She nuzzled her lips against his bare shoulder. 'Thank you with all my heart, darling. It was the best present of all.'

Lorenzo reached to put on a light, then propped himself on an elbow, gazing down at her in astonishment. 'But I have not given it to you yet.'

'Oh.' Jess blushed vividly. 'I thought—'

'Ah!' His eyes glittered. 'I see. You think I forgot—'

'Not at all,' she said tartly. 'You never forget. I

just assumed that this was where we began to leave everything in nature's hands.'

'You are right.' His lips twitched. 'When I said I wished to talk, this what I meant to say. But in the end words were unnecessary, no?'

She laughed. 'The demonstration was beautifully explicit.'

'Beautifully?'

'When we make love it's always beautiful, Lorenzo.'

'Ah, *mi amore*. How much I love you.' He slid out of bed.

'Where are you going?'

'Only to fetch something from my jacket.' Lorenzo dived back into bed, shivering, and Jess hugged him close, pulling the covers over them. 'Give me your hand, Jessamy,' he commanded.

She obliged, surprised, but Lorenzo shook his head.

'The other hand, *per favore*.'

Jess felt him slide a ring over her knuckle to join her wedding ring, and pulled her hand out from the covers to stare in astonishment at the exquisite oval diamond glittering on her finger. *'Lorenzo!'* she breathed.

'Do you like it?' he demanded.

She swallowed hard. 'It's—glorious!'

'Have you never wondered why I did not keep my promise?' he demanded.

'What promise?' she said blankly.

He lifted both her hands to his lips and kissed

them. On her right hand Jess always wore the heavy gold dress ring Lorenzo had given her to mark the first week of their relationship.

'When I gave you this ring it was not yet our *fidanzamento*, so I asked you to wear it as a token of my love until I had the right to give you another.' Lorenzo smiled down at her. 'Yet though we have been married for several months you have never mentioned this missing ring.'

'I thought you meant a wedding ring!' Jess reached up and kissed him in passionate appreciation.

Because Lorenzo's response was equally passionate, and more, some time elapsed before he spoke again. 'I searched for the perfect ring and did not find it,' he said at last. 'So I had one made to my own design, to give to you on this special day.' He smiled a little. 'But I could not do this downstairs with your family—not after Jonah had presented Leonie with the pearls in gratitude for his son, you understand.'

'Perfectly,' she said, a lump in her throat. 'Have I ever told you how much I love you, Lorenzo Forli?'

'It would give me great pleasure to hear it again.'

Jess told him so at length, both in words and kisses, then curled close, waving her hand in the air to admire the ring.

'Lorenzo,' said Jess after a while.

'Yes?'

'I also have a gift I wish to give you in private. But it's going to be a while before it's ready.'

'Is it another portrait?' he asked, mystified.

'No. But you'll have to wait until July for it.'

Lorenzo shook her gently. 'Do not tease me, *amore*. What is this gift that takes so long?'

Jess smiled. 'This is much easier to say since you made love to me. Now I know you've changed your mind, I mean—'

'Jessamy, for the love of God, tell me!'

'We're going to have a baby in July,' she said in a rush.

Lorenzo stared at her blankly for a moment, then she saw light ignite in his eyes and he crushed her close, telling her in his own expressive language just how beautiful and clever she was and how happy she'd made him.

'Then you don't mind?' she said anxiously.

'It is too late to mind,' he said, laughing. 'All my desperate restraint was useless, it seems.' He shook his head. 'I thought I had been so careful.'

'Fate decided otherwise. Do you see now why I tried to seduce you the other night in Florence?' demanded Jess. 'I was pretty sure I was pregnant, but I so much wanted—needed—you to make love to me properly before I told you. I was so angry and hurt when you refused me I came storming back here.'

Lorenzo's eyes narrowed challengingly. 'And if I had not made love to you just now, "properly", as you say, would you have still kept our child a secret?'

Jess shook her head. 'No, of course not, I was just keeping the news until we were together again. Besides, I only found out for sure yesterday morning, when I went shopping for a test kit.'

'Have you suspected this for long?'

'Of course I have. But I haven't been sick, or felt tired. I felt so normal it seemed best to make sure before I went public.' Jess smiled at him jubilantly. 'It's obvious I'm going to be a natural, like Mother and Leo, not to mention your own sister, where producing babies is concerned. So promise me you won't worry any more, Lorenzo.'

'I promise I will try, *tesoro*.' He held her close. 'And I confess that to see Leonie today, looking so serene and beautiful, has done much to allay my fears.'

Jess sniffed hard. 'It's such a relief to hear you say that, darling. And you needn't be there at the birth, if you'd rather not.'

Lorenzo gazed at her in astonishment. 'Of course I shall be there. Nothing in the world would keep me away.'

Jess smiled through tears of relief. 'But you can see why I waited until today to give you the news,' she said huskily. 'It's my extra-special Christmas present to you.'

'For which *mille grazie*.' Lorenzo cupped his wife's radiant face in his hands, and kissed away her tears. 'Until tonight I thought that your portrait was the perfect present, *amore*. But I was mistaken. To know that you are expecting my child is the greatest gift of all.'

THE DOORSTEP BABY

Marion Lennox

Dear Reader,

What is it about Christmas? Every year I say "bah humbug, no fuss this year"—a feeling that lasts until my husband and children haul home our pine tree, we hang up our baubles and I listen to "Silent Night" playing on a dinky little windup carousel we've owned forever. Straightaway I'm all misty-eyed and romantic, and it's downhill from there. Santa, count me in!

Christmas where I live in Australia is hot and dry, so every year I yearn for snow and icicles on my mistletoe. *The Doorstep Baby* has snow aplenty, and kids and dogs and mince pies—and the most gorgeous hero! In short, it has everything a perfect Christmas needs.

I hope you do, too.

Marion Lennox

CHAPTER ONE

'THE most gorgeous male I've ever known is spending Christmas in *my* bed!'

Despite her weariness, a twinkle appeared in Lia's green eyes as she tucked in the sheets. Father Christmas definitely had a habit of giving her weird surprises. This year her surprise was one handsome ghost from her past—which had its problems—but maybe even a ghost was preferable to some Christmas gifts she'd had.

What else had there been? She thought them through, her laughter fading.

Last year her mother had given her a six months' subscription to a diet plan. Her mother and her two sisters were willow slim, and Lia was—well, her mother described her as dumpy and mostly Lia agreed, though Lia's husband, John, had declared she was deliciously curvy.

John had been ignored by her judgmental family. Lia's mother and her sisters were tall, blonde and beautiful. Lia took after her father. She was small, dark and 'built for comfort, not for speed', and they'd never stopped trying to 'improve' her. Hence the diet plan.

It wasn't only her mother who gave her unwelcome gifts. Two years ago her grandfather had given her a case of vintage port and announced he was staying on until Easter to drink it. Since Grandpa treated women as doormats, by Easter she'd been heartily sick of Christmas presents.

Then, three years ago… Her twinkle vanished completely at the memory. That had been the year John had died and Sam had been born, all within days of Christmas. Some Christmas! For once her family hadn't arrived *en masse*, and it had been the only Christmas when she'd desperately needed them.

Before that, Christmases had been blurry affairs of too many relatives, weird gifts or no gifts at all, and far too much work. One stood out, though— the Christmas seven years ago when she'd found out Pete Barring had been two-timing her. Pete…the man she'd loved with all her heart.

'And now he's coming back,' she told a pillow, shoving it into its cover with a fierceness that threatened to send feathers flying. 'Toad. I hope he's bald and fat and his fiancée has warts on her nose.'

Despite her depression, she found herself smiling again at this vision. Fat chance. All the Barring men were fabulous—big and dark, with eyes that crinkled into pools of laughter and deep voices that made you sort of want to melt. They'd never had trouble attracting any woman they wanted. Pete's father had been a notorious womaniser with looks to die for. Ben, Pete's identical twin, had been more fabulous at thirty-two than he'd been at twenty-five, and Pete would look just the same.

'Will look the same,' she reminded herself. 'That's what I get for opening this place as a bed and breakfast. Unwanted guests. He'll be here tonight.'

'And I'll bet he's just the same conniving, cheating, two-timing…' She caught herself as she heard bitterness in her voice. It startled her. Heavens, she should be well over her affair with Pete by now, she thought. There'd been a husband, two babies and seven years in between.

All the same… I hope he's met his match in his fiancée, she thought, glaring down at her gorgeous bed just waiting for the happy couple. Poor girl. No one deserves a Barring male.

They were all so alike. Pete had done his best to break her heart before leaving for overseas, and when Ben, Pete's twin, had killed himself in a high-speed car crash, there had been three women at his graveside who'd all thought they'd been his girlfriend. Ben had two-timed every girl in the district, and over in the US Pete had probably been doing just the same.

'The Barrings are blots on the page of humanity,' she muttered, and glowered. 'And why he has to come here…'

'Mummy!' Her daughter's voice broke into her dark thoughts. Four-year-old Emma was calling her from downstairs. Tomorrow was Christmas

Eve, and Em's excitement level was rising by the minute.

'I'll be down soon,' Lia called. 'Is there a problem?'

'There's a baby lying on our doorstep,' Em said.

There was, indeed, a baby on the doorstep.

Lia came downstairs to find the front door wide open and Emma staring, open-mouthed, down into a carrycot. Lia looked down, and her mouth dropped open to match her daughter's.

The baby was tiny—two or three months old at the most. It was asleep in its cocoon of blankets, its dark little lashes fluttering slightly as if its nap had only just started, or was about to end. The baby had deep black hair, wisping into curls, and its tiny, rosebud mouth was pursed as if a teat had only just been removed.

It was the most beautiful baby, and there was no mistaking whose it was.

'It's a Barring baby,' Lia whispered, staring down at the sleeping child and trying hard not to let her insides clench. The likeness was uncanny— but no one had told her Pete and his fiancée were bringing a baby. They hadn't booked for a baby, she thought wildly. Pete's mother had made the booking and she'd just said Pete was coming with his fiancée.

Maybe Pete hadn't told his mother they had a baby, she thought, staring down at the little one in stunned silence. Maybe they meant to spring it on

Mrs Barring as a Christmas surprise. Margaret Barring would be ecstatic, Lia knew, even if Pete wasn't yet married. She'd lost Ben, but to gain a grandchild from Ben's identical twin...

But... The old lady had only returned a month ago from visiting Pete in the States. Surely she would have known of this little one's existence? This didn't make sense.

By her side, Em was hopping up and down in excitement, tugging Lia's jeans in urgency. 'Mummy, you didn't tell me a baby was coming. Where's its mummy?'

'I expect they've just put the baby down while they've gone to get their gear from the car,' Lia told her, resisting the urge to kneel and scoop the sleeping baby from its carrycot. Her son Sam was three now, asserting his independence, and she missed the feel of a little one in her arms.

But Em was still babbling. 'Mummy, there isn't a car behind the hedge. No one else is here.'

That caught her attention. For the first time, Lia looked further than the stone steps where the baby lay. The farmhouse was set back from the road, with a cottage garden surrounding the entrance. The garden was covered with snow—a winter wilderness. A winding path led through the hedge dividing the car park from the garden. The hawthorn hedge was bare, and you could see right through it.

Em was right. There was no car behind the hedge.

Frowning, Lia walked out into the garden and made sure. She reached the gap in the hedge and peered in all directions. The driveway was deserted, and so was the road for half a mile in each direction.

This was curiouser and curiouser.

'No one's come in the house while I was upstairs?' she asked Em. Surely she would have heard someone come in, and Woof would have barked.

'Nope.' Em seemed extremely impressed by this turn of events. She dug her fingers into her dungarees and looked four-year-old important. 'I would have seen. Just Sam and Woof and me are here, and Sam and Woof are asleep.'

Weird! Lia frowned, taking one last look around the garden—willing someone to appear. No one did. Finally she lifted the baby, carrycot and all, and as she lifted, an envelope fluttered to the ground.

The envelope was addressed to Pete Barring.

Much to Em's approval, Lia carried the cot into the sitting room and placed it by the Christmas tree. The fire had been lit for her expected guests, the room was the cosiest in the house and there was an armchair where she could sink down and take a few lungfuls of air. She felt like she needed them. For some reason she was breathless.

What on earth was going on? If Pete hadn't arrived, then what was his baby doing here without him? In fact, Lia hadn't expected him this early—his mother had said he'd arrive after dinner, and it was now only four. So... She could be faced with hours of childcare until Pete arrived.

The cost of that care, she decided, was reading his letter. Lia didn't usually open letters addressed to others. Neither, however, did she take strange babies into her home. There was no way she was doing one here without the other.

She read—and then read again.

Dear Pete,

Your brother, Ben, got me pregnant and I was stupid enough to think he'd marry me. More fool me. Anyway Ben's dead and I've got a new boy-friend. He's taking me to Australia for Christmas. Maybe for ever. So here's Ben's baby.

I called her Amy but I don't care if you change it. Looking after her is too hard. I want a life! I tried to talk Mum into caring for her but Mum doesn't want the kid and neither do I. So I guess it's over to you. Contact Mum if you want any information but she's all yours.

Happy Christmas.

Becky Worth

Becky... Lia stared sightlessly down at the letter. She knew Becky. Becky Worth was a local girl, but she was misnamed. Worth? Ha! There was no more worthless piece of baggage in the district.

Becky was gorgeous, but she was air-headed, conceited and out for all she could get.

Lia had seen her in town in the last few months and had noticed she'd been pregnant. With Ben's baby? Maybe there'd been gossip, but Lia was always too rushed to listen.

She was rushed now. She needed to get around the sheep before dark, she needed to feed the hens, organise dinner, do some Christmas cooking… She didn't have time to stare sightlessly into the fire. It was time for Sam to wake so she could get things moving.

The baby would have to come while she did her chores, she thought numbly. Ben's baby…

It was Pete's baby now.

Mum doesn't want the kid and neither do I.

The words echoed in her head, dreadful in their intent. As if compelled, Lia knelt on the rug beside the carrycot, and the baby's eyes fluttered open. They were gorgeous eyes. Barring eyes.

Pete's eyes. Her heart twisted within her, jabbing with remembered pain.

'Is it a girl baby or a boy baby?' Emma whispered, awed.

Somehow Lia made her voice work, but it came out as if from a long way off. 'It's a girl baby, Em. Her name's Amy.'

'Amy. That's a nice name.'

'Mmm.' Involuntarily Lia's fingers fell to touch the baby's tiny hand, which was peeping out from under the covers. Soft little fingers curled around her ring finger—and clung. Somewhere inside, something warm and fragile started to grow. Something insidiously sweet. 'It...it is a nice name.' The baby gazed up at her and the feeling grew.

'She's smiling,' Em whispered. 'Mummy, she's smiling at us.'

And she was. The little face was creased into a smile of absolute delight that these two strange beings had entered her world.

Mum doesn't want the kid and neither do I.

Dreadful! For a mother to say that... Her feelings were threatening to overwhelm her. The baby smiled and smiled, and slowly Lia's mouth curved into a smile right back.

'Oh, you sweetheart,' she whispered, and in that fraction of an instant a bond was forged, and it was a bond of absolute trust.

There was nothing for it. Lia lifted the little one from her cocoon of blankets and held her to her breast, cradling her in the protective way of mothers the world over.

Mum doesn't want the kid and neither do I.

Dear heaven...

At nine o'clock there was still no sign of Pete.

Somehow Lia had managed everything that had needed to be done—no mean feat when juggling a four-year-old, a three-year-old and a baby.

For a start it had been a squash to get them all

into the cabin of the tractor so she could check the sheep. The snow had come early this year, meaning that the romance of a white Christmas was tempered by the fact that the hay racks had to be filled and the sheep checked daily. With forecasts for bad weather, she'd brought the sheep down from the tops to the fells nearer home.

It'd cost to hand-feed them this early. She should sell them, she thought wearily. There was no money in them now. There was no money in her little farm at all...

Then there'd been dinner. She'd forgotten how hard it was to cook while cradling a baby, but Amy had refused to be put down. In Lia's arms she'd chuckled and chortled and enjoyed her world, but returned to her carrycot you could have heard her displeasure in Scotland.

Sam and Emma were dumbstruck with wonder. They clapped their hands to their ears when she yelled. They watched with awe as Lia heated the formula she'd found in the base of the carrycot, and they sat, riveted, as she fed the baby. Sam even held her bottle for a couple of magic moments, his small face stunned with the seriousness of his responsibility.

Then Em and Sam wrinkled two identical noses in delighted revulsion at the contents of one nappy. Finally they were stunned into breathless silence when, at the end of their bath, Lia dipped Amy in for her turn.

Bathtime was immediately extended. It seemed

Amy appreciated bathtime. 'She loves it, Mummy,' Sam whispered, and they were all entranced by her joy. Even Lia found herself chuckling. The strain of facing Pete later that night faded in the joy of this little one.

But it was exhausting. By the time Lia had all three safely asleep she was so hungry and so tired she could barely stand. She'd been up since five a.m. She needed bed.

But…her guests were yet to arrive, and there was still Christmas to be faced.

'Drat them,' she said into the stillness. 'Drat Pete for making me feel like this.'

And drat her family. Twenty assorted relatives were descending on the farm the day after tomorrow and they'd expect Christmas with style. Lia came back downstairs, ate Sam's rejected toast fingers—that'd do for her dinner—and started cooking mince pies.

Where was Pete, then? Where on earth was the toad?

'If he leaves me with the baby…'

'He doesn't even know the baby exists,' she answered herself.

'So I'll send Amy to him gift-wrapped for Christmas.' And then she thought of the baby's downy head and delicious smile, and she felt her heart kick. Hard.

'Concentrate on Christmas,' she told herself. 'This baby is none of your business.'

And then the doorbell rang.

Pete...

For one long moment Lia closed her eyes, dredging for courage. Then, slowly, she wiped her floury hands, hauled the apron away from her jeans and sweater and went to answer the door to her long lost lover.

It was harder to open the door than she'd expected.

Pete wouldn't recognise her, she thought grimly, her hand on the door and her courage somewhere in her boots. The girl of seven years ago had been bouncy, young and pretty. So, what had changed? Her glossy brown hair hadn't faded, but instead of a chic, expensive cut it was a mass of shoulder-length curls, badly needing a trim. Her green eyes had lost their sparkle—they were shadowed now—and the ravages of the past few years had left indelible lines on her face.

She was twenty-seven, and she felt a hundred.

No matter. It couldn't matter. Pete probably wouldn't even recognise her.

She took a deep breath, pinned a bright smile of welcome onto her face and opened the door.

He was just as she remembered—and more. Pete Barring... He stood before her, filling her doorway with his muscled frame. He was smiling in the way she remembered, with his gorgeous dark eyes creased from constant laughter, and he had exactly the same effect on her heartstrings as he had all those seven years ago.

So little had changed, she couldn't believe it.

He must have come straight from the airport. He was wearing his airline captain's uniform, softly grey and immaculately tailored, with white shirt and deep navy tie embossed with the airline's motif of outstretched wings. There was gold braid on his arms and his pilot's wings insignia on his chest. But underneath the uniform... His jet black curls needed a cut—hadn't they always? He looked wind-tousled and casually at ease, and he looked capable, strong and intent. In short, he looked every inch a man in charge of his world.

Her Pete...

She could hardly breathe. It was as much as she could do not to slam the door in his handsome face.

Instead, somehow she made herself pull the door wide. Seven years was a long time. She was a different woman.

'Mr Barring. Miss Shelby. Do come in. You must be freezing.'

It was her standard patter but it had the effect of stopping Pete in his tracks. He paused, and his smile faded.

There was a woman by his side. She was beautiful—of course. Lia might have wished for warts, but if there was one thing she'd figured it had been that Pete's fiancée would have to be gorgeous. There was no wart in sight here. Helen Shelby was just like Lia's sisters.

She was slim and tall and blonde, with cream trousers and a gorgeous cream duffle-coat accentuating the beautifully cut blonde hair falling down to her shoulders. She had the bluest of eyes, her make-up was perfect and her lovely smile was creasing into a pout as Pete's hand held her back.

'Helen, wait.' His attention was all on Lia. 'Do I know you?' The crease between his eyes deepened.

Lia was in the shadows, she realised. The porch light was on, and so was the hall light, but the hall light was behind her. Pete was at a disadvantage. She could see him but he couldn't see her.

'Do come in.' She was smiling like a fool. She stepped back, into the light, and Pete's smile died as if it had never been.

'Lia!'

For a moment neither of them moved.

She hadn't seen this man for years, Lia thought stupidly—blankly—and she'd thought that time would have made things fade. Seven years ago she'd been so in love with him that she'd thought she'd spend the rest of her life as his wife. Then…he'd betrayed her and he'd left to take up a job as an airline pilot in the US. She'd married her John and life had gone on.

For a while she hadn't thought it could. For a while she'd felt like her insides had been torn out.

That was how she felt now. She stood, her silly smile pinned on her face, and she felt like sinking into the floor.

Somehow she had to speak. The woman—Pete's

fiancée—was looking at them as if they were both dumb.

'Your name's Lia?' the woman said, looking from one to the other. 'Do you two know each other?'

'Yes,' she managed, and afterwards she could never figure out how she did it. 'I'm Lia Holt.'

'Lia Matherson.' Pete's voice sounded as though he'd just been kicked in the solar plexus.

'Lia Holt,' she said more firmly, looking warily into his stunned face. 'Didn't your mother tell you I married?'

'I...' He put a hand up and raked his deep thatch of hair, as if he were all at sea. 'I guess. I can't... But... Is this *your* place?' His words were suddenly explosive.

'Yes.' She'd had more warning than he'd had, she thought. She had herself more together. 'I guess you must be Mr Barring's fiancée,' she said to the woman. 'Mrs Barring has told me about you.'

This was Lia at her hostess-like best. She gave Pete her very nicest smile and he looked visibly taken aback. There was no way she'd let him see he'd unnerved her. 'Would you like to see the living rooms, or would you like to go straight to your bedroom and see downstairs tomorrow?'

'We'll go straight to our room,' Helen said, casting a strange look at Pete. 'Bring the suitcases, darling.'

'Oh, yes... Right.' He was totally flummoxed.

He didn't move. 'Mum didn't say this was your place,' he told Lia, his voice edged with the beginnings of anger. 'She just said she'd booked us into a bed and breakfast.'

'She tried the hotels first,' Lia said, still managing to smile her hostess smile. 'They were full. I don't usually take guests over Christmas but I did it as a favour.'

'Some favour,' he said explosively, and Helen frowned again.

'Darling, it's quaint. I'm sure we'll be comfortable.'

'I'm not staying…'

'There's nowhere else to stay,' Lia said calmly, 'short of putting up camp-beds in your mother's nursing home. I'm sorry, Mr Barring, but we're stuck with each other.'

He cast her a goaded look, and she managed to keep her smile intact. This was starting to feel…interesting. He'd hurt her so much, and to make him suffer a little was fine. He surely deserved it, and when he saw what was waiting upstairs…

'You don't need to spend time here, apart from sleeping,' she said, becoming more cheerful second by second in the face of his dismay. For years she'd thought he should suffer some of what he'd put her through. And now… For once a Barring male wasn't completely in control of what was about to happen. 'Why don't you collect your suitcases and come in to the warm?'

She adjusted her silly, bright smile and waited. Impersonal efficiency. It was the only way to handle this.

But he was still concentrating on facts. 'So you married,' he said at last.

'Y-yes.' She wasn't elaborating on that one.

'You have children?'

'Two.' Her fixed smile stayed in place. 'Maybe you'll meet them tomorrow. Emma's four and Sam's three.'

'They won't wake us, I hope,' Helen said, giving a shudder. 'I'm not into children.'

'My children won't wake you.' They wouldn't, either. Lia found her smile broadening. It wouldn't be *her* children doing the waking. She stood aside for them to pass. This was going on too long. She looked at Pete again, and her smile died. Maybe revenge wasn't so sweet after all. He looked... stunned. And he looked just like the Pete she'd fallen hopelessly in love with all those years ago. Gorgeous, but just a touch vulnerable under the outward strength.

It was an illusion. There was nothing vulnerable about this man and she had to get away. 'If you'd like to leave your suitcases where they are and bring them in later, I'll show you to your room.'

The room she showed them was the best room in the house. The master bedroom. Lia loved it. It looked south over the Yorkshire Dales and it had the most spectacular views in the world. Even on a bleak winter's night, like tonight, the moonlight cast a silver glow over the snow-covered fells and you could see for ever.

Fabulous.

It was also Lia's bedroom, but guests were willing to pay more for it so when the demand was there she moved downstairs with the children. She always felt a pang, showing guests in here. It was as if she were renting out part of herself.

When Margaret Barring had asked her to accommodate Pete and Helen she'd decided to put then in the twin rooms facing north. But...

'Get real,' her older sister had said, when she'd told her what was happening. 'What century are you working in? If they're engaged to be married they'll be sleeping together.'

'Maybe I shouldn't assume—'

'They've booked as a couple—right?'

'R-right.'

'Then treat them like one.'

So she had. She swung the door wide and waited for them to pass in. Helen went first, and then Pete, casting her a strange look as his body brushed hers.

Then he looked at the bedroom. 'But—' he said, but he got no further.

'This is lovely,' Helen interjected, bouncing forward to perch on the vast four-poster bed. 'Oh, Pete, there's even an antique crib in the window embrasure. How quaint. We can lie in bed and pretend to be an old married couple.'

Pete frowned. There was silence. There was even silence from the quaint antique crib.

And as for Lia... Her place was no longer here. So...

'I'll leave you,' Lia said firmly. 'Oh, and Mr Barring...'

'Yes?' Pete sounded as if he'd had all the breath knocked out of him.

'You might like to read this,' she said demurely, then handed him his letter and closed the door on the three of them.

Twenty, twenty-one, twenty-two...

Lia went downstairs, put the kettle on—and waited. Subconsciously she counted the seconds. He'd be reading the letter. And reading it again. Thirty-five, thirty-six... She put coffee in her mug.

There was a male exclamation. A woman's voice raised in shock. A man's low rumble, cut off short.

Sixty-four, sixty-five... They'd be checking out the crib right now. Meeting Amy. She poured in boiling water. Added milk.

Silence.

Amy was so much a Barring. Pete would be staring at her as if he were seeing a ghost. And thinking...what?

The silence ended. There were rough male footsteps, taking the stairs three at a time.

She tightened her hold on the mug, as if warmth could give her strength to face what was coming. And then the kitchen door flung open with a crash that almost took it off its hinges.

'What on earth…?' Pete's voice was thunderous. 'Is this a joke?'

'I beg your pardon?'

'There's a baby in our bedroom!'

CHAPTER TWO

LIA had had six hours to get used to the idea, and that made a difference. She had herself together—almost—and was able to face him without flinching. Carefully she placed her mug down and faced him from the other side of the wooden table. He'd hauled his tie off, and his top shirt button was undone. It made him look exposed—open to pain.

Which was a stupid thing to think!

'Yes,' she said calmly. 'Your niece arrived earlier.'

'My…' He took a deep breath. 'My niece.'

'That's what the letter says. She arrived about four this afternoon—abandoned on my doorstep. I thought of telephoning your mother or contacting the police, but in the end I thought you'd prefer it left to you.' She gave a determined nod and turned away to the stove. 'Excuse me. My mince pies are ready.'

There were further footsteps on the stairs and Helen stalked in—not quite as serene as she'd been five minutes ago. 'What's happening, Pete? Is it hers? I mean…it must be.'

Lia ignored them. Calmly she lifted her pies from the oven, and the smell wafted out over the kitchen. Gorgeous! She put another tray in, then

265

started lifting each cooked pie from tray to wire cooler—as if nothing were more important than her mince pies.

'Pete, is it her baby?' the voice said insistently. 'I assume—'

'Lia, is this some sort of sick joke?' Pete demanded again.

Still she refused to look up. If she did she might laugh—or cry, which was way more likely. 'It's no joke,' she said. 'I've read that letter. I'd say there's no joke in this at all.'

'You've read my letter?'

'The baby was dumped on *my* doorstep,' she said with asperity. Heavens, he was faced with an abandoned baby and he was accusing *her* of impropriety in reading his mail. 'Of course I read the letter. It made me feel ill.'

'But you—'

'This has nothing to do with me,' she said. 'I'm sorry, but I'm busy. If you'd like to telephone the police or anyone else, the phone's down the hall.'

'But, Lia...' It was a groan of absolute bewilderment, and she relented—just a little.

'I did one thing,' she admitted without looking at him, still concentrating fiercely on her pies. 'I telephoned Becky's mother. She's confirmed what the note says. Becky left for Australia this evening and no one wants responsibility for the baby. If you don't either, you'll need to organise adoption.'

Silence. Even Helen was silent at that. She stood

and gaped at Lia as if Lia were some two-headed frog.

Which was how she was feeling, Lia decided. She definitely didn't feel her normal self. She was scooping one mince pie after another from the oven tray in the motions of normal domesticity, but her fingers were trembling so much she could hardly hold the lifter.

This was nothing to do with her, she told herself savagely. Nothing!

But Helen had other ideas. 'She dumped it on you,' Helen said slowly. 'She didn't dump it on us. It's your lookout.'

Great! Lia thought this through and decided to ignore it.

So, it seemed, did Pete. He looked totally flummoxed but the anger was fading.

'The letter says it's Ben's baby,' he said slowly.

'You have no proof of that,' Helen snapped.

'I've heard,' Lia volunteered helpfully from behind her mince pie mound, 'that Becky and Ben were going out together a few months before he was killed.'

'They were an item?' Helen's voice was querulous.

'As much as any Barring male is ever part of an item.'

'What's that supposed to mean?' That was Pete, still looking flummoxed.

'Meaning Ben dated her sometimes.' It was desperately hard for Lia to keep her voice calm but somehow she managed it. 'He went out with a few women in the months before he died, but maybe... Maybe Becky was stupid enough to think he'd marry her.'

'How do we know it's not yours?' Helen demanded suddenly.

Lia's head snapped up, her green eyes sparking. 'Do you mind? I have two children of my own. Sam's and Emma's father is John Holt. My husband. The baby in your room is a Barring. You take one look at her and you must know that. Since I married I've never looked at another man, and if you think I'd ever be stupid enough—mad enough—to go near another Barring male—'

She broke off, gasping at the sound of her own voice. Heck, she was way out of control here. It must be shock or something. She took a ragged breath and flipped the last mince pie onto the cooler. Done.

And she knew what she had to do.

'I'm sorry,' she said coldly, and her voice was suddenly deathly calm. 'You two are paying guests in my home and I'm afraid my kitchen is out of bounds.' Somehow she dredged up a smile. 'There are tea and coffee making facilities in your room, and I've put equipment up there to heat a bottle. Now, if you'll excuse me... Please, leave.'

Despite being tired to the point of exhaustion, sleep was a long time coming.

Lia lay in the spare bedroom and stared up at

the ceiling, letting her tired mind absorb the events of the day. Somewhere above her Helen and Pete were sorting out their own problems—the arrival into their lives of one small baby. Those problems and that baby were nothing to do with her, she thought grimly. She had problems of her own.

She closed her eyes and willed herself to sleep.

There was a wailing above her head, and a man's murmur. The wailing grew.

An oath!

He must be in the spare upstairs bedroom, Lia thought, figuring out locations. Odd… She'd imagined Pete and Helen nursing their baby together.

She closed her eyes.

Another oath! And the wailing grew louder!

There was no sleep for anyone this way. Lia gritted her teeth and tried her hardest to ignore it. Ha!

OK. She'd help, but just this once—and only because she was concerned for the baby. She wrapped herself in her ancient dressing-gown and headed upstairs to investigate.

He was a man in trouble.

Lia had been right when she'd figured Pete wasn't in his allocated bedroom. At the end of the upstairs passage was a tiny box room—hardly usable by an adult but it held a bed suitable for a young child. The noise was definitely coming from there. She pushed open the door and her eyes widened in shock.

Pete must have been trying to sleep in the narrow bed, with the cot pushed in beside it. Now, though, he was wide awake and standing semi-naked, clad only in pyjama pants. On the bed, tiny Amy was bare from the chest down, dressed only in her matinée jacket and bootees.

It was obviously nappy-changing time. One was lying in a sodden heap on the floor. Amy was wailing and kicking, and the fresh nappy was clearly refusing to go on.

'Helen, I can't—' Pete heard her come in, glanced up and froze as he saw who it was. Now, however, was hardly the time for freezing. Amy's wails reached a crescendo, her tiny feet flailed the air and he swore and turned his attention back to what he was doing.

'Keep still,' he told her desperately. 'It won't go on if you kick!'

This was *not* a man in charge of his world.

Lia's lips twitched and then twitched some more.

'If you laugh,' Pete said conversationally, 'I make no promises as to what I'll do with the contents of that nappy.'

'Who me, laugh?' She smirked. 'I wouldn't dream of it. Do you need a nappy-changing manual?'

'I need help!'

She walked forward and peered down at what he was doing. Helpfulness personified. 'If you just fold the nappy into a triangle it won't hold much moisture,' she told him wisely. 'Even if you get it on…'

He glowered. 'So fold it for me.'

'Nope.' She grinned and scooped Amy into her arms, wrapping a rug around the baby's nakedness and holding her close. 'You fold it.'

Amy hiccuped and the wails stopped. Pete closed his eyes, took a deep breath and glared some more.

'I can't.'

'So learn. Take the top right-hand corner and—'

'Lia…' He practically groaned. 'Do it for me, there's a—'

'Good girl?' Her smile broadened. 'I don't think so. Where's Helen?'

'Asleep.'

'Lucky Helen.' This didn't make sense—when had a Barring ever had a woman who didn't run to his beck and call? But it was hardly her business. 'So there's only you.'

'Fold it for me, Lia. Put the thing on.'

'Nope.' She smiled sweetly. 'But I'll teach you how. You can read the formula instructions and heat a bottle?'

'Of course I can heat a bottle!'

'Then I'll teach you how to change a nappy and after that you're on your own.'

She might have smiled to his face, but it was harder to walk away than she'd thought possible. It seemed so wrong. If Amy had been hers she

would have cuddled her close, then taken her back
to bed with her and held her until they'd both slept.

That was what she told Pete to do—even though
the thought of him doing it made her feel weird!
Once Amy was safely nappied, she forced herself
downstairs, while her whole being was screaming
at her to return.

She couldn't. She couldn't afford to let herself
close to this man—or his baby.

So she lay in her downstairs bed and waited for
sleep, and listened to the fretting, the murmurs, the
squeak of bedsprings as Pete fed his baby... And
finally she listened to silence.

It was none of her business!

Lia must have slept a little. Toward dawn she woke
feeling as if she hadn't slept at all, but it was time
to rise and it was Christmas Eve.

Once such a day would have filled her with glee.
Once... In childhood. That was a long time ago,
she thought—before her father died—a time she
could hardly remember.

Reality was different. Em, Sam, Pete, Helen and
Amy were still fast asleep and she was so jealous
she could spit, but she couldn't afford jealousy.
Groaning, she hauled on her overalls, her threadbare pullover and her wellingtons, and headed out
across the snow-covered farmyard to the barn.

She had a cow to milk, and Pete found her there
twenty minutes later.

He entered the barn so softly she hardly heard

him. There was only one cow, separated from her calf overnight. Harriet-calf had become accustomed to the arrangement by now and was waiting calmly for milking to be over so her mother could be restored to her. Ernestine-cow was just as calmly standing in the bail, while Lia filled her bucket.

The milk was a foaming warm mass. The breath of Lia, of Ernestine and of Harriet steamed gently into the morning air, and the three were statue-still, apart from Lia's fingers kneading the teats. Pete came up behind her, touched her shoulder and she jumped sky high. If Ernestine hadn't been such a placid cow Lia would have ended up with milk all over the barn.

As it was, the milk was probably a milkshake.

'Do you mind?' she said crossly when she'd come down to earth and beached herself on her stool again. 'Creeping up...'

Then she paused as she saw what he was carrying. Amy was wrapped in her shawl and cradled against his chest. Pete was wearing casual clothes—jeans, a big khaki fisherman's guernsey and elastic-sided boots. He looked rugged and intensely male, and the baby in his arms was tiny in comparison, but he held her as if she was the most precious thing in the world. And the way he was looking at her..,

Something in Lia's chest lurched, and it wasn't from shock. 'You have...you have Amy,' she whispered.

'She won't settle. She was fine last night—as long as I held her—but I've just fed her again.' He grinned in triumph. 'And this time I got the nappy right.'

'Well done.' It was impossible not to smile.

'Thank you.' His smile faded. 'I was pacing in front of the upstairs window and saw you come out. I sort of hoped… I wanted to ask…'

'What?' Her smile died as well. This was obviously important.

'Lia… Are you sure this baby is Ben's?'

'Why?' Her lightness faded completely. 'Are you planning to reject her, too?'

'No,' he told her, anger surging at her note of accusation. His hands held his tiny bundle tighter, in a gesture of pure protectiveness. 'It's just… I've been watching her and thinking…and wanting so much for it to be true. For there to be a part of Ben left.'

And despite her hurt—despite her resentment of this painful ghost from her past—Lia felt her heart twist in sympathy.

Whatever else Ben Barring had been, he'd been Pete's identical twin. Once upon a time they'd been inseparable, and the pain of his loss was raw and exposed. Pete had loved his brother, his brother was dead, and this was his brother's child.

'She's Ben's baby,' she said softly, untying the rope and patting Ernestine on the rump to send her out of the bail and back to her calf. She rose, stiff muscles creaking. 'It fits with the time Becky and

Ben went out together. Trying to trap Ben into
marriage is the sort of silly plan Becky might follow, and the baby looks so like a Barring there's
no mistaking her.' She carried her milk over to the
shed door and then paused, looking back. 'Your
mother... She doesn't know?'

'No. Thankfully. Mum came to the US straight
after Ben's funeral, and she's only been back a
month. She's very frail. Ben's death knocked her
sideways. If Becky had landed this on her she
wouldn't have known what to do.'

'And you do?' Lia said softly—and waited.

He grimaced, staring at her with eyes that
weren't seeing her. 'I've learned nappies and formula fast, but...there's a lot of thinking to be
done.'

'Not by me,' she said. 'I have work to do.'

'Where's your husband?' he said suddenly, as
though John's absence had just registered. 'You
were up till all hours last night and then up again
on your lifesaving nappy mission. Why isn't your
husband doing this?'

'You haven't kept in touch with local news at
all, have you?' she asked, in a voice it was impossible to keep free from bitterness. 'John died
three years ago.'

Silence.

Pete had walked out with her, and now he
paused beside her in the yard. Their breath was
turning to mist before their faces, the two clouds
mingling in the still winter morning. Amy nuzzled

and whimpered and settled closer to Pete's chest, and by Lia's side her old dog, Woof, nuzzled against her leg, as if giving his own brand of comfort.

'I...' Pete seemed bewildered, at a loss for words. 'I didn't know. Car accident?'

'He rolled the tractor,' she said heavily.

'I'm sorry.'

'It was a long time ago.'

'But it still hurts.' His eyes creased into the beginning of a tired smile, and his smile was all about comfort. The anger between them had dissipated. 'Ben and I had been apart for seven years before he died, and it still hurts like crazy.'

'And now you have a part of him remaining.'

'Yes.' He cast a strange look down at the baby's tiny head. 'It feels...weird.'

'Good weird or bad weird?'

'Good, I guess.'

'And Helen? How will she feel about taking on an instant family?'

'We haven't got that far yet,' he said, startled. 'I mean...keeping her...'

'Someone has to keep her,' Lia said softly, and started moving again. 'If she's not to suffer, then that someone needs to make decisions fast. Now, if you'll excuse me...'

'Lia, I need to talk.'

'And I need to attend to my children,' she said, without pausing. She was slushing through the snow back toward the house as she spoke, milk pail in her hand and dog at her side. 'I'm sorry, Pete, but I'm afraid I need to leave you to look after yours.'

'My...?'

'Your child. Your family.'

Lia did a load of washing, prepared the turkey stuffing and made two trays of shortbread. Then she dressed the children, gave them breakfast and settled them in front of children's television. At eight she had her dining room laid for guest-breakfast.

A notice upstairs advised what time breakfast was. At the appointed time no one appeared so she rang her bell. Then she rang it again. Ten minutes later, Helen arrived, her face like thunder.

'You can ring all you like but he won't come. He's feeding the baby—again,' she snapped. She sat down at the head of the table. 'Do you have croissants?'

'Um...no.' Lia tried not to smile. 'I'm sorry. There's fresh juice, cereal, toast, bacon, eggs—'

'Coffee, then,' the girl snapped. 'Strong.'

'Yes, ma'am.' It was all she could do not to salute, but she'd been taking in paying guests for two years now and she knew how to bite her tongue. She provided coffee while Helen sat and brooded. There was no sound from upstairs.

'Maybe you could take something up to him,' Lia suggested as she refilled her coffee-cup, and was cast a dark look for her pains.

'Maybe I should just leave. I didn't expect to walk into this mess.'

'I guess no one could,' Lia admitted, not without sympathy. To come overseas with your fiancé and be landed with a baby... 'It's hard.'

'You have your own children, right?' Helen suddenly stared at Lia as if she'd had a thought.

'Yes.'

'So one more wouldn't make a difference? I mean...looking after it. We're planning to do some Christmas shopping this morning, you see. Pete's taking me into York, and there's no way I want to be saddled with a baby.'

Lia swallowed. The thought of tiny Amy was infinitely appealing. It would be so easy to say yes—and Lia always said yes. But... She had her own children, she had food to cook, she had animals to care for, and some time between now and midnight she had a pile of wrapping a mile high. She had to shop, too.

And, overriding everything else, this was a Barring baby. She couldn't get involved.

'I'm sorry,' she said. 'That's not possible.'

'Why isn't it possible?' The woman's anger was tangible. 'You dumped it on us. Surely you should take some responsibility.'

'Helen, that's not fair.' Pete's voice made them both start as he entered. Amy must be asleep again—at last. 'This isn't Lia's problem,' he said heavily.

'It isn't mine either,' Helen retorted, wheeling

on him. 'We came here to have some fun, and it's my holiday. There's no way I'm towing a baby around all day, but I need to go to York. I purposely travelled light so I could shop over here.'

'I'm afraid you'll have to take yourself to York,' Pete said wearily. 'There are things I need to sort out.'

'But I can't take myself. *These people* drive on the wrong side of the road!' She said 'these people' like she might have talked about a herd of unwashed barbarians, and Lia bit back a smile. Pete had a ripe one here.

But it *was* Christmas. She could be nice. To a point... 'I'm going into Churton,' Lia volunteered. 'I can take you that far.'

'Is Churton where your mother lives?' Helen didn't even acknowledge Lia's offer as she faced Pete. 'How big a town is it?'

'There are fifteen or so shops, a pub and a post office,' Pete said steadily. 'I'm going there myself to see Mum and break the news about Amy. Is there still a dress shop in town, Lia?'

Lia didn't get a chance to answer. 'Oh, right, a country town dress shop.' Helen closed her eyes. Things weren't going her way at all. 'As if I'd be seen dead—'

'Would you like some breakfast, Mr Barring?' Lia interrupted, figuring she wasn't enjoying this conversation so she'd start her own. 'I have juice, toast, eggs—fried or scrambled—or—'

'He knows what you'll have,' Helen snapped. 'Give him eggs on toast.'

And get out of here. The words were unsaid but they were implied. Lia flushed and did the smart thing. She got out of there, walking out of the dining room and letting the door swing closed firmly behind her. Very firmly.

Maybe warts weren't necessary after all, she thought grimly. She broke an egg into the frying-pan with such a crack that the pan ended up with more shell than yolk. She managed a reluctant chuckle, scraped the egg into the compost and started again. It was no use getting angry here.

After all, Helen might not have warts on her nose, but she was just the sort of lady Pete deserved.

The only problem was, Helen wasn't the sort of woman she wanted to see as Amy's mother.

Neither, it seemed, did Helen. Two minutes later the dining door close with a resounding crash and Helen stalked into the kitchen.

'Tell me how to call a taxi,' she snapped. 'I'm going home.'

Lia's method of coping with paying guests was to keep out of their way as much as possible and that was what she did now. She gave Pete his breakfast and a house key, and made no comment on the fact that he was staring into space while his fiancée was storming about upstairs, banging and thumping while she sorted belongings into his and her piles.

This was the coward's way out, she decided as she drove away from the farm, with Em and Sam belted in beside her. She didn't want involvement.

Or maybe she did—but involvement would lead to nothing but disaster.

Christmas shopping was dreadful. Lia had too little time, the shops were packed, and every person she met had heard of Pete's arrival and Amy's abandonment. It seemed that Amy's maternal grandmother had been spreading her troubles all over town.

'Is it true, Lia? Has Becky really dumped Ben's baby on Pete? Well, I always thought that girl was no better than she ought to be. And as for getting pregnant by Ben... You'd think she'd have more sense. Everyone knows what the Barring men are like.'

It seemed to go on for ever, with Em and Sam growing more fractious by the minute. By midmorning her list wasn't half-complete, but worse was to come. She walked out of the butcher's, her arms loaded with Christmas turkey, and ran straight into the biggest gossip in the district.

'Lia, my dear...'

'Mrs West, I'm sorry, but I don't have time to talk.' There was sleet in the air, and the children weren't enjoying themselves one bit. Neither was she. She had holes in her boots and her feet were soaked. Maybe her family might come good with a shoe voucher instead of a diet plan for Christmas, she thought humourlessly. Fat chance!

'Lia…'

Why Pete Barring had the ability to make her jump out of her skin she didn't know. It was all she could do not to yelp, and Mrs West's eyes widened in astonishment.

'Well, I never,' she breathed, gazing at Pete with awe as he approached them. In his huge greatcoat over his casual clothes, he towered over the diminutive lady, and the carrycot at his side looked almost ridiculously out of place against such a rugged male. 'If it's not Peter Barring. Oh, lad, you look the image of your poor brother. And you've not been home since he was buried. How's your mother, dear? Is she bearing up?'

'Thank you, yes, Mrs West,' Pete said politely. He turned to Lia, excluding Mrs West's quivering nose nicely. 'Lia, where can I buy nappies? And baby formula? And… I don't know.' He spread his hands in an age-old male gesture of please-this-is-too-hard-and-your-sex-is-suposed-to-be-good-at-babies appeal.

'Lanes Supermarket,' Lia said coldly, and hardened her heart.

'I don't suppose you could…'

'No.'

'Lia…'

'Don't wheedle, Pete Barring,' she said crossly. 'It doesn't become you.'

'But I'm good at it,' he said, and put on his very best wheedling expression. Her coldness evaporated. He always could charm her socks off, she thought desperately—even sodden socks like hers. It was all she could do not to laugh—but she didn't. He made her feel so unsettled that she felt like running a mile.

As well as that, the children were still tugging at her coat and they were miserable. She didn't blame them. It was starting to snow, the turkey was heavy in her arms and she still had her own supermarket shopping to do.

'Pete, I need to go.'

'Hey, maybe we can help each other.' To her surprise he stooped, crouching before Em and Sam. 'Kids, I'm really, really thirsty,' he told them, and he was addressing them only. Adults excluded. 'Do you guys know where we can find milkshakes?'

'Um...' This was too much for Sam who retreated, thumb in mouth, behind his mother, but Em knew no such qualms.

'Mrs Hill's,' she said promptly. 'She sells milkshakes and lollies and...and *lime spiders*.'

'Lime spiders?'

'They're green lemonade with ice cream and froth,' Em told him, and her small tongue came out and licked her lips at the thought. She sighed at the memory of bliss. 'If you stir spiders with your straw, then green froth comes out all over the table.'

Pete's eyes widened in awe. 'Hey, you know,

that's just what I had in mind. Wonderful. Is it warm at Mrs Hill's?'

Em's beaming smile stretched to her ears. This was looking very promising indeed, and she warmed to her marketing. 'Mrs Hill always has a fire. She has tables and chairs and sometimes Mummy takes us there for lunch.' She hesitated and then decided to be honest. 'Not very often, though. Mummy says we can't afford it.'

'Better and better.' Pete smiled and Lia could see her daughter capitulating before the massive Barring charm. 'So it'll be a Christmas treat for all of us. How would you two like to sit by Mrs Hill's fire and drink lime spiders while your mum finishes her shopping and buys my nappies? She can join us when she's finished.'

'Wow!' Em looked straight up at Lia, and the longing in her eyes almost made Lia want to laugh. Almost.

'Mummy, please...'

'I *love* lime spiders,' Sam announced, as though that put the seal on things, and Pete chuckled, a deep rumble that filled the cold air with a warmth that had nothing to do with the outside temperature. He straightened, and he smiled straight at Lia.

'Please, Mummy,' he said at his wheedling best, and he grinned down into her eyes—and it was all too much. She had to chuckle. For heaven's sake, he was a rat and she had to keep telling herself that, but he was one charming rat!

She shouldn't trust him. She *didn't* trust him,

and yet…shopping without the children…and all she had to do in return was to buy a few baby needs…

Bliss!

There was no choice. 'Yes, please,' she said before he could change his mind. 'They're all yours.'

And that was that.

'Well,' Mrs West breathed as Pete propelled his small charges lime-spiderwards. 'Well, I never. Isn't he the most gorgeous—?'

'He's just like his brother,' Lia said, half to herself, and Maud West cast her an odd look.

'Didn't you go out with one of the Barring boys when you were a lass? Which one?'

'Goodness knows,' Lia told her, her laughter fading, and she couldn't stop a note of bitterness washing into her words. 'They were interchangeable. One's as bad as the other.'

'But now one's dead,' Maud went on, and you could see exactly where her thoughts were headed. 'And t'other has a babe to look after. His poor mother can't do the caring. So… He'll be in need of a good woman.'

'Lucky him. He has a fiancée.'

'Henry Webster's taxi took that one to Manchester airport this very morning,' Maud said. 'I met Elspeth Webster just ten minutes ago and she was full of it. Seems the young lady doesn't like the idea of a babe, and she has friends in London she's heading for. So that leaves him alone. But he'll be staying with you over Christmas now, won't he, dear?'

'I suppose he will,' Lia said doubtfully. 'He's here to spend Christmas with his mother.'

'Well, that's just lovely.' Maud beamed. 'That's just what you want for Christmas. A good man.'

'A good man!' Lia drew in her breath. This was crazy. Her turkey was starting to drip and her hands were cold where they clutched the damp wrapping. Her feet were freezing and her world was crowding in on top of her. 'Mrs West, the Barring boys might qualify as gorgeous, but neither of them could ever be classified as good. Not in a million years!'

An hour and two full supermarket trolleys later, Lia and Woof arrived at Mrs Hill's. She still couldn't believe her luck. Supermarket shopping with the children was usually a nightmare and she'd accomplished it at almost the speed of light.

And now she was finished and the children were having a ball.

Mrs Hill ran the village café, but it was more than that. Confined to a wheelchair, May Hill had decided early if she couldn't get out to the village then she'd make the village come to her. She'd bought her little shop with its living quarters at the rear and had then knocked out the dividing walls. She'd kept her counter and her lolly jars and had put in just four tables and chairs 'because who can talk to more than four groups of people at a time anyway?'—and she'd proceeded to hold court.

She was equipped accordingly. The children had her building blocks out and were building a not very miniature version of the Empire State Building. There were traces of lime-spider over all four tables. May had her wheelchair up to the cleanest of the tables and was cuddling Amy, and after one look Lia could tell Pete was being subjected to one of her famous inquisitions.

May beamed at the sight of her, the kids groaned and built faster, sensing she might tear them away, and Pete rolled his eyes and rose to greet her. She could see relief washing over him in waves. Inquisition ended.

'I'm sorry I took so long,' she said guiltily, hauling off her boots at the door. Her socks were dripping. 'Have the children been good?'

'Excellent.' May smiled her widest smile. 'But look at your poor feet. You must have holes in those boots, lass.'

'I—'

'I'll bet you do. And what are you doing about it? When was the last time you spent money on yourself?' May's interrogation was turned straight at Lia.

'You can't spend what you don't have,' Lia said shortly. 'May—'

'I know. I know. Leave you be. I'll make you coffee, love, and it's all on me today, because it's

288 THE DOORSTEP BABY

Christmas.' She headed for her coffee machine
and...

'I'll just hold Amy,' Pete said, and made a dive
as Amy slid sideways on her lap.

'Oh...' May's beam didn't fade as Pete caught
his precious bundle. 'I guess you're right. Maybe
I shouldn't pour hot water with a little one on my
lap. Lia, dear, would you like coffee?'

She'd kill for a coffee but...

But what? It was warm in here. Lovely. And
Pete was here with the children... For heaven's
sake, the atmosphere was seductive in its charm.

'I need to go,' she said reluctantly.

'Nonsense,' May ordered. 'You need a break.
Hang up the "closed" sign, Peter. I have guests.'

Pete raised bemused eyebrows and did just that,
but May hadn't finished bossing. 'Lia, stick those
feet in front of the fire and let them dry. Now we
need to sort Pete out.'

'I...' Pete's eyebrows rose even further. 'I beg
your pardon?'

'He's stuck for Christmas, Lia,' May told Lia
bluntly. 'He's in a mess. With a babe on his hands,
and his mum expecting him to take her to dinner
at some fancy restaurant. Well, I've been thinking,
and there's only one thing for it.'

'I'm sorry?' Lia didn't have a clue what was
going on. She sat with her soaking feet stuck out
towards the flames and tried not to look at Pete.
Or Pete's baby. Or Pete holding Pete's baby as he
settled at the table again.

He looked just the same Pete she'd loved all her life, without stopping. The pain was just there.

Concentrate on May…

'He needs to come to you,' May was saying. 'I know it's unfair, but there's no help for it. You'll have to have Pete and his mum for Christmas dinner.'

CHAPTER THREE

IT TOOK two cups of coffee before May had it sorted, and even then Pete was still arguing. Lia wasn't. She'd been almost struck dumb.

But unfair or not, what May was saying made sense. She'd used her interrogation to good effect and could now give Lia a summary.

'He's in a hole, Lia. His girlfriend's gone to London, his poor mother's in a nursing-home and he's booked Christmas dinner at the fanciest restaurant in the North of England!'

'I can still take her,' Pete interjected.

'Not to that place, you can't,' May said firmly. 'It might be the best, but they don't admit babies. So what are you going to do with your Amy?'

'I have no idea,' Pete said blankly. 'I mean... I'll take her, of course. I'll just have to change restaurants.'

'Fat chance.' May hooted with derision. 'Everywhere that serves Christmas dinner was booked out months ago.'

'But I can't—'

'And if you were thinking of asking Lia if she'd look after Amy while you took your mum out, I'd say fat chance of that, too,' May went on, as if she hadn't been interrupted. 'I'd run you out of town rather than let you load that onto her. This girl is overwhelmed with the biggest lot of no-good family you ever met in your life. Her mother—'

'May, that's not fair—'

Lia's interjection was drowned out. 'Not fair! Huh! Your father was a fine man, Lia Holt, but he married a woman who has more hairspray than brains, and your two sisters—and that brother of yours—are cast in the same mould. And as for your grandfather and your uncles and aunts and those no-good cousins of yours…they use you, Lia. They always have and they always will.'

'May, don't.' Lia's voice caught in distress and May fixed her with a look.

'I know. Your heart's too big. All I'm saying… Well, I'll bet they're all coming to you tomorrow, I'll bet no one will raise a hand to help, and here's Pete desperate for somewhere to take his mother. At least he could milk your cow, cart hay, carve your turkey and help you with the washing-up.'

'Sort of like…pay for his pudding,' Lia managed, with the hint of a smile returning. Honestly, May was incorrigible.

'That's exactly what I mean.' May turned her attention full on Pete, regarding him as she might an interesting insect. 'Look at him. He's gorgeous. Would you really have him spend his Christmas in the street?'

Pete grinned at that, his sense of humour caught. He turned on his very best wounded Labrador look, and the look was enough to make Lia burst out laughing.

'Oh, for heaven's sake. That's enough,' she told him. 'If you look like that, they do a very nice Christmas dinner at the local welfare hall.'

His soulful look grew wider. 'You'd send me to welfare?'

'Yes!' Lia said, and her laughter suddenly faded as their eyes caught and held. All of a sudden it was really hard to breathe.

'Lia…' Pete's hangdog expression disappeared, and his expression grew serious. He really did have a problem. A whole heap of problems actually, one of whom was snoozing in his arms right now, but the immediate one was his mother's Christmas dinner. 'Lia, I'm sorry, but May's right,' he admitted. 'I'm in a mess. It's not me I'm asking for. It's for my mother.'

'But…you lived here permanently once.' Lia's voice was slightly breathless. She was being backed into a corner, and she didn't like it one bit. 'Surely you have friends in the district?'

He spread his hands and shook his head. 'I haven't spent any significant time here for seven years, and we have no family. Sure, Mum has friends, but there's no way I'm presenting her with a new grandchild and then asking which of her friends will invite us both…us three…for Christmas.'

'Pete—'

'Lia, I have no business asking this,' he said

softly, and his eyes met hers and held. 'I surely don't want to. But May's suggested it and she's right. I need your kindness.'

'So does half the district,' May said, jeering kindly. 'You wait and see what happens tomorrow. Lia has the world's biggest collection of no-good relatives. You won't even be noticed among the crush lining up at her place for free food.'

Pete's eyebrows rose and the twinkle returned. 'So I'll be in a welfare line after all. Gee, thanks!'

'How many are you having?' May demanded of Lia, ignoring him.

'Twenty.'

'There you go, then,' she said triumphantly. 'What's a couple more? And Amy won't eat much.' She turned back to Pete and poked a decisive finger at him. 'So off you go and introduce your niece to your mother, boy, and tell her you're taking her out to the world's best restaurant for Christmas dinner. To Lia's. If I know Lia, she won't let you down.'

'May...' Lia was practically speechless, but May wasn't listening.

'That's that, then.' She wheeled herself forward and pushed Lia's coffee-mug closer. 'You drink that, my girl, and then get out of here. If I'm not mistaken, you have work to do. You have Christmas to prepare for. But at least now you'll have someone with you tomorrow who'll bother to say thank you.'

*   *   *

'You don't have to do this.' Out in the snow a few minutes later, with a child on each side, Lia prepared to head back to the truck. Pete detained her with a hand on her shoulder, turning her to face him. Out of May's hearing he could be direct. 'If you really are having twenty people...'

'May's right. Two more won't make a difference.' She was back under control now, her voice formally polite.

'Honest?'

'Honest.' She gave a wintry smile. 'I need to go. I'll see you back at the farm.'

'I do need to see my mother.' He hesitated. 'I've already seen Becky's mother. She says there's no doubt that Amy's Ben's baby.'

'Did you really think she wasn't?'

'No but...' He hesitated and then sighed. 'It's a mess.'

'Yes,' she agreed—and waited.

His face hardened as he looked at her. 'But not your mess?'

'That's the one.' Somehow she made her voice flippant, when for some strange reason all she wanted was to burst into tears. 'I have a mess of my own waiting for me at home right now. I'll see you when I see you, Pete Barring. Goodbye.'

The rest of the day passed in a blur.

Christmas was crazy. She'd tried not to leave everything to the last minute, but every year the Christmas workload increased.

Why couldn't someone else put on Christmas for a change? she thought bitterly, staring down at her workworn hands and conjuring up visions of the beautifully manicured hand of every other woman in her family. Them? Put on Christmas? As a family they were the best bunch of work-shy emotional blackmailers she'd ever met, and she shoved her stuffing turkey-wards with unnecessary force while she thought of them. 'Drat them all.'

'Hey, watch it. You'll do the poor guy a damage.'

Lia jumped and glowered. Pete! She might have known. He spent his life creeping up on her.

'What do you want?' she snapped with more force than she'd intended, and he blinked.

'To help.' He looked down at what she was doing. 'Isn't that too much stuffing for one small orifice?'

'Not if I stuff hard enough. It's a very large orifice and, anyway, the size of the orifice is immaterial. There's a cavern in there.'

'Any more stuffing and it'll ooze out the other end. We'll have neck ooze.'

'I'll truss.'

'Very wise.' He nodded his approval. 'Trussing is good. Can I truss for you?'

'I can truss my own turkey, thank you very much.' She tried to push back an errant curl with a floury forearm. It sprang back over her eyes and Pete obliged by leaning over and tucking it behind her ear.

'Better?'

'I… Yes.' She practically flinched. How did one little touch have the power to unsettle her? 'Where's…where's Amy?

'Upstairs. Asleep.'

She hadn't heard him come in but, then, she'd given him a key. He was a paying guest. He had the right to come and go when he pleased. Still, it unnerved her.

He unnerved her.

'Where are your two?' he asked.

'Sam's asleep, and Em says she has presents to wrap. I've given her Christmas paper and Sellotape, and she's sticking everything within a ten-yard range. With luck she'll be occupied for an hour—but it might take an hour to unwrap her afterwards.'

'So…we have the house to ourselves.'

'Yeah, right.' She scowled again as she looked up to find him watching her with eyes that held the faintest trace of remembered twinkle. Good grief, he was laughing at her! To her astonishment there was still that look in his eyes that told her— despite her stained apron, despite the swipe of flour on her cheek and despite the shadows under her tired eyes—he was seeing her as every inch a woman.

'Hey, I've still got Woof,' she said, a trifle desperately. 'And if you're thinking of a spot of seduction on the side here, Pete Barring, I don't have time.'

'Hey, I wasn't thinking of seduction.'

'The Barring men always think of seduction. Even in their sleep.'

His face closed. 'You're thinking of Ben.'

'Am I?' For the life of her she couldn't keep the bitterness from her voice. Why? What had been between them had been seven years ago, for heaven's sake. To be bitter now...

It was totally inappropriate.

Lia looked up and found him watching her strangely. The twinkle had faded. 'I...I'm sorry,' she said, hauling herself back to playing hostess. 'That was a stupid thing to say. I guess I've just been thrown—with Amy and all.' She took a deep breath. 'Pete, I'm sorry about your fiancée.'

'Helen was *not* my fiancée.'

Her eyebrows rose at that. 'Really?'

'Really.'

'She didn't say that last night. Neither did you, if I remember correctly.'

'Last night I was too shell-shocked to say anything,' Pete said bluntly. 'Helen and I have gone out together a few times. She offered to look after Mum while I was on duty in the States, and...maybe I didn't realise until last night that Helen—and Mum—assumed so much. Anyway, last night killed it. Dead. Babies aren't Helen's scene. Lia, will you stop stuffing that dratted turkey?'

'No way. This turkey is all that's between me and disaster.'

'Surely—'

'Pete, I have a list a mile long of things to do before dawn,' she said. There was no time in her life for the emotion she was feeling. Or anything else for that matter. 'So leave me to it.'

'I'm not leaving,' he said, his voice gentling. 'Remember? I'm here for the duration. Let me help.'

'I don't need—'

'Lia, I want to help.' His voice turned to a growl and she stared up at him, shocked into stillness.

I want to help...

No one helped. Ever! And no one looked at her like this!

He smiled, and she looked away fast. Concentrate on work!

'You...you could shell peas,' she said weakly, and she motioned to a huge pile beside her.

His eyebrows rose. 'You have fresh peas? In Yorkshire?'

'It's Christmas. My family always have fresh peas at Christmas.'

'Aren't they expensive?'

'Yes,' she snapped. 'They're expensive. And, no, I can't afford them, but if I don't have fresh peas Grandpa will take one mouthful of his frozen ones and start reminiscing about how Grandma always organised the best, and how she'd move heaven and earth to make sure her family had a wonderful Christmas. He'll blow his nose.

'Then my mother will burst into tears and say

he mustn't expect the young ones nowadays to care so much for traditions, and my sister Sally will say how she could have got fresh peas if she'd had Christmas in London, and why we choose to live in this dump she doesn't know, but if I was stupid enough to marry someone who—'

That was enough! She broke off on an angry gasp and went right on back to turkey-stuffing. And all of a sudden Pete's hand closed over hers, preventing her wrist from leaving the turkey.

'Hey, Lia...'

'Don't touch me!' She couldn't pull away. Short of thumping him with the turkey, she was stuck!

'Aren't you getting a bit overwrought here? This is only a family Christmas after all.'

'Yes. It's only Christmas. And you're right. They're only my family. And I hate it all.' She gave her wrist an angry wrench but he didn't release it.

'You hate Christmas?'

'Yes. There's nothing about it I like. It's work, it's more work and it's memories.' She closed her eyes and, unbidden, the sight of his face came back to her. Christmas Eve seven years ago. She'd hauled off her ring and flung it back at him... 'I want nothing more to do with you. Never! Never again, Pete Barring, so just go!'

She remembered his look of utter disbelief that she'd taken his betrayal so seriously—his face white in the moonlight, staring at her as if she'd been someone he'd no longer known. And then he'd turned and walked out into the snow, and she hadn't seen him again. Until last night.

Was he remembering, too?

But his face was still gentle. 'May said your husband died just before Christmas three years ago.'

'I... Yes.'

'That must be hard.'

It was. The memory of John was still with her. Her John—a big, gentle man, limping with his bad leg which had been with him since his teenage illness. He'd been twenty years older than Lia and so grateful she'd married him. Sure, she'd married him on the rebound, but he'd known it. His farm had been impoverished, her family had thought she'd been a fool for marrying him, but John had loved her. He'd accepted her growing love for him with quiet pleasure, and she'd never regretted her marriage for one minute.

His death had stilled her world, but it hadn't made her feel as she had when Pete had walked away—like part of her had been ripped out.

'It was hard,' she repeated dully.

'Your family looked after you then?'

'Are you kidding?' She shook her head in disbelief and there was no way she could keep the bitterness from her voice. 'No way. I... The night John died... I found him trapped under the tractor and tried to lift him free but, of course, he was already dead. It was stupid. Futile. Anyway, I went into early labour and spent Christmas in hospital.

Without exception my family decided to fly to London because my misery would spoil their Christmas. If May and her daughter hadn't stepped in to take care of Emma, I would have had to leave my baby daughter with a welfare organisation until I was well again. That's my family for you.'

His brow furrowed in disbelief. 'And still you give them Christmas?'

'They expect it,' she said shortly. 'And it's too much grief if I don't.'

'Hmm.'

'Don't sound like that,' she snapped.

'Like what?'

'I don't know. Judgmental. They're the only family I have.'

He looked at her for a long moment. And then he smiled. 'So we shell peas?'

'We shell peas.'

'And what else?'

'We peel potatoes, we chop fruit because Uncle Herbert doesn't like Christmas pudding, we set the table, we wrap twenty assorted presents for relatives we don't like. Then we milk the cow, we feed the sheep—'

'Hey, wait a minute. We?' he said weakly, and she caught his look of horror.

She shrugged. 'OK, I mean me. But you did offer.'

And, to her amazement, the twinkle came back into his eyes.

'So I did,' he told her. 'Very well. Let's organise

you a Christmas to remember. There's only one condition.'

'Which is?

'This year, you can't hate Christmas.'

'Pete—'

'This year, I'm in charge,' he told her. 'If you've been organising Christmas for the past few years and you still hate Christmas, then you can't be doing a very good job. So therefore this Christmas is on me.'

'I—'

'No argument,' he told her sternly. 'Just shut up and enjoy it.'

So they worked on, but somehow the load was shifted.

Pete took over all the hard manual work and brooked no opposition. 'Because you need rest if you're to enjoy tomorrow,' he told her, propelling her into the armchair before the fire.

'Feed my niece,' he growled when she protested. 'That's woman's work, woman. Let me do man's work.' He squared his shoulders, beetled his brows and flexed his muscles until Em and Sam giggled at such a manly figure. 'Come on, kids. Let's do what a man has to do.'

'You don't know what to do,' Lia said weakly.

'I was born and bred on the Dales,' he told her. 'It's my heritage you're doubting, lass. I want the keys to the tractor. Tell me where the sheep are, what you're feeding them and where I can find it.

And what the head count is. I'll find 'em, I'll feed 'em and I won't come back until they're all accounted for. I've been digging sheep out of snow-drifts since before you were born.'

He had, too, Lia realised. Until his father had taken off when he'd been eighteen, he'd lived on a neighbouring farm. He'd know.

Bliss. Lia sat back in her armchair with Amy in her arms, and she almost sagged in relief.

So off they went—man, kids and dog. For once the children didn't protest about the feeding ritual. They bounced after this strange, wonderful man, and they came back red in the cheeks from exercise and squeaking with laughter.

'Pete made us tell him every sheep's name, and he thinks Dora should be called Snozzle because that's what she sounds like.' Em was hopping up and down on one foot with excitement. 'He made us count them, and Sam got threety-three and I got nine. But Pete says there's ninety-three—is that right, Mummy?'

'Ninety-three sounds great to me,' Lia said, and her relief grew. None of the shearlings had decided to return to the tops, then. She'd brought the flock down because the forecast for the next few days was dreadful, but sometimes the shearlings didn't like the shift. There was sweeter feed under the snow on the tops than the hay and supplements Lia fed them in the valley bottom, and the young sheep hadn't experienced how bad the tops could be in foul weather.

'Pete put Woof on the sheep's back when they were at the racks, and Woof ran all the way along from sheep to sheep because that's what his dog used to do when Pete was our age,' Em was saying. 'And he threw us up into the hay and we rolled and rolled...'

And Lia, sitting dreamily before the fire with the sleeping baby in her arms, could hardly believe that the hard work had been done.

Then, while she still sat there—'because my niece needs a cuddle and you're a person who looks like she needs cuddling back'—Pete and the children laid the table for Christmas dinner.

It was a different table to the one Lia had lain year after year. She'd kept it formal, knowing that the slightest deviation brought criticism down on her head like nothing else could, but Pete would have none of it.

'No hats?' He was astounded. 'Of course there must be hats. Em, where's the Christmas paper? There's far too much tinsel on this tree. Rip it off at once. We need tinselly hats. Sam, you're in charge of glue. Em, you're in charge of scissors. Let's get this production line moving.'

And the finished table looked brilliant! The hats were huge cones in every colour of the rainbow, with tinsel trailing down like tails. The tree then looked a bit denuded so they donned their boots and macs—Lia coming this time as Amy was asleep—and headed outside on a berry hunt.

Then they hung berries over every gap in the

Christmas tree and Pete stuck a vast bunch in the middle of the table.

'That means my mother won't be able to see anyone at the other end of the table,' Lia protested, but Pete shook his head.

'That's why we're wearing hats. Em, let's write big labels and stick them right up the top of the hats like flags, so if someone wants to talk to your grandma they can just look over the berries until they see a flag called "Grandma".'

'Grandma won't wear a hat,' Em said, shocked. 'Why ever not?'

'She has boofy hair,' Em said, thinking it through. 'She pats it all the time, and she piles it really high.'

'Then our flags will be even higher than Grandma's hair,' Pete said. 'This plan gets better and better.'

Then they ate, and to Lia's dismay Pete attacked the Christmas ham. 'Uncle Harold likes carving it at the table,' she protested. 'That's his job. He does it every year and he'll be upset if it's not whole.'

'Uncle Harold's been outvoted,' Pete said firmly. 'I'm darned if I'm eating baked beans on Christmas Eve just to pander to Uncle Harold's penchant for ham-carving.'

'Pete—'

'I'll chop a huge platter while I'm at it, then we can eat as much as we like and no one will know the difference. Apart from Uncle Harold. And we're eating some of your mince pies...'

'Pete!' He was taking over her world, overwhelming her with his organisation.

'Do you ever get to eat your mince pies?' he demanded, and she flushed. Goodness, no. She was always far too busy to taste her food, and her mother and uncles always took the leftovers away with them—'because it's so sad to go home without taking a little bit of Christmas with us'. But…how had Pete guessed she never got to eat them?

'So it's ham and mince pies and red lemonade and champagne.'

'Red lemonade and champagne! If you think I'm using tomorrow's drinks…'

'You don't need to.' He hiked outside to his car and returned, laden with bottles. 'This is my contribution to tonight's feast. Isn't it lucky it's cold outside? The champagne's already chilled. And…I have chocolates!'

'Chocolates!' Sam and Em were pop-eyed. 'For us? For now?'

'For us and for now,' he said firmly. 'Who could deserve them more?'

And who could argue with that? Not Lia. She was speechless.

Eventually, with their stockings hung over the fireplace and with longing backward looks, the children were finally herded to bed. Lia expected Pete to stay behind but he did no such thing. Amy was still awake, replete but cooing gently in his arms. Pete carried her into the children's bedroom and sat on Em's bed while Lia found their Christmas storybook and perched on Sam's.

'There's no need for you to stay,' she said, flustered by his presence. 'You'll have heard this story before.'

'I've heard this story for thirty-three years now,' he told her softly. 'Some years it seems more real than others. This year...this year somehow it seems special. If you don't mind, I'd like to listen.'

So he sat, as Amy snuggled sleepily in his arms and seemed to listen. Em and Sam heard the Christmas story for maybe the first time, unless they remembered it from last year—which was doubtful because, like Amy, they were fast asleep before the story finally ended with the Christ child being born in that long-ago stable under a starlit sky.

As they drifted into sleep, Lia's voice drifted on into the night. She was strangely reluctant to finish—to let go of this magic moment of stillness and peace—and Pete sat and looked down at his own infant as she read, and his face grew grave and his gaze turned within.

Finally she fell silent. It was hard, though, to break the moment. She laid the book on the bedside table, and when she looked up Pete's eyes were resting on her face.

'Why did you send me away?' he said softly, into the Christmas magic, 'all those years ago?'

'Pete...'

'I wanted to marry you.'

'Did you?' Her chin tilted, and the spell was

broken. 'The Barring men don't make good husbands, though. Or fathers.'

He flushed, his face darkening. 'So you threw me over because of my father and my brother?'

She shrugged. This was history. Water under the bridge. So much had happened…

There was nothing to be gained now by being accusing, or telling him just how deeply she'd been hurt. This was still a time of peace. Of reconciliation even.

'Maybe I…I was too upset at the time to explain properly,' she managed. 'But, Pete, that was so long ago. Girlfriend and boyfriend—that's all we were. Surely we've moved on since then.'

'We were more than that.'

'No.' She shook her head. 'I was too young. Too silly.'

'I was twenty-six. Hardly a teenager.'

Maybe that had been the trouble. He'd been older than her and so much more worldly—zooming off, training to be an international pilot, while she'd stayed and done her nurse's training and had come home every weekend like a dutiful daughter. She'd been so naïve, taking his faithfulness for granted, while he…

She gave herself a fast mental shake, and rose on feet that seemed suddenly to be unsteady. 'I… You'll have to excuse me,' she said. 'I have more work to do.'

'More…?'

'My Father-Christmassing.' She managed a smile. 'Goodnight.' And she fled.

CHAPTER FOUR

LIA might have known it wouldn't work. Pete couldn't be dismissed with such ease. Ten minutes later the kitchen door opened and he appeared again, his smile back in place.

'Caught,' he said, as she shoved what she'd been wrapping behind her back. When the door had opened she'd thought it might be Em or Sam. 'What are you hiding?'

She gave a mental shrug. This man was unsettling her no end, but part of her liked the fact that she wasn't alone on Christmas Eve. Playing Santa by herself wasn't much fun.

'A Fireygo.'

'A *Fireygo*?' he asked blankly, and Lia grinned and produced Sam's toy. It was a gleaming red fire-engine, with eight little tin firefighters lined up along each side. She put it on the table, pushed it forward and it made the most satisfactory noise. Bells rang, sirens wailed and the tin firefighters bobbed back and forth as if they were running on the spot with eagerness to reach the fire.

'Just like the real ones,' she said. 'It's what Sam says he wants more than anything else in the world. A Fireygo, he calls it, and it had to be just right. If you knew how many fire-engines I've tested in the Christmas cause.'

'Days and days of testing Fireygos,' Pete said, stunned. He lifted the little vehicle and examined it from all angles. 'It's magnificent. Why didn't I come earlier? I can't imagine any more desirable occupation in the world. Piloting jet aircraft pales in comparison. A Fireygo tester! Fantasy stuff! What else is in our pile?'

'A drum.' She sent the instrument spinning across the table toward him. 'Will you wrap it?'

'Not until I've drummed it. Is this for Sam, too?'

'Nope. It's for Em. She fancies herself as a drum-banger, and heaven help the neighbourhood. I'm giving the cows and sheep earplugs for Christmas. Sam's getting a chanter to go with it.'

'A chanter,' he said blankly. 'As in…'

'A chanter from bagpipes.' She grinned, a tiny frisson of excitement mounting inside her. Usually by this time on Christmas Eve she was so exhausted she hardly remembered what she'd bought for the children, but tonight she was rested, she wasn't alone and tomorrow was under control.

And Pete was here.

She couldn't think about that. He was still a Barring…

'Sam wants to play the bagpipes,' she said, and Pete looked astounded.

'Sam's only three.'

'Yep, and he saw bagpipes on the telly when he was two and he *wants* them. A neighbour plays and she's shown Sam her pipes, so Sam knows already that the first thing to do is to learn to play the chanter—the melody-pipe without the drones or bags.' She turned and searched through her pile and found what she was looking for. 'Here it is.'

He looked at the instrument, stunned. 'He'll never play it.'

'He will.' She smiled. 'Eventually. I'll teach him.'

'You can play the bagpipes?'

'Of course I can play the bagpipes. My grandma was a Campbell, remember? From the right side of the border. I used to spend my holidays...'

He was no longer listening. He picked up the chanter and proffered it back to her. 'Play something.'

'Like...?'

'"Jingle Bells".' He grinned and lifted Em's drumsticks. 'With accompaniment.'

'You're kidding.'

'Nope.'

'We'll wake the children.'

'Nothing short of a bomb will wake those children. And one of the good things about living on a farm...'

'Is that there are no neighbours in hearing range. Poor cow. Ernestine doesn't have earplugs yet.' She smiled back at him, light flooding through. She shouldn't be feeling like this, she thought, but all of a sudden she didn't care. She lifted the chanter to her lips. 'OK, Pete Barring. You asked for it.'

'And I seem to be getting it,' he said in a voice that wasn't quite level. 'One way and another, I seem to be getting more than I bargained for this Christmas.' He held the drumsticks poised. 'OK, Lia Holt, alias Lia Matherson, alias McDougal McOnachy. Give it your best.'

They didn't stop at 'Jingle Bells'.

They sat in the flickering firelight under the Christmas tree and they played every Christmas carol they knew. By the end of their recital Lia was in a bubble of laughter, and Pete's drumming was confident, consistent and *very* loud. Each carol had him drumming louder. Lia's pipe-playing increasing in volume accordingly, and finally she laid down her chanter in laughing defeat.

'I need my bags,' she said weakly. 'I can't drown you out without bags.'

'You don't own bagpipes? I though you said you can play.'

'I did.' She hesitated and reality hit home. She rose and looked down at him for a long moment, then wordlessly returned to the kitchen, put the chanter down and started to wrap. Reality had returned. 'I sold them.'

'Because you're broke?' He followed her out and stood, watching the angry thrust of her fingers with the Sellotape.

'Because I'm broke.'

'I see.' He didn't. 'But you can still afford to buy peas...'

'Pete, butt out.'

He held up a hand placatingly, and started wrapping Em's drum. 'OK. I know when I'm not wanted. And, Lia...' He smiled. 'You might be broke, but you play a mean version of "Jingle Bells". Grandma Campbell would be proud of you.'

And that was that. They were silent while they wrapped, but this time the silence wasn't strained. It was as if by playing together they'd achieved team status. A link had been forged.

Or re-established.

'Now for Father-Christmassing,' Lia said at last, as the final gift was wrapped. She ventured a look at Pete and smiled. It wasn't anyone she'd make this offer to, but he was part of her past after all. 'Want to help?'

'Try and stop me. I see myself with a white beard. Ho, ho, ho, let's go.'

So, while the children slept, they tiptoed through the house—which was crazy, given the amount of noise they'd been making only an hour ago, but somehow tiptoeing seemed right. They piled gifts under the tree, they stuffed stockings at the ends of beds, and Lia took a bite out of the shortbread while Pete nobly offered to drink the milk that had been 'left for Santa'.

It was indeed a noble offer. 'All the Santa Clauses I know drink beer,' he announced, staring morosely into Santa's milk.

'Em's call,' Lia told him, choking on laughter

at the look on his face after his first swallow. 'She decreed milk. You want to tell her she's wrong?'

So he drank his milk—or Santa's milk—and Lia watched while he drank, and she was feeling weirder and weirder. But as well as weird, she was feeling... Nice. Warm. And special. Like something missing in her life had somehow, miraculously, been restored.

'You have a milk moustache, Pete Barring,' she told him. As he straightened from putting the empty glass on the hearth, she leaned forward with a tissue to wipe him clean.

Mistake. On a scale of one to ten this ranked right up there about number nineteen. The moment she touched his lips she knew it was a mistake. Although she used a tissue—although her fingers didn't actually touch his mouth—it was as if the link that had been re-established had hardened and strengthened in that one fraction of an instant, and it had grown from a fine thread to a chain of pure iron.

Her fingers stilled.

The whole world stilled, and suddenly she didn't have a clue what was going on. She looked into his face, and his eyes were searching hers—and his hands were coming around to hold her waist, pulling her against him.

'Lia...'

Dear heaven, what was happening? She hadn't touched a man in three years. She hadn't wanted to!

She wanted to now. There was no way in the world she was pushing him away. All the barrenness and the pain of the last three years built up to the point where to push him away was a physical impossibility. She wanted no truck with this man, but her soul ached for comfort.

No! It wasn't comfort that she wanted. Her soul—and her body—ached for love.

And on this magic Christmas Eve, with the fire crackling in the grate, the Christmas lights twinkling and the mistletoe hanging just above their heads, she took what was offered with all the warmth she possessed. He bent to kiss her and he found her lips warm and responsive, her breasts pressing against him and her hands coming up to hold his head to hers—to deepen the kiss.

All the longing and want and misery of the last three years was released in that kiss, and there was no beginning and no ending. There was just…now.

Seven years disappeared, just like that. She remembered as if it had been yesterday the first time she'd kissed this man, but remembering was foolish as she didn't need to remember. Because it was just as it had been. The feeling was the same. Like they were two halves of a whole coming together—that here was her home. This was her man, and she was melting, becoming one with him, and to tear herself away would rip her heart from her chest.

Pete…

She'd loved him so much. He'd broken her heart

and he'd break it again if she let him, but surely it couldn't hurt to take just this moment of loving, this grain of warmth—of pretence of things that could be—before the realities of her harsh world hit home all over again.

This was her Christmas gift to herself—to let herself believe in this one kiss.

And somehow she did. Somehow she let herself believe that he needed this kiss as much as she. And belief was easy. His hand was caressing her cheek, the other was pressing the small of her back so her breasts were crushed against him—just the way she wanted them to be.

His kiss was fierce and yet gentle, possessive yet wondering. It was so sweet—so wondrous—that it enflamed the desperate longing until she thought she'd burn with desire. Her lips parted and she welcomed him, pleading with her entire being that he deepen the kiss.

She hardly recognised the flood of sensation coursing through her body. Had she felt like this before? Never with John, she knew. Although their love-making had been wonderful, it had been peaceful—joyous but calm.

But this… Maybe seven years ago she'd felt like this when Pete had kissed her—she must have—but she couldn't remember. The places they were travelling now had gone past remembrance.

She'd moved past the realms of desire she'd felt as a raw twenty-year-old. Her body was a woman's now, with a woman's needs, and her arms had been empty for far too long.

Pete... Her love...

Her life!

There was a crackling behind them and then a dull thud. Light flared as a log rolled forward out of the fire.

They had to move. They knew it but it was as if each was as reluctant as the other to let go. Their lips slowly parted and Pete's hands held her body to him while they turned to see the damage.

The log had rolled onto the hearth. Maybe it could just lie there...

Sparks shot outwards onto the rug, and the Christmas tree was close. They'd moved the screen while they'd been Father-Christmassing. Mistake.

'I'll put it back,' Lia said in a voice that was none too steady. But she didn't want to. She didn't want to break this moment.

There was the odd matter of the carpet, and the Christmas tree could catch at any minute. Pete saw the danger as clearly as she, yet his hands held on for just a fraction of a moment longer, as if he were holding the last faint traces of a dream.

And when he'd put the log back on the fire, and she'd knelt and readjusted the firescreen, she looked up and found his eyes closed and a look on his face that could almost have been pain.

'I...' She gave herself a fast mental shake, and stood. She felt unsure now. Her defences were right down. She knew that if he took her in his arms again she'd have nothing to fight with, and did she want to fight? No. Her body was screaming its need, and this man was so close, and she'd been alone for so long…

But he was opening his eyes, and things had changed. There was a distance that hadn't been there before. Subtle and yet real.

'I'd best… We'd best get some sleep,' he said, and the look on his face forbade any re-establishment of what lay between them. He'd remembered himself—remembered who she was. 'I'll just…I need to check on Amy.'

He didn't want her.

'Yes.' Lia's voice was a croak.

Amy was asleep in Sam's old pram in the hall where they'd settled her for the afternoon, rather than heading up and downstairs every time she needed them. Somehow Lia made herself move. 'I'll check my own…'

So they walked together out into the hall, their bodies just faintly brushing against each other, and Lia was so aware of him that every nerve in her body was screaming. She wanted to turn and fold herself into his arms again, make him hold her, let what was between them blossom and grow until it reached its own sweet destiny.

But she couldn't—not now that his face had closed and he held himself rigid, and when his body brushed hers he seemed to withdraw.

He stopped at the pram and she paused as well, gazing down into the tiny baby's face. She was so beautiful. Suddenly it was as much as Lia could do not to cry. Amy was nothing to do with her, yet she ached to hold her. She was part of Pete…

And Pete was looking at Lia again, looking at her strangely, with eyes that were suddenly speculative.

'You love babies, don't you, Lia?'

'They're not hard to love. And this little one…she's beautiful.'

'I…' He hesitated, looked down at Amy and then looked again at Lia, as if he'd come to a decision. His voice was forcefully businesslike. 'I've been thinking. I wanted to say this before…before what just happened between us, and if I don't say it now I never will.'

'Mmm.' As a response it was inane, but there was nothing else to say. It was as if there were two Petes—the one she'd held a whole two minutes ago, and the one who was talking to her now. The Pete who was looking at her as if she were a stranger.

Her whole body felt numb.

'It'll be hard for me to keep Amy,' he was saying in that odd formal voice. 'Without being married, I mean.'

Dear heaven, what was he going to say? The world seemed to stop—but then it started again as Pete's voice cut across her panic, his voice flat and devoid of any hint of passion.

'This farm's in financial trouble, right?'

'I…' She was so off balance she felt giddy.

But he was back to normal—almost. He was no longer looking at her. All his attention was on Amy. 'You don't need to confirm it. You can't tell me that flock of sheep out there is viable. Even running this place as a bed and breakfast, you must be struggling to make ends meet.'

'Pete, I don't...' Her mind just wasn't working.

'I'm in trouble, too,' he said, still in that strange, businesslike voice, 'but it's not financial.'

'I don't—'

'I took Amy to see my mother this afternoon,' he went on, ignoring her interruption. 'Mum... well, she's had a dreadful time. All her life's been hard. Dad was hardly a model husband. Ben and I didn't get on and I had to move away. Especially after you and I split—' He broke off, a trace of emotion creeping in, but somehow he forced his voice flat again. 'After Ben died Mum tried to move to the States, but she hated it. This is her home—but she misses us all so much.'

'I know that.'

'And now...here's her grandchild. Like a miracle, there's a piece of Ben left.' He sighed, flexed his fingers straight and then curled them into fists. His voice grew tighter—strained. 'Mum loved Ben like he was the moon and the stars, and to have a piece of him back...' He shrugged. 'As I said, she sees it as a miracle. She held Amy on her lap and she cried her heart out. Yet...'

'Yet she can't care for her.'

'No. But neither can I, and I can't put Amy up for adoption. It'd break Mum's heart.'

'It'd break yours, too,' Lia said softly, and watched his face.

'Ben and I weren't friends.'

'But he was your family,' she told him, acknowledging the truth of what she saw in the pain behind his eyes. 'Your twin. He pulls on your heartstrings even though there was seemingly no love lost between you and now he's dead. It's like me buying fresh peas for Grandpa. My family might treat me dreadfully but they're still my family. You can't knock them back and you hope they'd do the same for you if you were in trouble. Even if you don't believe it.'

'Ben wouldn't have done it for me.' Pete winced, and she could see he was trying to think it through. 'I know that. But...'

'But you can't give her up.'

'No. But I can't work and keep Ben's baby at the same time.'

'You don't think you could marry Helen?'

'Helen is a friend,' he said explosively. 'Nothing more. One of the women I saw...'

'I'd imagine there must be a few.'

His eyes narrowed in anger. 'What do you mean by that?'

'You kiss without thinking,' she said harshly. 'You make love without emotion. Like all your family.'

'What on earth do you know about me, Lia?

You threw me over seven years ago and you haven't seen me since.'

'Leopards don't change their spots.'

'So I'm like Ben and my father because I was born into the same family. You didn't have the courage to trust yourself, to trust what you knew of me. You had to judge me by others.' He broke off, choking back angry words, and thrust his hands deep into his pockets. 'Look, this has nothing to do with what I'm thinking now. What I've worked out—'

'I don't want to know.'

'Just listen,' he said, exasperated. 'Shut up and listen for a change. And keep your judgmental tongue under control.'

'OK.' She glared. 'Say it. But say it fast because I'm going to bed.'

'I want you to look after my baby,' he said.

Silence.

The silence stretched on for so long that the grandfather clock in the hall started booming midnight and finished its chimes before Lia found the words to reply.

'I told you,' she said at last, in a voice that sounded close to breaking. 'I'm not taking on your responsibilities.'

'This is a business proposition, Lia.'

'Oh, for heaven's sake….' Her anger was threatening to choke her. 'Amy's a baby. She's not a commercial enterprise.' She stooped and let her hand drift to Amy's soft cheek in a gesture of protection. Pete saw the caress, and he nodded in satisfaction.

'It wouldn't be hard to love her,' he said. 'If you let yourself.'

'Pete, this is…'

'Ridiculous? Is it? What else am I to do?' He shrugged. 'I've been thinking all day and I can't come up with a better solution. Amy's been thrust on me like a lightning bolt and I can't figure out an easy answer. But my problems are these.'

He held up one finger after another, his face set and firm. He was talking business now, Lia thought bleakly. Not emotion. The crazy nonsense before the fire was over.

'One, Amy is Ben's baby. There's no way I want her adopted into a strange family where there's no connection with me or with her grandmother.

'Two, I'm comparatively wealthy. I'm in my thirties. I've been flying commercially for years and I make good money. I can afford to keep Amy in any way she needs, but I don't want to employ a strange nanny—especially when I go off for days at a time, flying, and I can't keep a constant check on her. OK, I can get a desk job but I'd hate it and I'm not experienced in looking after babies. I'd still have to employ a nanny during the day.

'Three, you live here, close by my mother— Amy's grandmother. If Amy lives with you we can make arrangements for my mother to see her often. You have two great kids already, you love babies and you need money. So…if I undertook to keep this farm going, if I take it on as a business proposition and employ a man to help…'

'Have you any idea how much that would cost?' She was practically gaping at him, but he didn't bat an eyelid.

'I do, he said bluntly. 'I tried to keep our farm going when Dad left, remember? Now, though, it would give me real pleasure to know that you and your children could stay here and keep a stable base for Amy.'

'But you'll marry,' she said slowly. 'You'll want her then.'

'I'm not a marrying man. I don't get attached.' He didn't look at her and there was a hint of steel in his voice.

'But if you do… Or if her mother wants her back…'

'We'll worry about that when it happens.'

'No!' She drew a deep breath. This was crazy and it was a life they were talking about. A child's life—Amy, who was even now stirring in her sleep as if she knew her future lay in the balance.

'I know what will happen,' she said. 'You'll leave her here and the kids and I will love her to bits. Then Becky will want her back—'

'I'll adopt her. Sure, you'll need guarantees, Lia. I'll make it as watertight as I can.'

'You can't guarantee to always leave her here. She's not a possession.'

'You'll have to take my word on that. Trust me.'

'Trust!'

'I know,' he said, and his voice was suddenly harsh. 'It's not your strong point, is it, Lia? But I'm asking you to trust. I'm asking you to open your heart.'

'For a baby.'

'For Ben's baby.'

'It's unfair.'

'Yes,' he agreed calmly. 'It is. But I'm offering financial stability for all of you in return. That's a fair exchange, Lia.'

'I don't—'

'Think about it,' he said urgently. 'You'd have to cope with seeing me. I'd be here often to see her. I can base myself in Manchester and do the short-haul European runs. But we'd have to find some way of overcoming the chemistry between us.'

'The chemistry…'

'The fact that I can't look at you without wanting to take you to bed,' he said honestly. 'It's the way I've always felt about you, Lia, and the fact that you don't fight back makes it impossible. But it's only physical. You've made that clear, so I have to learn to keep it under control. I'll do that. For Amy's sake.'

'Pete…'

'Don't make any decisions tonight,' he told her, and he placed a finger under her chin and forced her to meet his eyes. 'Think about it over Christmas and let me know. I understand all too well that you don't trust. But I'm not asking you to trust me. I'll have it all drawn up watertight before solicitors. I'm offering you a future here, Lia, and I'm trusting you with my…my niece. Think about what you'd be refusing if you turn me down.'

How could she sleep after that?

There was no possibility, and Lia lay awake until the small hours, going over and over Pete's crazy proposition. It was utterly stupid!

Stupid…

Above her head she heard Pete settling the baby, and then settling himself into the big bed. He'd abandoned the box room now that Helen had left, so he was now in *her* bed and that thought didn't settle her at all. The knowledge of where he was had her wide awake and staring sightlessly at the ceiling, as if she could will herself to look through it.

Could she look after Pete's baby?

The proposition was crazy!

Yet what was the alternative? Upstairs was one baby who desperately needed a mother, and Lia knew her heart was big enough to take her in. She'd always wanted a big family. Kids, a farm, a husband…

She had kids now. She had a farm—just. But soon she wouldn't have a farm, she acknowledged. It was too small to be viable. There was no way John had been able to buy life insurance. He'd scraped and saved to buy the farm because he'd loved it, and while he and Lia had both worked they'd been able to manage. But now... It had been growing clearer all this year that she couldn't keep it. Which left her where?

Heading to the city and finding someone to look after the children while she went back to nursing? No! The thought of leaving this place made her feel physically ill.

Pete's proposition would solve that.

But the downside... She saw it too clearly. She'd learn to love this new little one and she'd break her heart if anything happened. She'd grow too attached.

And Pete would come...and she'd have to act as if she were indifferent, and that would break her apart as well.

It was far too difficult. And it was Christmas. She rolled over, put her head in the pillow and willed it to be Christmas Day already.

She wanted this to be over.

CHAPTER FIVE

'HE's been!'

Lia blinked and opened one eye as a small body landed on top of her with a flying thud. Followed by another small body.

Followed by Woof.

Woof was wearing a Santa Claus hat.

'He's been, Mummy! Father Christmas has been! And our bedroom is full of balloons. Our house is full of balloons.' Em was bouncing up and down on her mother's stomach, while Woof tried to lick Em's face. 'Go away, Woof, that's my toffee-apple.' The little girl pushed the collie away, and Woof turned his attention to licking Lia. 'You should see our bedroom, Mummy. There's balloons and balloons and balloons…'

Sam and Em were wearing Santa Claus hats.

Lia's eyes were wide open now. They were so wide open they practically enveloped her face. 'Down, Woof! Who let you in? And what are you doing on my bed?'

Santa Claus hats… Balloons…

The Father Christmas she knew hadn't delivered balloons.

But balloons there definitely were. Clutched in each small hand were bunches of brilliantly col-

oured balloons, there were balloons attached to
Woof's collar, there were balloons out in the hall
and floating in around the children's heads. They
were gold and scarlet and brilliant green, and they
were filled with helium and floating high. Some
had yellow tapes attached to small hands or collars,
and others were floating free.

One flew ceilingward while she watched. It
caught a splinter of wood and popped with a bang
that made both children squeal and made Woof
dive under Lia's bedcovers, his balloons trailing
after like a tail.

'There's millions and trillions of balloons,' Em
shouted, grabbing for a Santa hat that was threatening to slide onto her nose.

'And licorice allsorts,' Sam said, wide-eyed under his own hat. 'In the stocking on my bed there's
licorice allsorts. I've eaten six already, and there's
lots more.'

'And Santa gave me a toffee-apple,' Em said
triumphantly, leaning forward to kiss her mother
with a slurpy kiss that said, yes, she definitely did
have a toffee-apple—or rather she'd had a toffee-
apple, and it was no wonder Woof was interested.

'Where did you get a toffee-apple?' Lia was
stunned.

'From my stocking,' Em said patiently, as if Lia
were silly for not guessing the obvious. She
bounced up and down on the bed in her pink pyjamas, sticky-mouthed and Santa-hatted, a four-
year-old supremely contented with her world. 'And

there's piles and piles and *piles* of presents under the tree.'

'Mountains,' Sam said smugly. 'Some say "Sam".'

'And we think you should get up. Pete said it's breakfast in fifteen minutes and then a rest because he's pooped and has to get his strength back for the fest—festivities, and then *presents*...' She paused for breath.

From the front room came the sound of Christmas carols being played at full volume from the radio. 'We wish you a merry Christmas, We wish you a merry Christmas...'

A man's voice joined right in, in a booming rich baritone. 'We wish you a merry Christmas and a happy New Year!'

Pete...

And around her bedroom door came the singing Pete—complete with his very own Santa hat, and carrying Amy in his arms. The baby was dressed in a bright red jumpsuit and with her own small Santa hat on as well.

Lia stared in total bewilderment. She was starting to feel decidedly under-dressed. And decidedly confused.

'Ho, ho, ho,' Pete said sternly, beetling his eyebrows. 'Why are you bare-headed, Mrs Holt? This will never do.' He handed a heap of red and white felt to Em. 'Emma. Dress your mother immediately or she'll suffer Christmas consequences. Lia, you have fifteen minutes to get yourself respectable.

You can take your hat off while you wash but if you spend any more than three minutes bareheaded today then you'll go up in a puff of Christmas smoke. In fifteen minutes I want you present and correct at the Christmas breakfast table.'

'I can't...' She stared wildly about her. 'Pete... The cow... The hens... I have to milk...'

'Ernestine-cow has been milked and been given a double quantity of Christmas chaff. I'm instructed to present you with her Christmas compliments, along with a bucket of extremely creamy milk. She's re-established with Harriet-calf, and they're settled to enjoy Christmas without human intervention, thank you very much. As for the hens, the girls have presented you with thirteen Christmas eggs and many fine squawks of the season. Any more questions? You're wasting time.'

'Time...' She stared down at the bedroom clock. It stared right back at her. Seven o'clock! She gasped and sat up as if she'd been stung.

'Seven... I set it for five-thirty!'

'And a great deal of trouble I had unsetting it,' Pete said blandly. 'I'd sneak in and you'd wiggle or mutter or blink, and I'd have to sneak right back out again. Finally at three-thirty Amy had her last feed and you were snoring like a chainsaw...'

'I don't snore!'

'Snoring,' he said definitely, and smiled, and the smile in his dark eyes had her heart doing handstands. What had he said? He'd come into her room while she'd been asleep? Good grief! 'You were definitely snoring, Lia Holt. So I succeeded in my mission and you're now nicely rested, just like the doctor ordered.' He turned his attention to Sam and Em. 'OK, Twerp One and Twerp Two. Let's hit breakfast. And, Woof—are you under there?'

Before Lia could stop him, he hauled back Lia's bedclothes to reveal Woof's black and white nose. Plus Lia. But he was looking at the dog. 'It was only a balloon popping,' he told him sternly. 'Get used to it. There's bacon in the kitchen if you can risk a few more bangs.'

To Lia's amazement, Woof looked up at him for all the world as if he understood exactly what was being said. He cast an apologetic look at his mistress and abandoned her forthwith. Bacon...

He bolted. Em and Sam whooped and took themselves off kitchenwards, and Pete turned to go.

Then he stopped and turned back, devilment in his eyes.

'Are those your very best nightclothes, Lia Holt?'

Lia flushed bright pink. Her very best... They were John's old flannelette pyjamas, lacking in buttons and drawn in around the waist with a piece of frayed cord. She had better things to spend her money on than sexy nightwear.

But...

'They're incredibly sexy,' Pete told her, and

suddenly the smile slipped and Lia knew he meant exactly what he'd said. He took a deep breath as she hauled in the two sides of her pyjama jacket in an instinctive movement of defence.

His twinkle faded completely. Something was between them that neither understood—and it wasn't laughter.

'I'll not come in here again,' he said, and he closed the door behind him and practically bolted.

What on earth was happening?

Lia stood under the shower for a very long time—far longer than was sensible, given that hot water was expensive, but she had to fight for some measure of control.

She affected him—and he affected her in a way she didn't understand. Or maybe she understood all too well. She'd fallen in love seven years ago and she'd never fallen out again.

So she looked at him and she wanted to love him for ever. He wanted her, too, but in a different way. He looked at her and he wanted to make love to her.

But they were two completely different things, she told herself. Love...and lust. Combined, they'd be fantastic but there was no talk of love here. Once maybe, but he'd been unfaithful, and his talk of love had been a nonsense.

Pete was a Barring. She knew the way the Barring men worked. They moved from woman to woman. So, sure, she affected him, but there'd be other women in his life who he felt exactly the same about.

'So get Christmas out of the way, put him out of your house and your heart and get on with your life,' she told herself severely. 'And don't be so stupid!'

There were strawberries and pancakes for breakfast.

'Pancakes, pancakes, pancakes,' Em shouted as Lia walked through the door.

'Jeans,' Pete said, looking at her from tip to toe, and his tone said he disapproved. 'What about wearing something pretty for Christmas?'

'You don't see anything pretty under an apron,' she retorted, flushing. She wasn't used to people looking at her as Pete looked at her.

How long since anyone had actually taken any notice at all of what she had on?

'Surely you have a dress? Em, does your mother have a dress?'

'There's a really pretty yellow dress hanging in her wardrobe,' Em said. 'She never wears it.'

'Em, that's—'

'Your best dress?'

It was the dress she'd married in. She and John had slipped away to the registry office in York. She'd bought her dress and she'd loved it, but she'd only worn it the once.

'Yes,' she said, subdued. 'It's my best dress.'

'A Christmas dress?'

'I suppose…'

'Then put it on before our guests arrive,' Pete told her, smiling, and it was just impossible not to smile back. 'I promise, you won't need your apron. Meanwhile, have some pancakes.'

'Pete, the kids will be ill.'

'Not them,' he said. 'We have a deal. Two pancakes and a bowl of strawberries each, then a rest on their bed for an hour before presents under the tree. Nothing else to eat until lunch. Them's the rules.'

'Pete has ser—serious rules,' Sam announced, looking at his mother for confirmation. 'He says Christmas is always better if you use rules because otherwise you throw up. Pete threw up when he was three, and he can't even remember the rest of his Christmas after that.'

'I don't want to know,' Lia said faintly. 'Information overload here.'

'I don't blame you. It was my darkest hour,' Pete intoned in a dirgeful voice that made her choke on laughter. 'I've been telling them the dreadful tale, asking them to carry the warning on to generations to come. An hour on the bed and nothing else to eat until lunchtime isn't a huge price to pay to avoid such a catastrophe.'

'What's a catastrophe?' Sam demanded, breathless with horrified awe.

'It involves cats and apostrophes,' Pete said.

'And throwing up?' Em demanded.

'Definitely throwing up.'

'I'll 'bey the rules,' Sam announced, and tackled his pancakes like there was no tomorrow.

And then, to Lia's stupefaction, the children went calmly back to bed. Sure, they wouldn't sleep, but their lollies were put aside and they lay and sent balloons back and forth, and discussed at length what could be in the much prodded and poked presents under the tree. Pete's catastrophe had been averted.

Meanwhile, Lia was permitted—grudgingly—to don her apron, the turkey was wrapped in bacon and put in the oven, the pudding put on to boil, the vegetables were prepared, the brandy sauce was made...

And Amy had her first taste of something that wasn't milk.

'Brandy sauce is hardly the first thing a baby should taste,' Lia protested, but was drowned out.

'It's definitely the first thing she should taste. Look, she loves it.'

She certainly did. Amy tasted, her eyes widened and she beamed, and her little mouth opened like a baby bird wanting more. Lia headed around the kitchen and snatched the little one out of her uncle's arms before he could do some real damage.

'Pete Barring, have you no moral principles? Feeding a baby brandy sauce!'

'It's gorgeous,' Pete said, helping himself to a spoonful. 'We both think so. But...more brandy, I think. Try it.' He held out a spoonful and, her arms full of baby, she had no choice but to taste.

It certainly was good—or maybe it was just the combination of Christmas, and too much laughter, and her arms being full of beaming baby and…and Pete. She looked up at him and her smile died.

Silence.

Dear heaven. What…?

'It's time,' a voice said anxiously at the door, and Lia swivelled as if she'd been shot—to see Em and Sam standing hand in hand in the doorway. 'Pete said when the big hand was pointing at the nine…'

'So I did. It's present time,' Pete agreed. He gave Lia one last long look, then swung Em up in one arm and Sam up in the other. 'Yes! It's present time. Right now!'

It was a very silly, very happy hour. Amy lay in a pile of Cellophane and rustled with every move. This was a wonderful new sensation! She lay and looked and looked, and the noise and colour and laughter all around her was more than a two-month-old baby could ask of her world.

And Em and Sam could ask no more either. Em found her brand new satchel full of thirty-six colouring pencils and three different sets of drawing paper, and Sam found his Fireygo, and they were almost pop-eyed. Then they found their chanter and drum. The noise level escalated in an instant, and Woof barked in sympathy and Amy chortled with glee until Lia almost wept with laughter.

She almost wept, full stop.

This was what Christmas was all about. Happiness and noise and kids and warmth...and love.

And then she picked up a last present which had somehow materialised from the pile. She'd put in a few things for herself so the children would see her opening gifts—a pile of new teatowels, a couple of pairs of socks...

But this... She hadn't bought this. It was large and wrapped in bright red Christmas paper and had a green bow, and all it said was,

To Lia, From Santa.

Mystified, she opened it and found a big white box, and in the box were...

Boots.

Not just boots. Beautiful boots. They were Italian by the look of them, and by the trade name on the box. They were made of the softest grey leather, and every inch of them screamed quality. They were superbly shaped to the ankle with demure decorative stitching and invisible zips at the side. Stunned, Lia slipped her hand inside and found they were lined with the finest fleece.

They were just plain gorgeous! She'd never seen boots like these in her life! But... She put them down and stared at them as if they'd bite her. 'What the...?'

'Try them on,' Pete said mildly. 'Let's see if Santa can guess correct sizes.'

'Santa...'

'Put them on, Lia.'

So she did, giving him sideways glances of absolute confusion, and Em abandoned her drum and came across to run her hand down the fine leather.

'They're so soft,' she said, awed. 'They feel lovely. Mummy, they've got fluff inside!'

They certainly did, and they slid onto Lia's feet as if they'd been made to go there.

'You...' Lia's voice broke in a whisper. 'You did this?' She stared at Pete as if he'd just landed from Mars.

'Santa did this.'

'And...how did Santa know my size?'

'That's for Santa to know and for you to guess.'

'Pete...'

It wasn't the boots that were making her feel like this, she thought numbly. It was the thought!

No. It was the boots. She'd never had someone give her something she wanted. In the New Year she'd intended to buy boots but they'd have been the cheapest she could find. Now... She stuck a beautifully booted leg out before her and she felt like bursting into tears.

'Don't you like them, Mummy?' Em said anxiously, and Lia closed her eyes.

'I love them. But...I can't take them.'

'They're not a bribe, Lia,' Pete said gently. 'Regardless of what you decide, they're a "Happy Christmas" present. From me to you.'

She tilted her chin. 'Pete... I haven't... I can't...'

'You're giving my mother and my niece and

myself a Christmas,' he told her. He crossed from where he'd been standing before the fire—benevolent genie distributing largesse—and stooped and kissed her gently on the forehead. 'That's my Christmas present to you. Enjoy your boots. You deserve them.'

Then he hesitated, as if torn.

'I'd best be off,' he said slowly. 'I'll be back in an hour with my mother. Will you be OK by yourself—until then?'

'I... Of course.'

But he couldn't help himself. She was so lovely, sitting on the floor with her ridiculous boots, and her eyes welling with tears, looking as if she'd been handed the world. It was crazy—there was no way he intended getting involved—but he stooped again and this time he kissed her on the lips.

'Merry Christmas, Lia,' he whispered. 'You deserve the best.'

It was just as well he had an excuse to get out of the house. He needed time to cool off. Pete drove toward Churton and found himself slowing before he reached the village, dragging out the time before he arrived at the nursing-home. Giving himself time to think.

Amy lay sleeping in her carrycot in the back seat. He glanced over at her and his gut twisted. She was so small. So defenceless.

That was a bit like how he felt about Lia.

'You haven't thought about her for seven years,'

he told himself harshly. 'For heaven's sake, Barring, go take a cold shower.' Because all he could think of was Lia. He hadn't slept last night, and some of it had been because he'd had to stay awake to play Santa, but the rest of it had been because in the bedroom beneath him had been a woman he'd ached to hold with every fibre of his being.

'It's just physical,' he told himself with a desperation he no longer believed. It was starting to snow and he opened the car window to let the sharp wind in. Amy murmured and shifted, and he wound the window up again. He'd forgotten...

That he had a responsibility.

He had to forge her a future, he told himself harshly, and a sexual relationship with Lia would mess that future right up. Amy needed Lia. He needed Lia, but in a business sense only. As a woman who'd care for his niece.

Nothing more.

Why? he asked himself and he knew the answer.

Because once before—once only—he'd walked down the path his heart was sending him now and he'd been shoved away with an iciness that still left him cold. He remembered that Christmas Eve...

He'd remember it all his life, and never again would he feel like that. Never!

In two days he was due to fly out of Manchester back to the States. 'You'll have this organised by then,' he told himself. 'So...stay calm, level-headed and friendly. Keep Lia on side, keep your hands off her and don't let your emotions come into this. Talk her into keeping Amy. That's all you want.'

Liar!

'Lia.'

Lia opened the door and blinked. Margaret Barring stood beside her son, her face wreathed in smiles. Lia hadn't seen her for years. After Pete… Well, broken engagements often severed more ties than the ones between the couple. Lia and Margaret had been friends then, but not since.

The difference in Margaret between now and then was stunning. She'd once been a lovely woman, but in the last seven years she seemed to have shrunk. Withered. A philandering husband and the death of a son had taken their toll. She'd aged shockingly and the hand she held out to Lia trembled with infirmity.

'Margaret, come in.' Somehow Lia forced the shock out of her voice and stood aside to allow Pete to usher his mother into the warmth. 'You must be freezing.'

'Not now.' Margaret smiled and tears welled into her eyes as she entered the living room. 'Not now I'm having a proper Christmas.'

It certainly looked 'a proper Christmas'. The children were playing peacefully under the tree, the drum and chanter having been put aside until 'after company'. Woof was snoozing by the crackling fire, the lights on the tree were twinkling and Pete's balloons were everywhere. 'This...' Margaret faltered. I can't tell you how much I appreciate this.'

'It's all my pleasure.' Lia smiled and gave the elderly lady a kiss on the cheek, carefully avoiding looking at her son. 'It's lovely to have you here, Margaret. I'm so sorry you couldn't have your restaurant meal.'

'As if I wouldn't rather have this.' She gazed around and sighed. 'This is how it ought to be. Oh, Lia, I so wish you and Pete had married...'

Great! What wasn't needed here was sentiment. 'Now, don't you go throwing youthful indiscretions in our faces.' Lia smiled, keeping her voice deliberately light. 'I bet you didn't marry the first boy you went out with.'

'I did.' Margaret faltered. 'And I can't regret it.'

'And I can't regret my marriage either,' Lia said roundly, turning her attention to Em and Sam. Conversation at an end. 'Look what's come out of it. Emma, Sam...come and meet Mrs Barring.'

She was under control—just.

'Hey, I love your dress,' Pete said in an undertone as the children rose and came across the room, and suddenly she was in control no longer. She was wearing her yellow wedding dress, and she was feeling so self-conscious she wanted to bolt upstairs again. It was pretty and floating and altogether impractical. It made her feel about eighteen.

'I... Thank you.' He looked pretty good himself, she thought numbly. He'd donned a dark suit and a Christmas tie, with Santa Clauses tumbling downward, and he looked tall and strong and impossibly—hopelessly—handsome.

He looked like a Barring, and he scared her silly!

And then the doorbell rang. Thank heaven! Her moment of stunned hormonal silence was over, and Christmas was starting in earnest. The part she hated.

Only this time…it was different. This was a meal she dreaded, but right from the start Pete changed everything.

'Lia.' Her mother swept in on her Uncle Harold's arm, and presented one beautifully perfumed cheek for her daughter to air-kiss. 'Darling.' Then she stepped back and stared. 'What on earth are you wearing?' Her elegant nose wrinkled in distaste, the way it did every time Lia wore anything but jeans.

Just the same as always. But…

'It's gorgeous, isn't it?' Pete magically appeared behind her and his arm came around her waist in a gesture of protection that had Lia's body doing all sorts of strange things. 'Lorraine.' He smiled a benign greeting to Lia's mother and Lia remembered that Pete's reaction to her mother had never been anything but distantly polite. 'How are you? It's been years.'

'Ben Barring…' her mother said, stunned, and took a step back.

'It's Pete, actually. You must have known Ben died.'

'I... Yes.' For once her elegant mother was at a loss. 'I thought...'

'Yes?'

'I thought you were in the US.'

'I am, mostly. Now I'm here, with my mother and my niece. Lia's asked us to Christmas dinner. I hope you don't mind.'

'I... Oh, no.' Her mother recovered fast and practically fluttered, as she did every time a presentable man came within her orbit. In the old days Pete had somehow been eclipsed by Ben, but now... 'How nice.' She purred. 'Sarah will be so pleased.'

'Sarah?'

'You must remember my youngest daughter.' Lorraine handed Pete her coat and batted her false eyelashes. 'How fortunate. She was to have brought...well, she had someone coming with her but she's just telephoned to say his plane couldn't land. Apparently the weather's growing worse and they've diverted planes from Manchester. Without an escort she was in half a mind not to come, but...' She smiled and searched in her handbag for her mobile phone. 'I think I'll telephone her now and tell her it's worth coming after all.'

Then she turned to Lia again while she waited for the call to connect. 'So tell me why you're wearing that appalling dress. You must know it's years out of date.'

Lia took a deep breath. 'I like it,' she said.

'So do I,' Pete said, and Lorraine should have noticed the note of danger in his voice.

'Oh, well,' she said airily, ignoring Pete's growl. 'I suppose with the farm and two kiddies you don't have much time to think about your appearance. I'm just pleased I have two daughters who care about the things that matter.'

And she turned her attention to the phone.

'Would you like to tell me what's going on?'

Lia was in the kitchen, basting her turkey. Half an hour to go, thank heaven, and she could serve and then it'd be another step closer to finishing. Pete arrived by her side, picked up another spoon and started basting the other side. 'Lia?'

'I don't know what you mean.'

'Why do your family delight in putting you down?'

'They did it to my father,' she told him, basting with vigour. 'When he died they just carried right on with me.'

'Do you know that when they criticise you, you sort of shrink?'

'I...I don't take much notice.'

'Liar.'

She shrugged. 'No matter. Let's get this meal over.' She shoved the turkey back in the oven and turned to return to the dining room, but Pete caught her by the shoulders and stopped her.

'You're still wearing your apron.'

'So I am. Like a sensible person who's wearing a dress years out of date.'

'Nope.' He reached behind her for the ties and undid them, then slid the offending garment from her body. His hands were warm and strong, and she was intensely aware of them through the thin fabric of her dress. 'Show us you.' He flicked her curls back from her face. 'You really are lovely, Lia. I don't know what's been going on...'

'Lovely!' She took a deep breath. 'You have to be kidding. You've seen my mother. And Sally. And Sarah will be here any minute. That's lovely.'

'No. That's manicured. You're lovely.' He let his fingers drift in her hair. 'You know, I was so in love with you...' He stopped, catching himself.

Enough of that. All those years ago she'd made it very clear she didn't want him. But there were so many unanswered questions. 'Lia... This dress. Em just told me it was your wedding dress. Your mother was casting disparaging remarks about it, and Em said, "It's the one in the picture of Mummy and Daddy on their wedding day."'

'That's right.'

He frowned. 'So...the only dress you possess—apart from jeans—is your wedding dress?'

'I have a suit. For funerals and bank managers.' She managed a smile.

'Lia, what was wrong with John?' he said quietly, and perched on the kitchen table and waited.

Nothing. 'I...I need to get back. They... My guests...'

'Your guests are guzzling my champagne and enjoying it very much,' he told her. 'They're eating your savouries like they're going out of fashion, and they haven't even noticed you're not there.'

'They'll notice that you're not.'

'Too bad. Tell me about John.'

'He…' Lia shook her head. It all seemed surreal, standing here in the dress she'd married in, talking to the man she'd loved all her life about a different love. But he was waiting for an answer.

'John had polio when he was in his teens,' she started softly, staring down at her hands—staring at anything other than Pete. 'He must have been one of the last infected before immunisation became standard. He was an only son of farmers up on the border. His parents sold everything to pay for his medical treatment, including the farm, and when I met him he was determined to farm again. Only on his terms. No one would employ him, you see, because of his weak leg. He had residual breathing problems…so much wrong… It was mad to try.'

'But you loved him.'

'Yes.' She tilted her chin. That was the absolute truth. She'd loved John in a very different way to the way she'd loved Pete, but she'd loved him all the same. He'd fought so hard to return the care his parents had given him, and then, when they'd died and he'd met Lia, he'd had just a tiny sliver of a chance of personal happiness.

He'd found that happiness with her, though his

dream had cost every last penny they'd possessed, and she couldn't regret it for a minute.

'Your family disapproved?'

'Of course we disapproved.' Lorraine's shrill voice cut across Pete's question—of course. When had Lia's mother ever kept her nose out of her daughter's business? She stood in the doorway and glowered as she answered for her daughter. 'Of all the stupid, senseless things… Lia married him. Married him! A cripple. I mean, Lia doesn't have much going for her, but she had more than that. He was penniless and he bought this farm with her savings and with the money her father left her.'

'Mum…'

'I came to find Peter,' her mother said, giving her a cold look. 'I might have known you'd be banging on for ever about your personal problems. Lia, is dinner nearly ready? You know Aunt Grace is a diabetic, and if she doesn't eat by one she gets dizzy. She's starting to feel dizzy now.'

'Tell her to lay off the champagne,' Pete said drily. 'Lorraine…'

'Yes, Peter.' She tucked her arm into his, waiting to be escorted back to the living room.

He carefully untucked it again.

'I'm making gravy with Lia,' he said, turning her towards the door. 'We're having fun together and you're not included. You go and care for Aunty Grace, there's a dear.' And he patted her on the arm as one might have patted an elderly person in the early stages of dementia. 'Lia and I will fix dinner. You go back and join the rest of the old folk.'

And—for once in her life—Lorraine was stumped for words. She took a deep, gasping breath, Pete put a hand in the small of her back and propelled her out into the passage, and he closed the door behind her.

'You shouldn't have said that.' Lia stared at the closed door with her mouth ajar. What on earth had he done? 'Oh, Pete...'

'Why ever not? She was trying her best to hurt you. I just retaliated.' He grinned. 'A little. Nothing a good dose of Christmas punch won't cure.'

'But after that... She'll book in for plastic surgery by New Year.'

His grin deepened. 'I couldn't think of a better fate. Lia, your mother's a horror.'

'Yes, but...'

'She's your mother?' He grimaced. 'I know, but sometimes...' He shrugged. 'I loved Ben, too, but sooner or later, you have to walk away.'

'No...'

'She's trying to destroy you,' he said conversationally. 'Don't be a doormat, Lia, love.' His smile faded as he looked at her. She deserved better than this family. No matter how she'd hurt him. 'Now, let's get on with this dinner.'

Her mother wore a hat.

To Lia's total astonishment there was no argument at all about wearing the amazing Christmas hats Pete and the children had made. Before they tucked into turkey and trimmings, Pete rose and made a speech.

'Merry Christmas everyone,' he said, and he raised his glass in a toast. 'Now, before the next sip of champagne—or the next swallow of lemonade if you're under tippling age—you're required to don your hat. Last one to don their hats gets to wash the roasting-pan. Right. One, two, three—now!' And he held Lorraine's eyes with his, toasted her silently and with his free hand he placed his hat on his head.

Lorraine stared at him—mesmerised—and then, to the company's collective amazement, her mother perched her gaudy home-made hat on top of her bouffant hairstyle.

Stunned, the rest of the table followed suit—and in that one instant Lia's disapproving, critical family was turned into a party.

The hats were ridiculous—crazy—and putting them on seemed to transform people. Or maybe it was the champagne. Or maybe it was Pete himself who hauled the whole family into a bubble of laughter.

'Sally...' he said to Lia's silent older sister, who was staring in silent disapproval of her roast turkey. Obviously something like smoked salmon and caviar with maybe a truffle or two on the side would have been more satisfactory. 'You seem aloof.'

'I'm not—'

'But don't worry.' He contemplated her with his wicked, impossible-to-resist eyes. 'Be aloof if you want. The world needs more loofs. Do we have any more at the table?'

Ridiculous—the table collapsed with laughter, and Sally, who was still trying to be prim under her crazy hat, gave up trying and succumbed to his charm.

'Tell me what you think of the peas,' Pete quizzed Grandpa, and old Henry harrumphed and glared down at his dinner. This was his cue to say something disagreeable but, try as he might, it wouldn't come out. Two glasses of punch on arrival, followed by champagne, followed by the sight of his elegant family in silly hats had unnerved him entirely.

'They're damned fine peas,' he said at last, and waved a loaded fork in Lia's direction. 'Well done, girl.' And then he paused, overcome by the Christmas spirit. 'And you look damned pretty today,' he told Lia at last. 'Almost as pretty as your sisters.'

It was all Lia could do not to choke at this over-the-top compliment. She looked at Pete and found his eyes warm on hers, and there was no way her grandfather's words could hurt her. Pete's laughter forbade it. His eyes caught hers and held, and the laughter flashed between them, and it was Christmas, and it was just fine.

It was more than just fine. It was lovely.

Margaret Barring was sitting on Pete's left,
beaming and beaming. She had her granddaughter
cradled in one arm and was eating one-handed—
not because she needed to but because she couldn't
bear to put her sleeping granddaughter down. Em
and Sam were keeping watch on the baby—they
both showed that they thought Amy was theirs and
they weren't all that sure about sharing, but the
turkey was excellent and they put on hold any possible objections.

Everyone was happy. It all seemed…right.

Maybe she could take Amy, Lia thought
dazedly, and wondered just how much champagne
she'd had.

And then the doorbell went, and she remembered Sarah.

CHAPTER SIX

SARAH.

The laughter that had been bubbling in Lia since the donning of the hats died, as did the thought that maybe taking Amy and constantly seeing Pete was possible. Here was her gorgeous younger sister, ready to claim whatever she wanted.

Ready to claim what had always been her right.

Lia rose to answer the door but she wasn't fast enough. Sarah had rung the bell and had come straight in. Now she stood in the dining-room entrance, still wrapped in her wonderful crimson coat, her cheeks flushed from the cold, her gorgeous blonde hair splayed out over her scarf and her blue eyes alight with pleasure.

'Oh, it's snowing so hard out there,' she said, her soft laugh tinkling into the silence. If there was one thing Sarah was good at it was holding an audience. 'I so nearly couldn't make it. I expect we'll be marooned here for weeks.'

And then she turned to search the room, ignoring her family as she searched for one man only.

'Pete,' she said, as he pushed back his chair and rose, and she walked straight forward into his arms.

She kissed him.

Of course she kissed him—when had Sarah

never kissed a personable man? But this wasn't a kiss of greeting. This was a kiss of... wham!

She kissed him as if she owned him. Her arms came around his neck and held, her soft mouth locked onto his, and the whole table looked on as Pete was kissed with a passion that said Sarah was taking over just where she'd left off.

As she was, Lia thought dully, sinking back into her chair. And why should Lia mind after all these years? After all, Pete was just a Barring...

The kiss had to end—finally—but when it did Lia wasn't watching. She'd risen again and was starting to lift plates and clear.

'Hush, dear,' her mother said, putting her hand on her arm to stop the clatter. 'Isn't this just lovely?'

'Really cute,' Lia said, thumping a plate on top of another plate. 'A true romance, and not even any mistletoe in sight.'

'Don't sound so sour,' her mother snapped. 'You'll spoil it. Oh, children, don't stop...'

But the children had stopped. Pete held Sarah at arm's length and looked dazed. She gazed back at him with adoration, her blue eyes misting with emotion.

'Pete Barring,' she whispered. 'Oh, Pete, you walked out of my life seven years ago and left me bereft.'

'I'm...sorry?' Pete's voice sounded husky—as well it might. He'd been solidly made love to here.

Sarah's hands were reaching for his and holding on like she was staking her claim.

'I'm sorry, too. We so nearly made it.'

'Sarah, there's still some turkey left,' Lia said desperately, fighting for some sanity in the proceedings. She took Uncle Henry's plate from him and thumped it down on her pile with a force that made that elderly gentleman jump. 'But I'm clearing. Will I leave some for you?'

'I have something better than turkey right here,' Sarah purred, and Lia felt like throwing up.

'Yeah, well, take him outside and get on with it,' she said. 'It's putting the rest of us off our dinner.'

'*We so nearly made what?*' Pete said.

It was a stark, hard question, completely out of context with what had gone before, and it sounded off-key and ominous.

It sounded different to how he and Sarah looked.

The entire family was now looking at the couple standing hand in hand. They certainly did look made for each other, Lia thought, in a cover-page kind of way. Sarah's svelte blonde beauty and Pete's dark, rugged maleness. They were a perfect pair.

The family knew it. The children weren't interested—they didn't much like their Aunty Sarah, and kissing was boring so they whooped off to do a between-course present check—but the adults were riveted. Lorraine was beaming her satisfaction. The aunts, uncles and Grandpa were openly fascinated, and Margaret Barring was looking on with a resigned expression that said she'd seen it all before.

But something wasn't working. Pete and Sarah should be coiled together by now, turning to the rest of the table but with eyes still only for each other. That was the way Sarah's couplings worked. She couldn't bear her men to look elsewhere.

Pete wasn't looking elsewhere. He was looking at Sarah, but there wasn't the expression of slavish adoration on his face that Sarah demanded as her right.

'We nearly made what?' Pete said again, and his voice was flat and demanding.

'I…' Sarah looked up at him and fluttered her eyelashes. When that didn't make him smile she giggled. That didn't work either.

So, in typical Sarah fashion, she let her gorgeous eyes fill with tears. 'I would have come anywhere with you.' She had on her little-girl-lost look now, and she was acting in deadly earnest. 'I know you did the honourable thing…breaking up with Lia and going away…but I would have followed you. You only had to say the word. But now you're back…'

'Why on earth would you have followed me?'

That floored her. Her lovely mouth sagged open. 'But…we were in love, Pete, darling,' she said softly, and her clasp on his hands grew stronger. 'I know you and Lia were engaged but we couldn't help ourselves. And then, to be so honourable as to leave…'

She sighed and allowed one tear to slip. 'Oh, I understood your reasons but I suffered. Just ask my family if I didn't suffer. You can see, I've never married. But no matter. You're back now. Darling Pete…'

'I have never touched you,' Pete said blankly, his expression still stunned. 'Until now I don't recall speaking more than three sentences to you in my life, and I don't know what on earth you're talking about.'

Silence. More silence. And more silence still.

You could have heard a pin drop. Lia had ceased collecting dishes. She'd ceased breathing. The children had disappeared and all the adults were spellbound. This was an intensely private conversation, yet the entire table was agog—and Lia was so agog she was stuck to the floor.

It was Lorraine who broke the silence, her girl-like giggle sounding like a broken spring.

'Peter, for heaven's sake…' She stood, her chair scraping loudly on the polished floorboards. 'You and Sarah… Of course you've touched her. What a thing to say. She's right. My lovely Sarah was heartbroken. I always knew you and Lia weren't matched. When Lia and I came home that Christmas Eve and found you two together, it seemed so right…'

'Together…'

'You were making out on the settee,' Sally said

flatly from the other end of the table. Lia's older sister didn't enjoy these Christmas dinners, and she didn't like Sarah very much either. There'd never been much love lost between the beauties of the family. But she was enjoying this. 'You might not be able to remember it, Pete, dear, amongst all the women you've made it with, but Lia and Mother walked into a spot of love-making. Our little Lia just about went into a decline. Mother had to worry about her for almost an hour—until you left—and then she had to worry about Sarah instead. Talk about hysterics!'

'Sally!' her mother snapped.

'Lia, we need pudding,' Sally said, ignoring her. 'The children will start eating their lollies again.'

'We were…making out?' Pete was no longer even remotely interested in pudding—or lollies or anything else. He turned to Lia, and everyone else in the room might as well not have been there. 'With…Sarah?' He shook his head in bewilderment. 'I would never—'

'Three people saw you,' Sally said cheerfully. 'Lia, the pudding…'

'How did you know it was me?' Still he looked at Lia, and there was absolute horror in his voice.

'I…' Lia shook her head. 'Pete… Of course it was you. I mean…'

'Is that what you thought? That I was having a relationship with your sister?'

'You were.'

He took a deep, ragged breath, and pain washed

over his face in an expression that was almost un-
bearable to watch. 'No,' Pete said flatly, as if the
words hurt. 'There is no way in the wide world I
would ever have touched Sarah. Not when I was
engaged to you. Lia...' Another ragged breath.
'Lia, it must have been Ben!'

'Don't be funny,' Sarah snapped, her breath
hissing in as if she'd been slapped. 'As if Ben
would... Ben was engaged to Louise Enther.'

'The heiress to Daddy's millions.' Pete nodded,
his eyes still not leaving Lia's, horror being re-
placed by sick comprehension. 'I know. Ben tried
really hard there. He wanted that money. For the
four months until she ended the engagement he
tried every trick under the sun to make Louise
think he was faithful.'

'He wouldn't make love to me if he was engaged to Louise!' Sarah sounded outraged.

'But I could make love to you if I was engaged
to Lia?' His eyes were still locked with Lia's. 'I
don't think so.'

'No.' Lia couldn't make her mind think. But,
despite her confusion, memories were flooding
back. Pete, standing next to the settee as she and
her mother had burst in. Pete, semi-naked, laughing at her with those wicked eyes that had showed
not a trace of guilt, and then pulling on his
sweater...

'You were wearing the sweater I'd knitted you,'
she said faintly. It was stupid how some details

stood out. Or maybe every single detail of that ultimate betrayal had stayed indelibly in her mind.

'And that made me Pete?'

'I... You said... Sarah said...' Lia pushed a dazed hand up and swept her curls away from her eyes. This was crazy. 'I remember. You said, "Sorry, darling. One engagement ring doesn't make a chain!"'

'And you believed—'

'It *was* you,' she said.

'Ben,' Margaret said faintly. She looked sick. 'Dear God...Ben.'

'I'd have known,' Lia said wildly.

'If they wanted to fool me they always could,' Margaret told the room in general. 'And I'm their mother.'

Dear heaven...

Pete was shaking his head in disbelief. 'I've been blind,' he said. 'Stupidly, criminally blind. For seven years! Of course you wouldn't have broken off our engagement because you couldn't trust me. Not without cause. But if you had me—or someone you thought was me—in front of you, laughing at you. If you had your sister mocking you... That would have been unforgivable.'

And then he turned to his mother.

'I know you loved Ben,' he said simply, 'but my twin has done his damnedest to wreck my life. I'll never forgive him for this.'

And he walked from the room without another

word. There was a slam of the front door, the sound of an engine revving and then silence.

Nothing more.

Somehow she got through pudding.

Somehow Lia had to push herself to do what was expected—light the brandy on the Christmas pudding—try to smile so the children wouldn't have their Christmas destroyed—try to keep going. Just like she'd always kept going.

But underneath… Underneath something was starting to sing.

He hadn't betrayed her. It had been Ben. Ben, going to any devious length to have his way, including borrowing his brother's clothes, telling Sarah he was Pete, lying and lying and lying…

The noises of Christmas swelled and eddied around her—and other sounds, too. Sarah sobbing on her mother's shoulder and being patted dry, and Sally saying they were all the same, the Barring men, and Christmas hadn't been this interesting for years, and Margaret rising and coming around to put her arm around Lia's shoulder in silent support.

And placing Amy in her arms as if she knew that Lia was desperate for something to hug.

Something of Pete's.

Because amazingly, when Lia looked down into the baby's big brown eyes, it was Pete she saw—not Ben. As it had been Ben she'd seen all those years ago—not Pete. Twins—physically identical but so different inside.

Finally it was time to leave the table. Now was the time for everyone to head for the Christmas tree and distribute gifts—but Margaret rose and made it clear she wanted to say something.

'No presents yet,' she said.

'I...' Lorraine stared at her. 'What business is it of yours? We always have gifts now.'

'My son helped plan this Christmas,' Margaret said with dignity. 'And he's given you all a hat. Underneath every hat there are instructions—and instructions have to be obeyed before gifts.'

'What the...?' Grandpa said, and lifted his hat. And stared. 'Wiping,' he said. 'What the heck....?'

'That means drying the dishes,' Em told him sternly. She headed around the table and tugged at his hand. 'Pete said my instruction was the same as yours. Come on, Grandpa, I'll show you where to find the towels.'

The room held its breath. Whether it was the Christmas punch or the champagne or the feel of his little great-granddaughter's hand in his Lia didn't know, but all of a sudden Henry grinned.

'Wiping, eh? Well, that's a turn-around. Come on, then, you lot.' He turned to Lorraine. 'I seem to remember your mother organised Christmas teams. Let's follow our instructions and get back to our gifts.'

And what Grandpa decreed, Grandpa achieved. The rest of the family were left to follow.

Which left Lia watching her family do the clearing-away and washing-up. Stunned, she turned her hat over to find her instruction.

'Help Pete feed the sheep,' it said.

They would need feeding. She'd thought she'd be doing it in the dark after everyone had gone home, but Margaret was lifting Amy out of her arms and reading her hat instruction over her shoulder.

'My note says take care of my granddaughter,' she said. 'Go on, dear. Feed your sheep and come back to us.' She looked down into Lia's eyes and her own expression held a tremulous hope. 'Oh, my dear…'

He was already there.

At first she thought she was dreaming, but the tractor was out and Pete was hauling hay onto the trailer. Lia had pulled on overalls, mac and wellingtons. She and Woof arrived at Pete's side, and for a moment there seemed nothing at all to say.

The snow was falling on her nose, and the world was white and silent. Waiting…

'I didn't hear you come back,' she said at last, heaving one end of the hay bale he was tossing onto the trailer.

'I took off with speed,' he said softly, concentrating on the hay. 'Said a few swear words and burned a bit of rubber. Then I came back—but I didn't fancy facing that lot again.'

'I'm sorry, Pete.' Her voice fell to a whisper.

'Why?' He gave a curt laugh. 'My brother deceived you and lied to you. It was me who was to blame—me who was stupid enough to think that the one disagreement we'd had could have made you reject me.'

The disagreement...

She remembered it. He'd just been given his first international run with the airline. He'd been so proud and she'd been upset at the thought of him spending time away. 'Don't you trust me?' he'd said. 'Lia, if you're willing to marry me there has to be trust.'

And the next time she'd seen him it had been in Sarah's arms. And after that she'd thrown her ring at him and had said she could never trust him— not in a million years.

He'd thought...he'd thought she'd been talking about his job, and the next day he'd left to fly to the US. It had been his first international flight. He'd worked so hard to get there that she should have been proud, and instead she hadn't seen him again for seven years.

A gust of biting wind swirled around her ankles and Lia stood stock still, so mortified she thought her world should end right there.

'Let's get these sheep fed,' Pete said, glancing at her face and then away again. As if he couldn't bear it.

She didn't blame him. She'd accepted his brother's lies.

If you're willing to marry me there has to be trust.

The pain was almost overwhelming. She could hardly speak. Silently she climbed into the tractor cab with him. Woof scrambled up after her, and they made their way behind the farmstead to the hay racks.

The sheep were lined up, waiting. The Herdwicks were as tough as nails, bred to cope with these conditions, but they needed all the nourishment they could get in this freezing weather. Emotion had to be set aside as Pete hauled the feed into the racks and Lia counted. Despite the thoughts tumbling over themselves in her head, another worry surfaced. The flock seemed to be fewer.

She was right. She finished counting and stood silent, taking it in. It was no use recounting. She hadn't made a mistake.

'What's wrong?' Pete fed the last of the hay into the racks and came up beside her. He was still in his Christmas suit, but with his vast greatcoat over the top. The coat was charcoal grey, beautifully tailored, and it made him look—

No! Enough. Somehow Lia forced her thoughts to stay on her sheep. The feel of Pete beside her was building warmth—a burgeoning joy—but there were overriding fears.

Three years ago, on just such a Christmas as this, the sheep had been buried in snowdrifts. She'd been nine months pregnant and John had tried to do what she had to do now.

She couldn't think of that—of what had happened. 'There are fifteen sheep missing,' she told him bleakly. 'All the shearlings.'

There was no choice. Both of them knew it, and with one accord they turned and looked up along the scree.

How far had they got?

There were no tracks—there couldn't be in this weather as the snow would have covered them in minutes. If they'd left not long ago, with the racks being empty and the thought of the feed on the fell tops driving them on, then maybe...

Maybe not. There was no way they'd reach the tops. The weather here was bad. Higher, it'd be filthy.

And the tractor couldn't be used. John had tried that three years ago, and that was why Lia was a widow.

Not more death. Not this Christmas.

But Christmas was over, as of now. She whistled Woof to her side and turned her face into the wind.

'Tell them inside that I've gone up to find them,' she said. 'I can't afford to lose fifteen.'

'You can't go up there. Not in weather like this.'

'I'm going. They'll be buried.'

'They can survive in the snow. You know that.'

'Sometimes. I know.' She pushed snow out of her eyes, thinking of her lovely young shearlings. She couldn't bear it. 'But sometimes they huddle together under the snow and they suffocate. That's what happened last time.'

'Last time?'

'The Christmas John was killed,' she said bleakly. 'We... I lost a quarter of my flock.'

He looked at her for a long minute, and then his arm came around her shoulder.

'And John was killed, trying to find them?'

'Yes. With his bad leg he couldn't walk and I was nine months pregnant. So he took the tractor. But I'll walk now.'

There was a long silence. He held her close, imparting warmth with his body, and the bleakness of three years ago diminished in his presence. 'Come on, Lia,' he told her gently. 'We'll do this together.'

'I don't... You're not dressed...'

'For snow? I'm warm enough.' He shrugged underneath his big woollen coat. 'They can't have gone far.'

'Pete, I can do this on my own.'

'No, you can't,' he said gently. 'Because there's no way I'm letting you. You sent me away seven years ago, Lia, my love. Don't you think seven years' separation is long enough?'

She should have been freezing. Someone had once said that there was no such thing as bad weather, only inappropriate clothing—but Lia knew better. The winds across the scree blew straight from the Arctic.

But now...right this minute...she wasn't cold at all. She stumped on through the snow, Woof at her heels, and Pete's hand caught hers and held it as they walked. His warmth spread from the fingers up. It crept right through her body, warming her from tip to toe, and she could have gone anywhere—faced anything—as long as that link stayed unbroken.

They climbed straight up the fells in the direction she knew the sheep would have taken, their feet making huge craters in the snow. Pete strode strongly, his long legs steadier than hers, and he supported her as she stumbled. He was born and bred in the Dales, and it showed.

But where were they?

'Bring 'em in, boy,' Lia told Woof, and Woof looked up at her, puzzled, because there were no sheep in sight. But his nose obediently sniffed and she knew Woof was the only way they could find them.

'We'll go no higher than the top of the first fell,' Pete said into her ear. The wind was whistling around them, making speech hard. 'Any higher and we risk trapping ourselves.'

'I can't lose them...'

'I can't lose you.'

Cold? What cold? She couldn't feel a thing but the warmth of his hand, the brushing of his body against hers.

Finally they rounded the outreaching crag overlooking the farmstead. Instantly the wind cut out, blocked by the outcrop, and Woof put his nose down and sniffed. He headed away from them, to where the snow had blown in against the rocks in a vast mound. He sniffed and pawed, looked back at Lia and pawed again.

There was nothing there but a mound of snow. Nothing…

But…

'It makes sense,' Pete said, slushing his way forward to where Woof was sniffing. 'If they came up here they'd be weary of the wind by the time they reached this point. They'd cram against the rocks for shelter and then be covered.'

Yes! Lia was hardly listening. She was stumbling forward to join him. 'Good dog,' she told Woof, hugging him close. 'Good dog. If you're right there'll be turkey for you tonight.' And she fell on her knees and started digging.

They were there.

They were alive, but it was a miserable, bedraggled bunch of sheep who emerged into the fading daylight. One after another Lia and Pete dragged the shearlings out of their burial mound, shook them off and checked them for damage. Ten, eleven…

'They're all here,' Lia said exultantly. She hauled a big sheep out and Pete hauled another. The sheep tolerated being shaken free of snow, bleated their relief, broke free and then huddled behind Pete and Lia. They made no attempt to leave. Humans, it seemed, looked pretty good from the sheep's point of view. 'Thirteen, fourteen…'

'I bags the last one,' Pete said, but there was no way.

'First one to find wool gets an extra mince pie!' Lia dived snow-wards, and so did Pete, digging furiously like two children at the beach. The emotions of the afternoon for both of them were finding an outlet in sheer physical work.

They'd have to share their pie. They found her at the same time, uncovering an ear each, digging deeper in a race to reach her legs, laughing at each other's eagerness and then grabbing a front leg apiece and pulling her free. Their combined strength was too much—the sheep came flying free and Lia and Pete ended up sprawled on their backs in the snow. The sheep landed on top of them. She lay stunned for a moment, then bleated in disgust and scrambled off them to join her friends.

'She landed on me,' Pete said bitterly. 'She weighs a ton. That must mean something in the pie department.'

There was no answer. Lia lay flat on her back and smiled and smiled, and Pete rose and took her hands in his and pulled her up into his arms.

As he did, he glanced down at the snow he'd just pulled her from and his face creased into the smile she knew and loved so much. Without releasing her one inch, he turned her within his arms and gestured down to the image she'd left in the snow.

'Look at that,' he said. Where she'd fallen her body had crushed the newly fallen snow. Her outline lay crystal clear, a body with arms outspread, blurred where she'd reached forward to take his hands. It looked just like...

'An angel,' he said, and all the joy in the world was right there in his voice. 'A snow angel. A Christmas snow angel and she's all mine.'

Then he looked from the shape of the angel to where the sheep were regarding him in bedraggled astonishment.

'She's my Christmas angel,' he told them. 'She's your saving angel and she's mine, too. Now...if you guys will excuse us, there's something I need to do. Something very, very important.'

And then he kissed her.

His mouth covered hers, his body enfolded her completely, and he kissed her as if he'd never let her go.

He kissed her as if all their tomorrows were about to start—right now.

His Christmas angel. His snow angel.

His Lia and his love.

Their audience was not amused. They'd just had a traumatic experience and were not in the mood for this frivolity. One of the flock, braver than the rest, edged forward and nudged Lia's leg. They'd come up here for a reason. They were hungry!

'Stupid sheep.' Lia broke from Pete's hold—well, broke about two inches free—and her smile embraced every stupid sheep in the flock. It embraced the world. 'You might be a bit grateful.'

'They just want your attention,' Pete said thickly, and pulled her forward again. 'Very understandable, but you guys can wait. I'm reclaiming my own.'

'Pete...' She held him back—just a smidgen. There were things to be said before this went further. 'Pete, I'm so sorry. I—'

'Hush.' He put a finger to her lips. 'You're not to say it. No sorries. Not ever. Because we were both wrong. You for thinking I could ever betray you—but I know why you did it. And me for thinking you could ever reject me without a reason like the one Ben gave you. So we've both been foolish—and we've paid for our foolishness. We've paid with seven years. But, Lia...' He smiled, and his smile took in all of her, from her woolly cap to her overalled body, from her snow-tipped nose to her wellingtoned feet.

'But those seven years haven't been wasted,' he said softly. 'I have capital now that we can use to turn this farm into a wonderful home. You have your Em and your Sam, and your memories of John, and I have Amy.' He smiled down at her, and his smile made her heart flip right over. 'So...shall we put our seven years together? Marry me? Make a happy ever after for all of us?'

'Oh, Pete...'

'Just say yes, please,' he told her.

There was no arguing with that. 'Yes, please.'

He sighed, and pulled her against him, but this time he didn't kiss her. He simply held her close, with his heart beating against hers. His face rested on the top of her head, and in that moment it seemed like the absolute joining of two bodies. Two becoming one. It was a marriage of the most intimate kind, with sheep and dog as witnesses, and neither Lia nor Pete could have asked for more.

'Marry me,' Pete said again at last, as if he couldn't believe that she'd already said yes. 'Be my wife.'

'I think...I think I already am.'

And then, finally, they whooped and hollered down the scree, for all the world like two excited children rather than two mature adults who should have known better. It was still snowing but the wind seemed to have eased, or maybe it was just that it stood no chance against their united energy. Woof drove the sheep down before him, a ragged bunch just aching to reach the homestead and food and shelter, and Lia and Pete brought up the rear.

Hand in hand.

Heart in heart.

Down below, the sheep rejoined their companions with sheepish contrition. None was so weak that it couldn't shove its way into the racks. Lia watched them start to feed and she knew that her flock was safe.

Her world was safe.

'So we face the relatives again?' Pete said, holding her fast.

'We may as well.'

'Together.'

There was only one relative left.

Margaret was sitting placidly by the sitting-room fire, Amy in her arms. Em and Sam were playing at her feet. She looked up as they entered, and she beamed.

'Well, my children?'

'Well...' Pete leaned over and gave his mother a kiss. 'Wish us joy.'

'I wish you all the joy in the world.' Her smile was almost as wide as her son's. 'I couldn't have asked for a more perfect Christmas.'

'Who could?' Pete gazed around. 'What have you done with Lia's family?'

'Organised them out of here.'

'You...'

'I thought it was time they all went home,' she said placidly. 'So I told them the weather forecast was appalling and Lia had told me everyone was welcome to stay because the barn needed mucking out and she needed help.' She grinned. 'You should have seen them move. They grabbed their gifts and ran.'

'Bet they didn't leave any gifts for Lia,' Pete said darkly, and his mother shook her head.

'No. But they didn't take the food.'

'The food...'

'Lorraine said they always took the leftovers.' Margaret chuckled. 'So I said you'd stipulated this year that the leftovers were only for those who muck-raked the barn.'

'Margaret...' Lia was speechless.

'Well, I had to keep myself amused somehow while I waited for you two to stop canoodling in the snow.'

'We were not canoodling,' Lia protested. 'We were rescuing sheep.'

'Pull the other leg. It plays "Jingle Bells",' Margaret retorted, and Lia knew she'd never believe the reason for their absence—not in a million years. Lia stood in the crook of Pete's arm while Margaret rose stiffly to her feet, and suddenly she had a flash of brilliance. A flash of what could be...

'Margaret...'

'You'd best take me home now,' Margaret was saying to Pete, 'before we do get snowed in.'

'Margaret, do you really need to live in that nursing-home?'

'I don't... It's my home.' The old lady stared at her, and by her side Lia felt Pete stiffen. And then she felt the ripple of laughter and love running right through him, and she knew he'd guessed what she was about to say. They always had known what the other had been thinking.

'This place is a bed and breakfast,' Lia said softly as Pete's hold tightened. 'It's a little farm with a huge house. With Pete's support I won't have to take in guests. But I don't suppose you'd like to—'

'Live with us?' Pete finished for her, and before she could stop him he'd swung her up in his arms and spun her around, before setting her on her feet and holding her close. 'Lia, that's brilliant.'

'What's brilliant?' said Em, looking up from her Christmas gifts. 'Why is Pete's mummy crying?'

'I guess...' Pete looked at his mother's tremulous face and he smiled. 'I guess she's crying because she's happy.'

'Why is she happy?'

'She's happy because we're going to be a family,' Pete said, and he scooped Em up and swung her, too. 'An instant family. With a mummy and a daddy called Lia and Pete, a grandma called Margaret, a girl called Em, a boy called Sam, a baby called Amy, a dog, some sheep, some cows, some hens and whoever else might come along.'

'You mean...we should all live together?' Em said.

'That's exactly what I mean. I can fly out of Manchester on restricted runs, so most days I'll either be here all day or home in time for tea.'

'Or in time to milk the cow,' Lia teased.

He grinned and his hold on her tightened. 'Exactly. What do you say?'

'You mean you want to marry Mummy?' Em asked seriously, and Sam looked up from what he was doing and stared.

'I sure do.'

'Why?' Sam asked.

Pete stopped to consider. He was silent for a

long moment and then he placed Em back down on her feet. Turning to Lia, he took both of her hands in his and he smiled down at her. His love was clearly written on his face. They needed no vows. The vows had already been made, and they'd been made for ever.

'Because she's my Christmas angel,' he said softly into the Christmas night. 'Because your mother is my own perfect Christmas gift. My Christmas angel and my love.'